Love at First Set

Love at First Set

A Novel

JENNIFER DUGAN

AVON

An Imprint of HarperCollinsPublishers

HarperCollins books may be purchased for educational, business, or sales promotional use. For information, please email the Special Markets Department at SPsales@harpercollins.com.

FIRST EDITION

Interior text design by Diahann Sturge

Exercise equipment © Koson Rattanaphan; Oleksandr Panasovskyi/Noun Project

Library of Congress Cataloging-in-Publication Data has been applied for.

ISBN 978-0-06-330748-3

23 24 25 26 27 LBC 5 4 3 2 1

*To all my fellow disasters working toward
their happily ever afters . . .
This one's for you.*

Love at First Set

Chapter One

I've just finished checking in Mrs. Patel for her silver sneakers water aerobics class, and happily returned to my sketching, when my best friend, James, comes up behind me. He rests his chin on my shoulder, his mop of blond hair flopping into his icy blue eyes, and leans the bulk of his six-foot-something personal-trainer body onto the old, faded black office chair I'm sitting in. The chair squeaks and groans in protest. I try to elbow him off.

"No, not there." He snatches the pencil from my hand and hastily erases the words "cardio machines," moving them over closer to the windows of the giant square I've drawn. "Put them over here near the parking lot so they can at least people watch while they destroy their gains."

Meet James Manderlay, head of personal training at The Fitness Place. Twenty-eight, avidly anti-cardio—as evidenced by the "cardi-no" tank he's currently sporting—shockingly handsome per half our guests (which is how we refer to the people who slog here in their sweats to work out), and owner of well-defined abs, exactly one dimple, and a bank account full of family money, thanks to his parents and their sketchy business practices.

He's been my best friend since I moved to this godforsaken

town five years ago, nineteen and already desperate for a fresh start. I'd wandered into his parents' gym looking for a job, and found him on the ground behind the desk. When I asked him if he was okay, he explained he had just been dumped and was waiting for the universe to swallow him up. I nudged his leg and asked him for an application. (I don't have time for sentimentality. Not when a paycheck is on the line.) James had laughed and dragged himself up long enough to scrounge one up.

He said he appreciated my tough love.

I didn't bother asking what other kinds there were.

The Fitness Place didn't really need another employee, but James convinced his parents to bring me on and I worked hard to make sure they never regretted it. It took about a year for them to upgrade me from floater—which meant I did everything from stock towels in the locker room to reposition floor heaters on wet or snowy days to cut locks off jammed lockers—to gym attendant, which largely consisted of sitting in the workout areas and assisting people who don't know how to use the machines (awkward, because the number of people who think they are using a machine correctly when they are not even in the REALM of correctly is staggeringly high).

I'd rather pick gum from the gym locks, thank you very much.

Still, it was my job to make sure that nobody went viral for trying to use leg machines to work out their necks or for getting thrown off a treadmill because they mistook the speed for the incline setting and hit it up to warp.

By then the gym chain had really taken off—five locations and counting—and when the front desk manager left a couple years ago to run one of the new buildings, I got their job. The pay's decent—maybe most people wouldn't say so, but it's the most I've ever made—and bonus, it comes with a free gym membership instead of the lousy 15 percent discount they give to other employees.

The "manager" title is more for bragging rights than any sort of actual authority though. My duties include sitting behind the desk, scanning people's tiny key cards with my giant green scanner, and answering the phone fifty times a day for people asking to sign up for various personal training lessons with "dreamy James," as most of our senior population call him.

It might not be that glamorous, but I love it. The smell of the mats, the sound of weights clinking, the feeling of crushing your reps or knowing you're helping someone else crush theirs? There's nothing better. Nothing. It's the one place on earth I can actually make a difference, for myself and others. Right now, I have to do that within the existing framework of The Fitness Place. But someday, if everything goes right, I'll have my own gym and develop my own programming. Imagine how awesome you could make a place if you designed it specifically to be welcoming and accessible to all from the ground up.

In fact, I spend almost every spare moment I have sketching out my hypothetical future gym, which is what I was doing before James came up and forced his opinions about cardio on me. I know the odds of someone like me *actually* being able to own a gym fall somewhere on the scale between "never going to happen" and "uncontrollably laughing in my face," but still. It's all I've wanted to do since I was old enough to know what a gym was.

"Hey, I gotta ask you something." James flicks my wrist and then pulls the paper to the side. He scribbles "Lizzie's Killer

Gym" on the top, and then draws a stick figure in the center, careful to add large biceps to it after he's done. A little arrow points to it, labeled "James."

"Wait, why are you in the center of my gym?" I snort and pull the pencil from his hand.

"You wound me," he says. He falls backward to the ground and mimes being stabbed. "I got you a job and you won't return the favor? I guess I'll just lay here and *DIE THEN*."

I see we've come full circle.

He's still sprawled out behind me—refusing to tell me what he really wants unless I promise him a senior role at my imaginary gym—when Henry Meyers comes up, his beard trimmed and waxed within an inch of its life. He fixes me with a strained yet polite smile, one that says anyone without a mid-six-figure income is beneath him. He drops his keys on the desk, even though I'm already holding the scanner, and waits. Okay, then. I rummage through them to his gym card and lift it to the scanner, his BMW key tag nearly blinding me under the bright gym lights.

"Oh, Jamie!" he says, his smile going wide and genuine at the sight of my dumbass best friend still playing dead behind me. "I didn't see you there."

"Henry," James says, hopping up in one lithe motion. He flashes Henry his best chemically whitened smile and is it just me or is he flexing? I fight the urge to roll my eyes as I slide the keys back to the man in front of me.

"All set!" I say cheerfully, but they both ignore me.

Henry leans forward on the counter, positioning his arms to maximize his muscles under his too tight Nike Pro shirt. I glance between them, suddenly feeling like I'm stuck in an episode of *National Geographic: The Mating Rituals of the Hot and Wealthy.*

I snicker when James shows off his plumage, which in this case means stretching just enough that his "cardi-no" shirt rides up, exposing the very bottom of his six-pack, or eight-pack, or shit, I don't know, it could be a twelve-pack by now. I stopped keeping track of his gains somewhere around year three of our friendship, when his mom made him get formally certified instead of just hanging out here all the time and he started teaching bored stay-at-home spouses all day. This was more of a last-ditch effort by his parents to make him seem respectable than any real support of his interests—and even though he did exactly what she asked, she still seems disappointed.

His parents, especially his mom, Stella, intimidate me even on their best days. And I am usually not a part of their best days. Best days don't usually require the owners to be on the premises of their lowest volume gym, after all. When we cross paths it's usually because something major is wrong—like the time the sewers backed up into our locker rooms or the time an entire bus-load of seniors coming in from the retirement home got rashes from over-chlorinated pool water.

I somehow managed to get blamed for both. Who knew front desk managers were in charge of human waste engineering *and* properly administering pool chemicals?

No matter how much I tell James his mother hates me, he still insists I'm "reading too much into things."

I'm not. I know I'm not.

Just like I'm not reading too much into the way Stella puts

"just a" in front of "personal trainer" whenever she's introducing James to her "classy" friends.

But even so, James gets enough attention and swoons from his clients. He doesn't need me taking attendance every time a new muscle or vein appears on his body. Let the clients fawn; I'm just here for the late-night pizza-and-beer binges when one of them inevitably breaks James's heart by being like, ya know, married.

"I love your ring, Henry, is that new?" I ask, fake gushing over the platinum and gold band around his finger. It's not and I know it, and it earns me a kick to my chair from James, who is decidedly *not* preening anymore.

"Same old, same old," Henry says, jerking his hand back. Goodbye, pec cleavage, hello, reminder of holy matrimony.

"And how is the senator these days?"

Henry Meyers is married to Juliana Christiansen, a state senator at least twenty years his senior. I know this because she's friends with James's mom, Stella. And Stella loves to bring up that friendship in nearly every conversation—"The senator told me at brunch the other day . . ." and the like. Henry and the (state) senator have complimentary memberships to our club. James's mom thinks it's some sort of prestige to have her here sweating all over the equipment—which, by the way, she never wipes down after she's done.

"Oh, she's fine. You know, busy," he says, clearing his throat and shoving his keys into his gym bag. "Well, I have to go get ready for HIIT but it was great to see you, James."

"Always a pleasure," I say, even though he didn't mention it being great to see me. A scowl flashes over Henry's face so quick

I almost think I've imagined it before he rushes off to the locker room.

"What was that?" James frowns at me when he's gone.

"What was what?" I ask, blinking my eyes quickly to express peak innocence.

"You cockblocked me!"

"I think technically his wife, the senator, did that long before I could." I snort.

"Hey, if I don't crush your nonsense dreams," James says, gesturing toward my gym sketch, "you don't crush mine."

"Okay, right, except mine is not a nonsense dream."

James leans down close to my ear and whispers, "It is if you don't get off your ass, McCarthy."

And okay, I get his point, sometimes you gotta shoot your shot, I guess. Whether that means flirting with the senator's very hot husband or, like, actually doing something to achieve your dream job. Maybe he's *kind of* right; on some level, it is a nonsense dream. But I want it so bad I can taste it.

"I am off my ass," I say, and he raises an eyebrow at my very large, cushioned office chair. "Well, okay, maybe not right now I'm not, but in general. I'm thinking about putting in for that gym manager job at the new club."

James seems to consider this for a second. "You *are* the only worker who actually wants to be here," he says. Wow. His confidence in me is truly astounding.

The new gym is about forty-five minutes away—a bit of a commute, yes, but not bad, and with the raise that comes with it, I could afford a more reliable car. James's parents have been building it for the last six months or so and are *finally* talking staffing.

Sure, it's not quite owning my own gym, but it's close. If I got brought on as the general manager, I'd be the big boss. Everything would be up to me. Well, everything that isn't dictated by Stella and George, the actual owners, but still. They can't keep me here scanning key cards forever. At least, I hope not.

"You applying today?" he asks.

"No, but soon . . . ish."

"Uh-huh."

I fling a pencil at him and spin back around to check in the next client. "What did you want anyway?" I ask him. "You said you had to ask me something when you came over, ya know, before the temper tantrum, and the flirting with married men, and—"

"Right," he says, cutting me off. "I need a favor. A big one. I . . ."

I turn back to face him, confused why he trailed off, and am met with his infamous narrow-eyed smirk.

"Immediately no," I say.

"You don't even know what I'm about to ask!"

"I know nothing good ever comes out of your face doing that whole . . . thing." I wave my hand.

"Not true." James leans forward, his lips widening into a full-on grin. "In fact, I just realized that the favor I need from you would also be a favor *for* you."

I scrunch up my face. "You're making no sense right now. You know that, right?"

He holds up a finger. "What if I told you that I have an opportunity for us to spend time with my parents and turn you into a front-runner for that gym manager job in a way that a shitty résumé never would."

"I would be extremely suspicious. Your parents barely tolerate *you*, let alone me. Put us together and we're the Voltron of their disappointment and regrets."

"O ye of little faith," he huffs and pretends to walk away. "Fine, if you don't want to know . . ."

"Just tell me." I sigh. Even when I try to avoid his scheming, I usually get roped in anyway. If I ask now, at least I'll know what I'm up against.

James spins my chair around so fast it makes me dizzy. "You know how my sister's getting married next weekend?"

"How could I forget? Stella's had me wrapping wedding favors for weeks since I'm 'on the clock anyway.'" I roll my eyes.

"Okay, well, two birds one stone, then," James says.

"What?"

"Come to Cara's wedding with me; that's what I was coming to ask you anyway. Except now you wouldn't just be helping me. You can *also* use that time to dazzle my parents so they move your application to the top of the pile and, bonus, you get to enjoy the fruits of your labor." He leans in conspiratorially. "Those Jordan almonds aren't gonna eat themselves, you know."

"Nope, no way." If there is anything I want to do *less* than spend a weekend watching James's golden-child sister prance around at her Barbie dream wedding, I certainly can't think of it. It's bad enough my fingers are rubbed raw from all that tulle; she does *not* get my one weekend off this month too.

"Come on, please, please, please." James falls to his knees begging, as the next client reaches my desk. "This could be so good for both of us!"

"Will you get up?" I grit through my teeth.

"Lizzie, please! I—"

"Don't you have a class to teach, James?" Roger asks as he walks up, swinging his keys on a lanyard. He's the general manager of this gym, number 105 (because Stella insisted on calling the first gym 101, like she'd opened a hundred before it). While I'm used to people yelling at *me*, Roger is quite possibly the only person here—besides me, of course—brave enough to take that tone with James.

"Not for ten minutes, boss," James says, with a mock salute. Roger frowns.

"I don't like you hanging around the desk distracting Lizzie. What if someone complains?"

To his mother? I fight the urge to say. Fat chance.

"Wouldn't dream of causing any problems, Roger," James says, standing up. "And Lizzie, think about it, okay?" He starts to leave and then turns back to press his hands together and mouth the word "please" to me.

Shit, he is not going to let this one go.

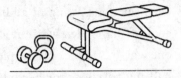

Chapter Two

It's my day off.

I should be spending it working on my résumé, but instead I woke up to three texts from James begging me to go to the wedding with him and, even worse, a dozen texts from my mom. She's complaining that her cable was turned off and her electric is overdue, which means it is now My Problem to Solve for Her™. Mom's problems have a habit of becoming mine, and I learned long ago it's easier to cut them off at the pass then hope they'll go away or, god forbid, assume she'll fix them herself.

She will not. It's never been her style.

Mom and I were broke, like broke-broke, when I was growing up. We lived in a half-abandoned town that didn't have much to show for it except for an empty Kmart, a Burger King, and a crumbling gym that boasted a $9.99 a month membership fee. Mom made friends with the woman who managed it, who was all too happy to look the other way when mom left me at the gym day care all day instead of just the one-hour limit.

While other kids were learning the alphabet, I was learning how to disinfect gym mats. We are not the same.

And it wasn't any better at home either. Mom's life has just been one long string of addictions, evictions, and choices that couldn't have been worse if she tried. And I've always been the one who has to pick up the pieces—whether that means sending half my paycheck for her bills or spending my only childhood scraping her off bar floors.

When you have a mother like Pattie, you figure out real quick that the only one you can depend on is yourself—and unfortunately, the only one *she* can depend on is you.

That kind of responsibility grinds itself into your DNA and becomes a part of you even if you don't want it to. Even my "fresh start" at nineteen only brought me twenty minutes down the highway. I couldn't *really* leave my mom—even though everything in me was telling me that I should—but I could get myself a little breathing room, at least.

Which is why I linger at my apartment for a while, instead of rushing right over. I even stop at the gym to get in a quick workout to steel my spine, like every weight I lift will make me stronger inside *and* out. No day can truly be shitty if you're crushing your PR or at least trying to, right?

I get cut off twice trying to parallel park near my mom's building, but I can't tell if I even really mind. I just circle the block aimlessly, waiting for someone to leave. It's totally fine.

But then my phone buzzes as I finally pull into a spot.

YOU COMING IN OR WHAT?

Shit. All caps. She's pissed. She must have been tracking me on Find My Friends.

When I bought her new phone—on my plan, no less—the man

at the store "helpfully" set it up for us. I think he thought he was doing me a favor: now I could easily keep track of my mom or whatever. I didn't have the heart to tell him she's way younger than she looks—a life of booze and god knows what else will do that to you—or that the only one liable to get tracked now was me.

LIZZIE

Thanks so much, Apple Store dude!

"Hey, Ma!" I say cheerfully as I walk in her door. "Smells good in here."

It doesn't. It smells like stale cigarette smoke and burned food, but she lit the sugar cookie candle I gave her for Christmas last year, so I decide to play along.

"Such a charmer," she grunts out around the cigarette dangling from her lip. "Took you long enough."

"I couldn't find a spot."

"Oh, 's that why you went to the gym?" she slurs.

Awesome! She's drunk before noon. Love this for me. I wonder if it would be weird if I just grabbed her bills and ran, like some kind of reverse home invasion—we don't steal things, we hook you up with 257 cable channels and counting!—but decide that it probably would be.

"I had to pick up my paycheck," I lie, because there's no sense arguing with her when she's like this.

My excuse seems to settle her, and she falls back against her oversize chair. "I'm missing my stories," she says and gestures to the black screen of the TV. "HDMI2" blinks lazily in the corner, waiting for input that will never come.

Well, until I pay the bill.

"What happened, Mom? I just gave you money a couple weeks ago."

She leans forward. "I don't go asking you how you spend your money. Now, take your coat off, stay awhile."

I do as I'm told, not bothering to point out that if I'm the one supplying the money then maybe, just maybe, I do have the right to ask.

Definitely not worth the argument though.

Things with me and my mom are . . . complicated. When things are good, she's actually kinda fun to be around. I can at least see where I get my sarcasm from, our visits turning into mini improv sets slash bitch sessions. But when they're not good—and things haven't been good for years now—she can strip you down to the bone with one withering look. You never know what version you're going to get until it's too late.

It's why I left in the first place, even if I didn't make it that far.

"How's work?" she asks, and a part of me knows she's just asking to make sure my hours are steady so that I can keep passing part of my check on to her. But I let myself imagine, just a little, that she's asking because she cares.

I'm halfway through telling her about this new training program I'm working on with James that I'm wildly excited about when she gets up and starts rustling through the papers on her kitchen table. She selects a couple and drops them into my lap.

Right. The bills.

"I called and if you pay before five, they'll turn my TV back on tonight," Mom says, with a look that makes me wonder if she thinks she's the one doing *me* a favor. "You can pay right at the grocery store. I asked."

I'm sure she did.

I sigh and pull open the first bill. It's her cable company and it's three months behind. Next comes electric. That number hurts to look at. I can cover it, but it's gonna just about wipe me out.

"Mom," I say, but she waves me off. She heads back into the kitchen and pulls a sandwich out of the fridge. Peanut butter and fluff, cut in triangles with the crusts cut off. My favorite from as far back as I can remember.

"I made you this, baby girl," she says, setting the plate on her coffee table in front of me. "Thought you might be hungry."

Is it manipulative? Yes.

Do I love that she made it for me anyway? Also yes.

I shove the bills into my bag and the sandwich into my face. It feels like old times, like good times if you squint.

Until she breaks this happy silence with an offer to text me the address of the closest grocery store. She pinned it on Apple Maps apparently, right after getting off the phone with the cable company.

"Just trying to be helpful and all," she says.

Right. Yeah.

At least this gives me an exit.

"I better head out, then," I say, giving her a quick kiss on the cheek before carrying my dish over to the sink. "The sooner I get there, the sooner you're turned back on."

She beams, and I know I said just the right thing. I hurry to pull on my coat and get out the door before she changes her mind.

Short and sweet.

Well, short and sweet and expensive, but still. I've made it out relatively unscathed, I realize, and relief floods me as I dart down the stairs in front of her building and onto the sidewalk. But just as quickly as the relief comes, it goes, leaving behind an aching loneliness that only seems to hit in situations like this.

When I was younger, I used to let myself wallow in it, just drown right in all the what-ifs. *What if Mom took care of* me? *What if Mom decided to get sober? What if Mom wasn't such a goddamned narcissist?*

It's pointless, though. I've learned the answers to those questions inside and out. She doesn't, she won't, and she always will be.

James texts me again as I'm getting into my car—a quick reminder that it's *Bachelor* night, and he'll be over to watch as soon as he finishes up with his last client later this evening . . . followed, of course, by another text begging me to consider being his plus-one.

As annoying as he can be, he's the closest thing I have to real family. If anything, this visit to my mom cemented it. James gave me a job and friendship when I had neither, and let me crash on his couch until I got my first paycheck instead of leaving me to sleep in my car. As impossible as it is to ever repay that, I'll be damned if I won't keep trying.

I stare down at his text for a beat, steeling myself before I reply.

> Alright, alright. We'll figure out the wedding thing tonight.

The wall of smiley emojis he sends back is blinding.

Chapter Three

"Have I told you lately how amazing you are?"

James is standing at my front door, holding out two bags of what smells like takeout from my favorite Chinese restaurant, Golden Bird. It's our weekly Tuesday night date to watch *The Bachelor*. Yes, I know it airs on Mondays, but I can't afford to pay my cable *and* Mom's, so I have to wait the twenty-four hours for it to hit my shitty, ad-filled Hulu plan. James, to his credit, never complains.

"This sudden burst of adoration wouldn't have anything to do with me agreeing to hear you out about this wedding thing, would it?" I take the bags from him and head into the kitchen with a smile. While this is a standing dinner date, I don't normally have a say in what we eat. Mainly because my tastes skew . . . shall we say *down* from those of Mr. "My Body Is a Temple" over there. If he's bribing me with Golden Bird, he must be truly desperate.

I arch my eyebrow at his answering grin, but then he pushes past me to where I keep my plates—a chipped hand-me-down set my mom gave me when I got my first apartment. They were supposed to be temporary, but I tell myself I keep them because I like them and not because I just can't bear to spend what little

money I have on something that nobody but me, and once a week
James, will ever see.

"I got you General Tso's Bean Curd!" he says in a singsong
voice, already heaping food onto my plate. He's careful to drizzle
a little—but not too much—of the sauce onto my sticky rice. In
this house we don't say "I love you," we say, "I have learned your
random food quirks and I support you."

"I noticed," I say, as he shoves the plate at me with the enthusiasm of a Labrador puppy freshly out of the crate.

He scoops some onto his own plate with an exaggerated flour-
ish and an "mmmmm, smells so good!" that couldn't sound more
fake if he tried. James has never hesitated to tell me that this isn't
real Chinese food. That he had real Chinese food during the two
years he spent traveling the world after college. That this is *knock-
off, Americanized fast food and it sucks*, thank you very much.

I may not have backpacked across most of Europe and parts
of Asia, but I know good food. Of which Golden Bird is the
pinnacle.

I know, I know, for someone obsessed with the idea of opening a gym, I eat like shit. And that's largely true. I like to eat
cheap and hearty and that doesn't usually translate to healthy.
But when you grow up the way I did, cheap and hearty is all you
know. I don't think I even had a vegetable that wasn't out of a can
until I moved out, and even then, they were always frozen until I
started hanging out with James.

I fully intend to have a nutritionist on staff at my new place. I
might even go to them. But, like, not on *Bachelor* night.

I follow James to my living room and we both plop on the

couch. It's a nice oversize one, way too big for my living room but way too comfy to pass up when James offered it to me for free. The dude gets a new couch annually. He says he gets bored. I wonder what it must be like to have the time and money to get bored of your couch.

I shove a giant piece of bean curd into my mouth, savoring it while James pulls up the show on my laptop and hits play. Curiosity about why he thinks this wedding thing is such a good idea wells up inside me, and I'm losing my battle to wait him out.

"Tonight, on the most dramatic season of . . ." the host blares on.

"So, the wedding?" I blurt out. "I thought you were going with—"

"Shhhhhh, Queen Cassie is speaking."

I roll my eyes. "She's obviously only there because of the producers! She's not even a real contender! Before I fully commit to doing this, I have a couple quest—"

"Shhhh!" he says, this time louder, his eyes fixed to the screen. But I notice his knee is bouncing, one of his only stress tells. I study his face for a second, and then decide to just go with it. He'll tell me what this is really all about when he's ready; waiting is what best friends do.

It takes two helpings of bean curd and three commercial breaks before he turns to me and blurts out, "Okay, so basically you'll be my date."

"What?" I sputter, because yes, as the only two queer people that work at The Fitness Place, we definitely did gravitate toward each other, but only in the platonic sense. James is gay, and while I'm personally an equal opportunity dater, beefcake boys like him are not my type at all.

James rolls his eyes. "Not my date-date, just like my plus-one slash shield me from family drama slash ongoing moral support. It's just . . . you know how my mom is."

"That sales pitch needs a little work. I'm not really getting the 'fun opportunity to dazzle your parents' vibe you've been promising. What's really going on?"

James rubs his face. "Do you even get how embarrassing it is to have to ask you to do this for me?"

"Wow, thanks for that," I say.

"I didn't mean it like that, I just meant . . ." He drops his head back. "Dana dumped me. Again. I didn't want to tell you because I know you were all 'exes are exes for a reason,' but yeah. And I already told my mom I was bringing someone, so . . .'"

I sigh and tug him in closer for a hug, resisting the urge to say I told you so. This isn't exactly out of the norm for him, and I think we both saw this coming from miles away. James is that perfect kind of pretty that has him cycling through relationships without even meaning to. He doesn't sleep around or anything, and he's definitely not what you'd call a fuckboy, but he is a total flirt without even realizing it (or when it comes to Henry-the-senator's-husband, sometimes *with* realizing it). Which means half the time someone wants to date him, it's because they think he's going to be just another easy fling, another pretty notch on their bedpost.

Unfortunately, James falls in love the way other people change their underwear. Five minutes in he's naming their future kids and debating the merits of daisies versus chrysanthemums for their inevitable hipster barn wedding décor. More often than not, his dates freak and end up ghosting him. Like Dana's done twice now, apparently.

And for as much as James pathologically wants to commit, I absolutely never ever do. Collectively, we make one well-rounded human. Separately, we're both kind of disasters. He's the brother I never had and always wished for.

We make quite the pair, a couple of queers, inching our way toward the wrong side of thirty, coming together once a week to watch people younger (in both our cases) and hotter (in my case) hand out roses that one of us would be desperate for (him) and one of us would puke if we got (me).

"I'm sorry about Dana," I say, ruffling his hair. "But there are plenty of other dudes in the sea."

"Are there, Lizzie? Are there? I'm twenty-eight! I'm practically one of those dried up corpses from that vampire show you forced on me."

So okay, maybe he wasn't kidding that time he said *The Vampire Diaries* gave him nightmares. I assumed it was the monsters, but maybe it was just his fear of being ancient wreaking havoc on his subconscious. My bad.

"You're hardly desiccated." I snort. "And if you were, we'd just get you some blood. Problem solved."

"Ha-ha, very funny. Seriously, Lizzie. I need you!" He pouts. "I'm in my hour of need!!!! I got dumped!"

"Okay, before this convo goes any farther, I would just like to point out that I believe marriage is a stupid social institution designed to trap women and treat them as commodities. So, by agreeing to accompany you, I'd be abandoning my moral fortitude."

"Noted," he says. "But remind me what part of your morals allowed you to stick your tongue down two different bridesmaids' throats that time we crashed a wedding in Newport?"

"Queer chaos trumps moral fortitude, especially when making out is involved."

James laughs. "Right, right, the morality of making out. Got it."

"And also, it's kind of weird that I've never even met Cara. Didn't she like run off to NYC to be a real estate lawyer and abandon your whole family? What's even up with that?"

"She's just been very busy!"

"For eight years?"

"I guess!" he all but wails. "I flew down that one time though!"

"But still, I haven't met her. And you're asking me to go to her wedding."

"As my friend-date," he says.

"Right, but on top of that, may I remind you that your parents are, you know, my bosses?! I know you consider that a feature, not a bug, but the way your mom has been stressed out about this wedding and how much they need to impress *the senator* . . ." I say. "You're trying to spin this as an opportunity for me too, but don't you think I might just piss them off more by being there?"

"What if I pay you, then?" he asks. "Name your price, seriously. I'm desperate."

"Holy shit, you cannot pay me to go to this wedding with you. What kind of person would I be if I accepted that?"

"Lizzie, please. I'm begging you. Do not make me face this alone. My mom will be trying to set me up with everyone and Cara will think I'm a fucking loser in the face of her *perfect* fiancé and *perfect* vineyard wedding. Did you know Max has political aspirations? Of course he does, they're the perfect power couple!" he spits out. "All I ever hear about from Mom is how they're so wonderful, and so smart, and how they're going to make the cutest babies. Fuck."

"I don't even know who Max is," I say but he ignores me.

"All my parents care about is that his family is *old money* and has *important political ties*." He groans. "Lizzie, don't make me go alone and sit there with all of those boring people. Please, please, please, I'm on my knees here."

He's not, but when I raise my eyebrows, he starts to slide down, like a repeat of last time is all that's missing from the equation. I shove him with my shoulder, and he sheepishly sits back up on the couch.

"What about taking Mina instead? If you're hell-bent on bringing a friend, at least they like her way more than they like me."

"In case you haven't noticed, Mina is like eight months pregnant. You're my only hope."

"Come on, man," I say, even though I can already tell I'm definitely going to give in, and I'm sure he can too.

I glance at the screen just in time to see Queen Cassie shoving her finger in another girl's chest. James is missing all the good stuff. James is making *me* miss all the good stuff.

"Have I mentioned yet that you'd be at the family table?"

"I thought you were trying to sell me on this, not make it sound even more hellish."

"I'm serious," he says. "You would have practically the whole night to show them how awesome you are. That's a huge leg up on the competition."

"James, I love you, I do, but I promise they are not going to want to talk about my promotion at their daughter's wedding. Nice try."

"Well, no," James agrees. "It's not like I'm saying pitch yourself for the job while she's walking down the aisle, but you would have so much face time. They'll get to really know you outside of the gym. Then when they go to look at your application they'll just be like 'Oh god, we already love Lizzie. Remember how great she was at Cara's wedding? She's hired!'"

I would hate his confidence if I didn't already love him for it.

"Goddammit." I sigh, because it's nice to have somebody who believes in me, but I'm not giving him the satisfaction of admitting that.

James's face breaks into a smile like he sees right through me. He stabs some bean curd with my fork and slips to one knee, holding it out like a ring.

"Lizzie McCarthy, will you accept this rose, er, tofu, and be my best-friend date to Cara's wedding?"

I laugh so hard I snort before taking a bite and chewing thoughtfully. "I guess, since you're so desperate and all."

He squeals and tackles me, right as a contestant shoves Queen Cassie into the pool.

Chapter Four

*C*ara's wedding is a destination affair at a high-end vineyard in the Finger Lakes that's become *the* upstate place for weddings. Unfortunately, being four hours away, it requires a two-night stay—one for the rehearsal dinner the night before, and then one the night of the wedding, something James helpfully left out until last night when he helped me pack.

I don't know that it would have changed my answer, if I'm being truthful. The way he's been a jumble of anxiety over this—I hate how he always feels like he's living in his sister's shadow. So no, there was no way I was letting him go through this alone. And besides, a free vacation to a place that doesn't suck, where I don't have to look at the laundry piling up around my apartment? I'll take it.

James had been pissed that his mom had booked a double for him and Dana versus the king suite that was available. He was insulted not by the cheapness, but by the coddling, as if they weren't going to sleep together anyway, or maybe even push the beds together if they wanted to get really wild. I think we're both grateful for that now, as we drag our luggage out of the back of his Audi e-tron.

Stella is waiting for us as we walk up the steps to the "inn," a large, mansion-type building situated in the middle of the property to accommodate wedding parties and the like. (Most of the guests are staying off-property, though, at an assortment of luxury Airbnbs that Stella handpicked to perfection.) There are only about a dozen rooms here, each one high-end and beautiful: the bridal suite, which of course goes to Cara; two king suites, one of which remains empty; and then an assortment of doubles and singles to accommodate those of us special enough to be considered inner circle, but not important enough for the level of class and comfort the others enjoy. No wonder James is salty.

Stella's face registers surprise as she sees me approach with her son. "Elizabeth," she says, even though I hate being called that. She grabs both of my hands warmly, while shooting her son a questioning look. "What a pleasant surprise. I didn't realize that you'd be joining us today." She spreads my hands apart and glances me up and down, like she's really taking in my appearance. "And you look so nice!"

I'm in my traveling clothes, which are literally some leggings and a sheer top over a tank top, but I don't know. I guess anything looks better than the stupid navy polos we have to wear at The Fitness Place. It's possible that Stella believed those were the only clothes I owned.

"Yeah, Dana couldn't make it and I didn't want to come alone," James says, sparing me any more of his mother's inquisition and pulling her into a hug. I step back, grateful to have his mother's laser beam eyes off me—and their look of *you don't belong here*—if only for a second.

She hugs him hard, leaning back to squeeze his chin. "You

wouldn't have been alone! You're with family!" Then she buries her face in his shoulder as if to emphasize the last word. James mimes shooting himself in the head and I swallow a laugh.

As if Stella isn't over-the-top enough in day-to-day life, Wedding Planner Mother of the Bride Stella is apparently ten times worse.

"Now let's get you checked in," she says, grabbing both of our wrists and dragging us up the beautiful wooden steps—lightly stained to look weathered, but in a somehow still pretentious way.

James compliments the lobby for being "farmhouse modern minimalist chic," but truly those words mean less to me strung together than they all do apart. All I know is that it's heavy on the wood and weird angles, and every chair in the lobby looks achingly uncomfortable to sit on.

Stella leads us to the counter, where a friendly faced attendant with a man bun and a name tag that reads *Ramón* is waiting for us, already typing away at the computer in front of him.

"Ramón. Ramón!" Stella calls as if he isn't already watching us. "Ramón, our next guest has arrived! My son, he's in the first-floor double." I wonder for the first time how long she's been in this lobby. If she's been haunting it like the telltale heart, if Ramón wants to take a hammer to her—

"Pleasure to meet you, sir," Ramón says, his eye contact lingering on James just a little too long.

"James, please," he says, "and the pleasure's all mine." And oh my god. Great. Perfect. I knew I was going to end up being the third wheel this weekend somehow, I just didn't think it would start at check-in.

"Ramón," Stella says and taps her fingers on the desk.

And yeah, I think Cara definitely had the right idea when she ran off to the city and never looked back.

What I can't figure out is why she bothered coming back for the wedding. From what I heard from Stella's incessant warbling around the gym, it sounds like she let her mom run the show carte blanche. Well . . . "let" might be a strong word for whatever happened here.

Ramón snaps his attention away from James long enough to swipe two magnetic key cards.

"James and Dana, I presume, two nights in our—"

"No, Dana is my ex-boyfriend. We broke up ages ago," James lies. "This is my best *friend*, Lizzie. My *platonic* soulmate that I have no romantic interest in. Filling in as my plus-one like a good *friend*," he explains, like Ramón really needed to know any of that. Beside him, Stella quietly scoffs at the idea of me being her son's anything, let alone best friend and platonic soulmate—not that James notices. It's fine. It's fine. And hey, at least it distracted her from James's other, bigger admission, that he and Dana broke up again.

"Oh, excellent." Ramón beams, passing us our keycards. "That explains the double beds."

"That it does." James smiles.

I take my card with an apologetic shrug. "Well, I'll just leave you two to it, then," I say, dragging my suitcase behind me. "Me and my platonic ass will be in the double bed to the right, watching HGTV, if anyone needs me before dinner."

Stella frowns at my word choice, but can't disguise being pleased at the fact that James is ditching me already. She looks back at where Ramón and James are still eye-fucking each other over a pseudo-marble countertop, and I wonder if she's trying to decide which is the lesser evil: me or a random hotel worker.

And suddenly this all feels like a colossal mistake. The kind of colossal mistake that leaves you feeling dizzy and nauseous. How am I supposed to schmooze someone who can't stand my presence? What am I even doing here? I don't belong at upstate vineyards or fancy weddings.

"You're reading into this too much," I say quietly, even though it sounds like a lie. It's James's lie—one he tells me every time I complain about his mother, one that he would tell me right now if I said I heard her scoff. Normally I hate that he doesn't take me seriously, but right now I desperately want it to be true.

I pick up the pace, my suitcase bopping into my heels as it gets caught and uncaught on the carpet. Who puts carpet in hallways? Well, I guess a lot of people, but that's not the point. The point is if you're going to carpet a hotel hallway you need to go with something light, something industrial and sturdy, not this fluffy shit I'm practically swimming in on the way to the room.

Finally, finally, I get to my door. Dragging my suitcase over with one final grunt, I press the card to the door scanner. It doesn't unlock.

I press it again. And instead of a green light and a beep beep, I get a red light and a buzzing sound.

I try it faster. And faster. And slower.

Scan, turn, push. Scan, turn, push ad infinitum while the door stays stubbornly locked.

I'm going to lose it. I am absolutely going to lose it. I kick the door and slide down to the floor. I'll just sit here for the next two days, or at least until James comes up with a working key to save me. No way am I going back and interrupting him and Ramón, and no way am I going to find Stella and beg for help. It's going to take a good long hot shower before I can wash the sound of her scoff out of my head. If I have to see her again right now, I'll scream.

I drop my head back against the door, eyes closed. Please just kill me now.

"Need help?" A woman's voice makes me jump.

I jerk my head and am met with the biggest pair of brown eyes I've ever seen. I instantly think of cows. Wait. I don't mean . . . Like she doesn't look like a cow, just her eyes are big and soulful and tender like cows'. In a good way. Hot cow eyes. Wait, that's weird.

I swallow hard and try to reset.

The woman pushes some of her long brown hair out of the way, tucking it back to reveal the cutest ears on earth. "Um," she says, licking perfect pink lips that have the most delicate cupid's bow I've ever seen. She raises her eyebrows, groomed and arched to the latest trend, as a small smile ghosts across her face. "Are you okay?"

And shit. Shit, I've been staring too long, categorically memorizing every inch of her face like I've never seen a hot girl before. Beautiful, I mean. Beautiful girl. No, woman. Shit. I'm the worst. At least I didn't call her "chick"? Fuck me. Reboot brain, reboot.

"Yeah," I say, whipping out my customer service smile. "Yeah, I'm great. Perfect, even. You're perfect. Nope! I did not mean that." I laugh nervously. "I meant me. I'm perfect, well, good. All set, great, even. Thanks!" I blush down to my toes when she raises a single eyebrow at me this time and, god, why do only hot girls have the ability to raise one eyebrow? Meanwhile, I'm over here like a gremlin with a unibrow.

"Do you want help?" she asks, eyeing my suitcase. "The key cards can be a little tricky; it took me a minute to figure it out."

I hand her the key card automatically, desperate to keep the conversation going. Who are you? I want to ask. A cousin? A friend of the bride? Does James know about you? Would you prefer someone like James to me?

She holds it up to the lock for a moment longer than expected, the light turning from red to green, before she turns the knob and blissfully pushes the door open with barely any effort at all. "There you go!" She smiles again, wider this time, revealing perfect white teeth, no doubt the result of years of orthodontia teen me could only dream of.

The sun from the giant window in my room cascades through the open door, bathing her in light. Her skin looks luminous, peachy against the soft pink of her lips, and I feel inferior to her pores.

I . . .

Am still staring.

"Well, thanks!" I say and grab the handle of my suitcase, which immediately rips off because of course it does. Kill. Me. Now.

"Oh no!" she says and bends down to help me, which provides another, not entirely unwelcome view.

I'm a monster.

"Oh, it's fine, it's fine, it does it all the time," I lie, practically ripping my suitcase from her hand in mortification. She seems concerned and I'm torn between explaining to her that I found this suitcase at a thrift shop for five bucks, so it's okay . . . and the idea of setting myself on fire and running down the hall, out the front door and all the way home. If I'm lucky, maybe I'd turn to ash and blow away before she noticed.

"Well, thanks again!" I say, giving her an awkward wave and then shutting the door in her face.

It's not until its safely locked behind me, and I'm taking the longest, coldest shower of my life, that I realize that I never got her name.

Chapter Five

"I really wanted you to meet Cara before dinner, but I guess she ducked out awhile ago to go for a run."

I lean my head out of my bathroom, where I'm trying to towel off my hair with an old T-shirt. "Yeah, it would be nice to, ya know, meet the bride before the wedding."

"Rehearsal dinner," he corrects, holding up two equally boring polos. Either one will work for what I'm gathering is going to be a sea of stuffy summer dresses and button-up shirts.

"Whichever," I say, before he gives me a little-lost-puppy-dog look. "The pink one," I amend, tossing the wet T-shirt at his head before heading back into the bathroom to brush my teeth. I've decided to let my hair air dry—it's too hot to straighten it today, even with the air conditioner on.

Also, I don't really want to spend the next fifty-seven hours doing my hair for people who won't be impressed by it anyway. I'm here for free food and to show Stella and George that I'm 100 percent the type of person you want running a gym—put-together and professional but not over-the-top. With my electric toothbrush in my mouth I lean closer to the mirror to check out a small bump that definitely looks to be the beginning of a zit on the side of my forehead. Perfect.

"At least she has hot friends," I say, around a mouthful of tooth-paste bubbles.

"Huh?" James asks, leaning against the doorframe. He's changed into the pink polo already, and why do guys, even ones as pretty as James, have the ability to get ready so quick? It's honestly bullshit.

I spit into the sink, spattering some on the mirror, which I wipe off with a wince. We've long ago given up any pretense of manners around each other, but spit spatter on the mirror is a hard limit for James. Something I learned the first time I crashed on the couch at his house after drinking too much, woke up long enough to puke and brush my teeth, and then was rudely awak-ened a few hours later by his most ungodly high-pitched shriek. I rushed into the bathroom to find him pointing horrified at the mirror. "Is that your *spit?*" he shrieked.

I never made that mistake again.

"I said," and I pause for effect, raising my eyebrows up and down in as corny a manner as I can manage, "at least her friends are hot."

"Her friends?" He grabs some of his pomade and quickly cre-ates perfectly crafted bed head—his trademark combo of messy and styled—in under a minute.

"Yeah, I met one in the hall."

"Weird," he says. "I didn't know she brought anybody with her from New York. She told Mom 'Max is all I need' when she asked about bridesmaids and stuff. Mom had to find people herself."

"It definitely wasn't an employee, so she must have."

"Huh." James narrows his eyes. "Oh god, are you planning to hook up with a bridesmaid this weekend? You are, aren't you? Lizzie!"

"Says the man who practically bent the hotel manager over the desk at check-in!"

"I wasn't coming on to him or anything! I was just . . ." He freezes at the sight of my face. It's my no-bullshit face. He says it scares the crap out of him. It reminds him of his third and final nanny, who he declared an utter monster because she made him and Cara clean their own rooms every night.

When they were thirteen.

"Fine," he says, wiping his hands off on a towel. "Maybe I was flirting *a little*."

"Thank you," I say, pulling out my eyeshadow. "But no, I'm not planning to bag a bridesmaid, no matter how hot. This weekend is all about putting my best foot forward with your family, no distractions."

THE BAR DOWNSTAIRS where we're supposed to meet for hors d'oeuvres while waiting for the wedding party to finish rehearsing is busy and warm. I grab a stool and am pleased when the bartender tells me it's an open bar all weekend. I can't even imagine what that must cost, but I'm also not going to let it go to waste. I order up a Dark 'N' Stormy and look around.

I knew this wedding was pricey—Stella went on and on about sparing no expense—but I guess it didn't really hit me until the bartender reached to the top shelf just how expensive it was.

Before I can even thank him, a smiling waitress is in my face with a beautiful tray of food.

Toto, I don't think we're in Kansas anymore.

I take the napkin she offers, and then pile up the shrimp. It isn't until she gives me a weird look that I realize I should probably take less, but when I go to put some back, she jerks the tray away as if I was trying to poison them.

"It's quite all right." She smiles and then heads back toward the kitchen. "Plenty more where that came from." Her voice sounds polite, but her face looks strained. This is going swell.

I chug my drink like it's a shot and drop it down onto the bar louder than I mean to. A few people turn to look, and I scan their faces, hoping for a glimpse of the woman from earlier. If I can find her, maybe I can strike up some awkward conversation so at least I won't have to sit here in a puddle of embarrassment alone. She's probably at the rehearsal though, with the other bridesmaids.

I should go back to my room.

Ideally until tomorrow, but at *least* until it's time to eat and I can hide behind James again—assuming he's not in some dark corner making out with Ramón.

They'll probably be engaged in a month.

I read an article about that once: that weddings are a great place to meet people, that a lot of couples come out of them. They have a better winning streak percentage than the entire *Bachelor/ette* franchise, but then again, what doesn't?

I stare down at my phone, wondering if I need to tell someone before I leave, when the bartender slides a fresh drink in front of me. I down that one nearly as fast, sadly eat a couple shrimp, and then fire off a text to James:

> Heading up to the room for a bit. Text me when it's time for dinner.

I go to stand up and realize I don't think I have any cash to tip the bartender, who has since slipped me a third drink before walking away. He's trouble. Trouble but attentive. I dig through my purse, searching for the emergency ten-dollar bill I keep stashed at the bottom. I upend my bag in the process, makeup flying everywhere, along with ten thousand receipts and more tampons than any sane person would carry. Still, no cash.

I scramble to scoop everything up, ignoring the bigger issue, which is that I can't leave, not without tipping, but I also *don't* want to be sitting here with a pile of tampons and guilt-inducing shrimp when James—and hopefully the woman from the hallway—comes back.

My phone lights up with a text from James:

> Heading over now. Stay put and I'll see you in five.

And, oh god, I'm definitely buzzed. Three Dark 'N' Stormys in less than an hour will do that to you. Okay, best foot forward, best foot forward, I can do this.

I look around at the mess I've made and realize this is the

extreme opposite of best foot forward. In a panic, I grab the napkin that's still full of shrimp and shove it into my purse, along
with the tampons and the stray receipts that are still fluttering
around. I may not be able to sober up before they get here, but at
least I can hide some of the evidence.

I snap it shut just as they walk in, noticing the bartender giving me a weird look. But if he wants that lone wrinkled dollar I
just found under my pile of receipts, he better keep his mouth
zipped.

"James!" I say, a little too enthusiastically, my cheeks burning
from embarrassment and alcohol. But the game must go on. The
show is afoot. Or something. Oh god, I'm buzzed. I have to shake
it off. I have to dazzle them. Stick to the plan. Operation "charm
the hell out of my bosses and maybe they'll remember me when
promotion time swings around" is a go.

"Stella! George," I say, leaning forward to air-kiss their cheeks
as they come closer. See, I can be fucking delightful.

James tilts his head, his eyes going a little squinty as if he's
trying to figure something out. But there is *nothing* to figure out.
This is me on my A game. Even if I my head feels a little sluggish
and loud and my skin feels hot and flushed. I'm *fine*.

"I see you've been having a lot of fun," Stella says.

"Yep!" I pop my *p*. I don't mean to; it just happens. "I was
waiting for you guys to finish rehearsing. Are you done?" I lean
forward in a way that I hope looks conspiratorial. "Are you rehearsed?"

"We're rehearsed, all right." James smiles. "I think Cara was
sweating worse than you are right now."

I smack his arm, but then rub my hand over it in case his mom is looking. I flash Stella what I hope is my soberest smile and keep talking.

"Where is the birthday girl anyway?" When James stares at me, I realize what I just said. "Bridal girl, I meant. Bride girl? Is that—"

"Bride?" James asks. The bartender sets a fresh glass down in front of my empty one, but James snags it before I can with a quick "Oh, thanks." I pout, but he gives me a look that tells me I'm probably not pulling off my sober act as well as I thought.

"I'm sure she's around her somewhere," George says. "It's her big weekend after all! Probably just went to freshen up."

"Speaking of freshening up," I say, sensing an opportunity, "I have some ideas for freshening up the gym."

Stella's eyes narrow and James shifts nervously beside me and yes, maybe it's the alcohol giving me the courage to pitch right here and right now, but—

"She has so many great ideas," James says, talking over me. "Maybe we can talk about them later! When she's got some food in her! Or even better when *we're not at Cara's wedding?*" He looks at me urgently, but whatever he's trying to tell me doesn't compute because I've pulled off the perfect segue and now it's time to close the deal.

"Or we could do it now!" I spin on my stool to show them what a fantastic idea I think this is.

James frowns. "I don't think—"

"You should give me the promotion!" I blurt out with a smile. A tiny, sober corner of my brain starts shrieking but I ignore it.

Stella and George's faces freeze in polite horror. "We don't really need to talk about that now, dear," George says, patting my arm gently as he and Stella start to walk past me.

"No, wait." I kick up my foot, trapping them behind my outstretched leg. "I want to. It's fine. I mean, dinner doesn't start yet, right, so we could just talk about it over drinks. I have so many ideas. We could add new classes! I could . . . I could also help with the design process inside. Just because James convinced you to put the cardio bunnies near the windows doesn't mean that people who lift heavy don't want a view too. You think only runners like birds? No! And that's the kind of innovative thinking you need for your team. Bird-watching! A plus."

Stella flashes me a pained smile and turns to walk the other way, but I shoot my other leg out to form a double barrier. Success! They are now fully trapped. "We can and should talk it out right now." I grin.

I think James tries to stop me. I *know* the bartender makes cutting motions against his neck. But it isn't until the shrimp waitress walks by, her face twisted up in equal parts disgust and concern, that it full and truly hits me what I'm doing.

And oh, oh god. I've ruined it. I'm going to be sick.

"I have to . . . I have to go!" I say, jumping up and rushing toward the bathroom.

"Lizzie!" James calls, but I shake him off and I run.

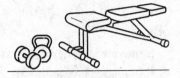

Chapter Six

I forgo the bar bathroom for one farther away, down the labyrinthian hallways and in the back of the building, where I'm sure no one will find me. The urge to get sick has passed, but not the urge to be somewhere far, far away from that rehearsal dinner. I even let the bathroom door slam shut behind me for good measure.

I make my way to the sink, porcelain and deep set into a dark mahogany vanity that uncomfortably reminds me of a giant monster opening its jaws, and set my hands on the edge, eyeing myself in the mirror.

My hair is disheveled, its unruly waves toeing the line between beachy and unkempt, while my eyes are glassy and bloodshot. A smear of mascara has found its way to the side of my temple. I look deranged.

I let myself imagine for one quick second that I could just flush myself down the toilet. Dive deep down the drains and come out somewhere with the sewer alligators and other monsters. Somewhere they won't judge me because we're all disasters. A clubhouse with an entry sign that reads ONLY TRUE FUCKUPS NEED APPLY.

I'm about to flick the faucet on and scrub the makeup off my face—there's no way I'm heading back to the rehearsal dinner now—when I hear the tiniest sniffle. And then another. And another.

Someone is in here.

Someone who's definitely trying not to let me hear them cry.

I turn the faucet on, giving them some privacy, but curiosity gets the better of me and I lean over to peer beneath the stall door. A lone pair of extremely high heels, the delicate gold straps in stark contrast to the dark wood all around us, peeks out from beneath the stall at the far end of the room. I would cry too if I had to walk in those.

I stand back up and lean against the counter. I'm tempted to turn the faucet off and just leave, but that seems like breaking some kind of code. Drunk girls don't leave other girls to cry alone in the bathroom, right? Isn't that the point? And besides, I might suck at a lot of things, but I'm the world's best hype woman. Ask James.

I walk to the front of her stall, and not sure what else to do, I raise my hand and knock gently.

"Occupied!" she snaps.

"No, I know," I say, my hand falling down. "But . . . are you okay in there?"

"What?"

"It just, it sounds like you're crying."

"It's allergies," she says, her tone cold through the closed door.

"Okay, then," I say. "Look, I was just trying not to be in violation of girl code, but I can see you're fine, so ignore me, I guess." I walk back toward the faucet and turn it off, fully intending to leave her be, when the stall door clicks open.

"What girl code?"

I fall back a little when I realize it's the same hot girl from the hallway earlier. Her eyes are red and puffy in a way that's definitely more tears than allergies. "Um," I say, swallowing hard because she is somehow so, so cute, even now, and I—

"'Um'?" she asks, wiping her nose with a tissue. "You knocked on my door and invoked girl code. I expected more than an 'um.'" My face must look panicked because she shakes her head. "I'm kidding, relax."

She walks over to the sink and washes her hands, her immaculate French manicure disappearing under a mountain of bubbles as she does. She looked good in a ponytail and workout gear earlier, but now, with her long hair piled on top of her head, her makeup all done up—somehow still perfect, despite the tears; what *is* her secret?—and that silky pink dress that hugs her body like it was made for her . . . I'm in lust. Head over heels. Sign me up to be the cliché date bagging a bridesmaid, I don't even care. James can have the hotel manager; all I need is *her*.

"You're staring," she says, drying off her hands.

"You're so pretty," I blurt out before I can catch myself. In full gay panic, I switch gears and detour right into my hype routine. "Where did you get that dress? I mean, stunning. And your makeup? Flawless! Despite the, uh, allergies."

She eyes me, still sniffling, and I snap my purse open—the perfect excuse to look away before she realizes I've gone all heart eyes on her. "I have extra-soft tissues in here somewhere. Beats the toilet paper you're using." I dig around deeper, only to pull out a napkin full of shrimp. Perfect. Wow. I love my life.

"Is that . . . ?" Her face contorts into a pained expression.

I stand frozen with my handful of smuggled crustaceans. "Unfortunately."

"I'm going to need to hear the story of how you ended up with a purse full of shrimp, you know that, right?"

"I'll share my sob story, if you share yours."

"What makes you think I have one?"

"Most people don't hide in out-of-the-way bathrooms to deal with their *allergies* if they don't."

"Fair point." She hops up onto the counter and swings her feet as she smiles at me. "But you go first."

I hold out the napkin to her as an offering, but she shakes her head. I shrug and pop some shrimp in my mouth before throwing the rest away. The woman laughs, which makes my stomach twist in a good way. And I know with absolute certainty I'm double drunk now: not just on alcohol, but also on the butterflies that I've been mainlining since I saw her face again.

She sits and waits, the pink satin gleaming against her faintly tanned skin. How is she not afraid of stains or wet spots or any of the other thousands of things that would definitely plague me if I attempted anything half as daring as *sitting* on a bathroom counter?

"You zoning out on me?" she finally asks and I blink the world back into focus.

"Sorry, sorry. I had a bit too much to drink tonight—which, long story short, is how I wound up in this bathroom with a purse full of shrimp, just in time to hear your allergies kick in."

"Why did you drink so much?"

"Open bar." I shrug and she raises her eyebrows.

"You're here for the wedding, then?"

"Isn't everybody? I think Stella booked the whole place. What are you? A bridesmaid? Cousin? How'd you get wrangled into coming to this shitshow?"

"Something like that," she says softly, "but it's your sob story right now, not mine." She waves her hands for me to continue.

"Fine. I came here with my friend James, who's like . . ." I sigh, trying to figure out how to put our friendship into words. "He's the best even if he makes the worst life choices sometimes. He's basically a brother to me." She makes a face, but I move on. "Anyway, I said I'd come with him even though I don't even know the bride. I figured I might as well, it's all I've been hearing about at work forever and—"

"At work?"

"Yeah, so the bride, Cara, I guess? Her parents own a bunch of gyms, and I work at one. Her mom's constantly coming in all tense, barking at me to do this or that for the wedding since she's 'paying me anyway.'"

"She does not!"

I nod solemnly. "She definitely, definitely does. I didn't even mind that much at first though, because I thought it would win me brownie points."

"Why do you need brownie points? Isn't doing your actual job enough?"

"Nothing is enough for Stella. Which is the main reason I'm here, to get more face time and win her over."

"Meaning . . . you came here to suck up?"

I nod a little too hard, the alcohol still making my brain feel cloudy. I tell her all about the promotion that's opening up and how James is helping me. I tell her about his plan to get me here and how it would help both of us. I thought she might judge me for using a wedding to schmooze, but she doesn't. She seems more focused on James than anything.

"That's really cool of him," she says, like it hurts her to admit it. "I'm surprised he—"

"He's not like his parents, if that's what you're thinking. He's great."

"I wasn't thinking anything," she says, but I can tell she's lying. "But if tonight is the big night, why are you hiding in this bathroom eating shrimp?"

"I'm getting to that!" I sigh. "Look, you gotta understand, I really want this to work out. It's not just a paycheck to me. I actually fucking love gyms. I love the people, I love helping them get healthy and stay healthy. I love when women come in and they think they can't lift heavy and then they see me lifting and I don't know, like—you can be strong *and* feminine, if you want to be, right? It's not either/or." I flex my bicep. "Like maybe some people don't think this is hot, but it is. Strength is hot. Strength isn't just for dudes. I'm tired of feeling like I'm a traitor for skipping the elliptical and grabbing the weights. I want to foster a robust woman's lifting program, but I'm not into women-only gyms. I get why people do like that, but I want it to be a safe, welcoming space for everyone. I don't want to feed into the idea that we have to hide ourselves away from the guys."

She beams at me, and I blush.

"What? Do I have shrimp in my teeth or something?"

"No," she says, "I just love how passionate you are. I haven't felt that about anything in a long time."

"Blame it on the booze?" I lie, embarrassed, because I can get this fired up about it any time and maybe that's a little weird. I flexed my arm at her, for god's sake.

She narrows her eyes. "No, it seems pretty legit."

"Yeah, well, too bad I sabotaged myself, then."

"How though? Dinner hasn't even started."

I check the time on my phone, ignoring the ten thousand texts from James. "It definitely has," I say. "James is freaking out."

"I think we still have time to get there, if you want."

"Uh, no. I definitely do *not* want."

"What did you *do?*" She laughs, but I can tell she's not laughing at me; more like we're in on the same terrible joke. She leans impossibly close, her tongue darting out to wet her lips. For a second, I let myself wonder what would happen if I just leaned forward and—

No, stop it. You're better than this. Or at least you need to try to be. You cannot make out with a crying woman in a bathroom when you're wasted. This isn't senior year. Act like an adult. A *real* adult!

"It's the alcohol," I say. "I may have had a drink or three while I was waiting for them to come out. So, by the time the time they did . . ."

"You were blitzed with a purse full of shrimp?" she helpfully supplies.

"Yeah. But that's not even the worst of it."

"It gets . . . *worse?*" she all but shrieks, covering her mouth to hide the laughter.

And maybe it's the booze, or the way her skin is pebbling up from the coolness of the marble she's sitting on, or the way the light keeps catching in her eyes. But I realize there is nothing I want more in this world right now than to keep the smile on her face and the laughter on her lips, so I tell her. *Everything.*

"You trapped Stella and George between your *legs?!*"

I peek from between my fingers and nod.

She laughs so long and hard that I can't decide if I want to crawl into a stall and never come out or listen to that sound forever. But when she blurts out an "oh my god, you're fantastic," I'm positive I'm exactly where I want to be.

I blush again, shaking my head and staring at the floor. "Yeah, and that's how I got here. And if I wasn't 99 percent sure that I left my key on the bar, I'd be heading straight to my room to hide after this. Forever."

"I, for one, am really glad you decided to hide here instead."

"Me too," I say, moving even closer to her. "Alright, you've heard my horror story. You gonna tell me yours?" I lean my hip against the counter. We're only a few inches apart now, and I can smell her perfume better—lilacs maybe, and a hint of something citrusy. It reminds me of the lemon trees that my grandma used to grow outside on our deck during the summer. I used to think those trees were my favorite scent in the entire world, even though they had to live under grow lights in my basement every winter. But I was wrong.

She leans into me, bumping her arm against my shoulder, and I fight the urge to lean right back. I wonder if she feels this infusion of butterflies too. The way she lets her skin linger against mine says she might.

But then her throat clears, ending the moment. "I still haven't heard about the shrimp though."

She's deflecting, but I roll my eyes and tell her that part too. Our bodies are inching closer and closer when she says, "Let me see if I got everything: you got drunk at an open bar, robbed a shrimp waitress, and then tried to kidnap my—the bride's parents?"

I tilt my head. "It was less of a kidnapping and more of a hostage situation, to be fair."

A smile spreads across her face. "Right, yeah. To be fair."

"And I did try to put some of the shrimp back."

"You didn't!" she yelps, absolutely horrified.

"Yeah, that was the waitress's reaction too. Thus, the whole hiding-them-in-my-purse thing. Destroy the evidence and all that."

"Okay." She laughs. "Thank you. I needed that." She hops off the counter like she's going to leave, and I reach for her arm without thinking. Her skin is warm and soft in the palm of my hand.

"Your turn, remember?"

"Wow, you really do work out," she says, looking at where my hand meets her forearm. I let her go, embarrassed.

"Sorry, I—"

"No, fair is fair. This is what I get for hoping you were too drunk to remember."

"Never. Now, your sob story," I say, tapping her cheek, which is thankfully dry again. No more tears tonight, not on my watch. "Go."

She takes a deep breath. "Okay, I was dragged here by someone else too. And at this point I'd rather be anywhere else."

"Oh, are *they* the friend of the bride, then, not you?" I ask, playing the pronoun game. I don't exactly want her to have a girlfriend . . . but her having a boyfriend wouldn't get me any closer to knowing if she was firmly in the "dudes only" camp. At least a girlfriend would confirm we're somewhat on the same team.

"He's close with the bride." She frowns.

Okay, *he*. Well, that doesn't necessarily mean anything. She could be bi, or pan, or . . . I could be misreading everything, as usual. And just because she came with him doesn't mean they're *together*-together, right? I came with James and look how that works. He's probably in some security room making out with the hottest hotel manager I've ever laid eyes on right now.

I decide to press my luck. "Have you guys been together long?"

"I guess. A couple years but—"

Fuuuuuck. Okay, switch gears. Supportive friend. Supportive friend. Supportive friend. Supportive new friend that you definitely don't want to lick the lipstick off of.

Friendship. Nothing else.

She narrows her eyes as if she can see inside my head. "But I don't think he's the one. He hasn't been for a long time."

"Oh," I say softly.

"But what can I do? I can't break up with him at a wedding!"

"Why not?"

Her eyebrows hit the ceiling. "Don't you think that's kind of a dick move?"

"I don't know, aren't weddings like massive hookup spots? If you can *start* a relationship at a wedding, I don't see why you can't *end* one."

She looks at me like she's not convinced, and her eyes start watering again. And no, no, no, no, no, I just got her to stop.

"Look, if this guy was it for you, you wouldn't be crying in the bathroom with the drunk shrimp lady. Like, be better than that, c'mon."

I don't know if it's my buzz or the stress or the fact that she's so pretty and smells so good, or some combination of all of that, but I want to wipe her tears. I want to wipe her tears and make her laugh and kiss her until she forgets all about whatever loser guy sent her hiding in here in the first place.

But I know I can't. I don't have a ton of moral hang-ups but dating people in relationships crosses a line I'm not comfortable with.

"Okay, new plan," I say and take a deep breath. "Do you want to talk this out more or do you just want to go straight to a hype session? I can tailor my bathroom speeches to whatever you need."

"I think just the hype," she says with a sniffle. "I can't take any more allergies right now; my mascara is barely hanging on as it is."

"You look perfect," I blurt out.

"Wow, you switch to hype mode fast."

"Yeah," I lie, because that was all 100 percent me. "You're beautiful, you're perfect, even your elbows are cute," I say, in for a penny, in for a pound.

"My elbows."

"You must have a very distinguished moisturizing routine, and I'm envious." I tap my elbow and raise it to her face. "You see this elbow? This is a pauper's elbow." I hold up my fingers. "And look, calloused hands. I'm terrible at moisturizing, and my hands are all toughened up from lifting."

"But lifting is cool though!"

"Yeah, but this isn't about me. This is about you and your perfect elbows and how anyone would be lucky to have you. If he's not making you feel good about yourself every day, then dump his ass. Now. Don't wait until it's you trapped at the altar with a momzilla forcing employees to tie Jordan almonds in tulle for you. You deserve someone that makes you happy."

I pause to make sure she's still paying attention and she is. She looks so serious, nodding along with me as I rant: "You deserve someone who wants to make every day of your life the best day of your life, whether that means some stupid grand gesture or just grabbing your favorite candy bar when they stop to get gas. Someone who doesn't just know how you take your coffee, but the movies you like, the songs; someone who wants to know what makes you tick. Don't settle for anything less. Listen, I've known you like five minutes, maybe seven if we count you helping me get in my room, and I can already tell that you're really goddamn great. I don't know the particulars of your situation, mainly because you broke our deal and won't tell me." That gets another tiny laugh out of her. "But if you're not getting that from whatever guy dragged you here? Don't be like me. Don't sit behind the gym counter of your life when you're meant to be in front of it."

And okay, maybe that metaphor made more sense in my head, but I'm doing my best here, thinking on the fly and all, three sheets to the wind.

She wipes at her eyes again, and then wraps me in the tightest, warmest hug. "Thank you. I needed to hear that," she says, looking at me out of the side of her eye. "I just . . . I wanted 'okay' to be good enough. But I think I deserve more than okay? Maybe? I don't even know what I'm even saying right now."

"Dude," I groan, dropping my head back. "You do. You definitely do. People settling just robs other people of their perfect match, you know? Think of it like that: What if you two *both* have someone else out there waiting for you, but you're stuck with each other, being just okay? You'll hate his horror movies; he'll hate the fact that you wear socks to yoga. And one day you wake up eighty and your whole life was wasted on something that was just frustratingly okay."

"First all of, they're yoga slippers, not socks!"

"I knew it."

"What?"

"I knew you were too good to be true. Yoga is meant to be done barefoot. I'm banning you and your socks from my gym. It was nice meeting you, but you're dead to me now."

She rolls her eyes, but this time her smile feels genuine.

"I should get going, but you've given me a lot to think about." She tilts her head as if searching for my name, but I don't think I ever gave it to her.

"Lizzie," I say, holding out my hand. "I'm Lizzie."

"It's nice to meet you, Lizzie," she says, shaking it. "And I hope you come to the dinner, if only to save me."

"When you put it like that," I say. "Hey, if everyone's watching you dump your boyfriend, maybe they'll forget all about my little hostage-taking faux pas."

"Undoubtedly." She smirks, pulling the door open.

"Wait," I say, holding the door for her. "You didn't tell me *your* name."

"Oh, it's Cara," she says with a smile before disappearing down the hall.

And oh. Oh shit.

Chapter Seven

ames. James!" I shout, running up to him. Now that the bride-to-*hopefully*-be has arrived, the dinner itself is properly starting. The crowd moves from the bar to the reserved dining area, pushing me back as I try to shove my way through

The thick mahogany tables spill into the center of the room, heavy chairs topped with ornate cushions to give the space a rustic yet modern feel. In the middle of the table, interspersed with gorgeous floral arrangements, is the most delicious-looking bread I've ever seen. God, I'm hungry.

Focus, Lizzie, focus.

"James!"

He spins around and greets me with a relieved sort of smile. "Lizzie, thank god! You weren't in our room. I've been looking everywhere for you!"

"I'm here." I wince, my eyes darting to where Cara is standing with her boyfriend. No, *fiancé*, I correct myself. "And I think I really fucked up."

"You had too much to drink, it happens. Your timing could have been better, but we'll figure it out. I'm sure tomorrow you can take another stab at it. Just lay off the open bar."

I shouldn't bristle at that—he's absolutely right—but I do.

"Well, excuse me for getting nervous after being left alone all afternoon."

His brow furrows. "It's not my fault you decided to make friends with a bottle of rum, but if it makes you feel better to blame me, then go for it."

"What? No. I wasn't . . ." I sigh. My head is jumbled now, panic lacing through the once pleasant buzz of butterflies and booze. And, oh shit, the look Cara is giving to her intended right now is decidedly not good. She catches my eye and gives me a quick thumbs-up.

Fuck. FUCK.

"I can take it," he says. "If you want to be mad."

"James, no, this is serious! I—"

"They aren't going to write you off because you got drunk at a wedding, Lizzie, relax. Blocking them with your legs was weird but they'll get over it. I'm sure it's going to be okay."

"I'm not talking about—"

"Seriously, deep breath, Lizzie, it's not the end of the world, I promise." He pulls out my chair and gestures for me to sit beside him. Cara and the man who she's *supposed* to be marrying take their seats across from us.

I drop down, waiting for her to look up at me again. The second she does I widen my eyes and gesture to the side. She stares at me, a lost expression on her face. I jerk my head to the side harder, doing my best to indicate that she should meet me out in the hall, but she continues to give me a confused look . . . until her partner pulls the menu out of her hands, distracting us both.

"I wasn't done with that," Cara says, trying to pull it back. "I haven't decided."

"I'll take care of it, babe," he says, running his eyes down the page in front of him. It's a limited menu, no doubt painfully and deliberately selected by Stella and the chef over a thousand Zoom meetings. Speaking of, George and Stella take their seats beside Cara, looking at their soon-to-be son-in-law approvingly.

"Very romantic, Max," Stella says, leaning over Cara to playfully tap the groom on the arm.

"George sets the bar high." Max beams, his over-whitened teeth practically glowing even in the soft dinner lights. "I have big shoes to fill."

Both George and Stella simper at this, while Cara glares at her napkin.

"James," I whisper. "I have to talk to you about—"

"No more business talk till you're sober," he says, in a voice that's firmer than I'm used to. And I guess that's fair; for all he knows this is his sister's blissful wedding. He probably doesn't want to miss a thing. Or more like he's doing his best to come off as a doting, involved brother. I'm clearly not the *only* one trying to suck up.

James and Cara aren't all that close in real life—not that I'm an expert on sibling dynamics, being an only child myself. But I know they don't talk that often, and he's only flown out to see her once in the entire five years I've known him, and mostly because it lined up with some event in the city and he needed a place to crash. He's flown out way more than that to meet his ex in Vegas, though, so does that one visit really even count? I always assumed siblings ranked above repeat exes in terms of commitment.

Whenever he's talked about Cara, especially lately with this "perfect wedding" on the table, there's always been a weird undercurrent of competitiveness there . . . which is probably why he doesn't seem to notice how unhappy she looks right now. But still, it's hard to believe she never confided in him even a little. Cara couldn't have just bottled it all up until it exploded out of her in a dingy bathroom, could she?

Okay, so maybe the bathroom wasn't dingy and "exploded out of her" isn't really the image I'm going for, but the sentiment remains.

She looks miserable and not a single person here seems to notice but me.

I glance down the table at the pile of guests and realize for the first time that there's hardly anyone her age. No bustling, laughing bridesmaids or groomsmen, just a few stray cousins filling in. No giggling friends in the background. It's mostly her parents' friends here today. Max seems to have a few guys that keep punching him in the arm as they walk by, but where are Cara's people?

"Cara, how'd you pick this place?" James asks, smiling. "It's awesome."

"Oh, you know I had to help her with all of that," Stella says, patting her daughter's arm. She reaches for the breadbasket with her free hand, chuckling a bit. "No carbs for you, dear. You have a dress to fit into tomorrow."

Cara shoots her mother a strained smile and then looks at the bowl of bread wistfully. I'm torn between telling her to flip her mom off and eat the goddamn bread and being glad she *isn't* doing that, which means the wedding is probably still on. Right?

Our eyes meet again.

"Lizzie," James says, nudging me with a little smile.

"Yes?" And then I realize the waiter is standing over me. "I'll have, um, a water, please, and, um . . ." I glance down at the menu—I've been too busy staring at Cara to actually look at it until now. "The steak," I say, because it's the first thing printed there.

"You don't like . . ." James says, but there's no time for whether I like or don't like food right now. I need this waiter to leave so I can get back to trying to smooth things over on every front. Sorry, Cara, but getting on Stella's good side trumps girl code when there's bills to pay.

"Are you excited for the big day tomorrow?" an older lady a few seats down asks Cara. An aunt maybe?

Cara shrugs. "This is really Max and Mom's deal. I've never been big on splashy things," she says in a tone that almost sounds like she's just realizing that now. "It's almost funny how little of me is in here."

And, oh god, what have I done. I have to fix this. I have to fix this immediately.

"Sure, but it'll be great," I say. "I'm sure you and Max will be *very* happy. Forever. Tomorrow's just the start." And okay, not the most elegant of deliveries, but hopefully I got the point across that she's definitely not supposed to take anything I said to heart. When I not-so-subtly implied that she should dump her boyfriend, I thought she was talking about, I don't know, a Tinder hookup that had passed its expiration date. Not a goddamn fiancé twenty-four hours from the altar.

"Cara, meet Lizzie," Stella says, a pained smile on her face. "You'll have to forgive her; she spent a little too much time with the bartender while we were at the church. She works at one of our gyms."

"I'm the front desk manager," I say, feeling proud of myself for managing not to slur even a little.

Beside me James folds and refolds his napkin nervously.

"Oh, we've met," Cara says.

James looks at me and I bite my tongue, trying not to snap *this is what I was trying to tell you about!!*

"Oh, really?" Stella asks.

Cara smiles. "Yes, we—"

"Cara helped me get into my room when my key card wasn't working," I cut her off. Beside me James lets out a little chuckle, probably remembering I called her "hot" before I knew who she was.

"And then Lizzie repaid the favor by giving me some great advice." Cara smiles.

"No, I didn't." I smile back, my jaw clenching.

"Yes, you did. Don't be modest." She reaches for the breadbasket, nabbing the last roll and taking a giant bite. And no. NO. "Mmm, this bread is so good." She smiles.

"What kind of advice?" James asks, tearing off half of *my* roll and popping it into his mouth. I instantly wonder if you can kill someone with that fancy bent butter knife this hotel uses. The edge is supremely dull and rounded, but I do lift, and with enough force . . .

Cara reaches for the butter. "Oh, we were just talking about—"

"How cool it is to be married," I blurt out. "Which you will be, tomorrow, and it'll be great! And, uh, which mascaras she won't sweat or cry off during the *big day*. When I'm at the gym working hard, I . . ."

Stella sets her glass down and James stares at me like I have two heads. Across from me, Cara scrunches up her eyebrows.

"Right, well," Stella says, breaking the awkward silence. "No hard work here, Max and Cara are meant to be. It's even their wedding theme," she says, and oh yes, the monogrammed "M+C meant to be" ribbons I've been tying around tulle baggies for weeks. How could I ever forget?

I try to meet Cara's eyes again, but she avoids me, diving into a deep conversation with her great-aunt.

"I think you should not talk anymore," James says, with just enough of a smile to know that he's teasing.

I groan. "I'm really crushing it this weekend."

"It's fine. At least know we know that you can't handle three drinks in an hour. That could be helpful in the future."

"Right," I grumble. "I'll remember that next wedding. But James, seriously, I need to—"

"James!" a booming voice calls.

"Uncle Dennis!" James hops up to hug the man walking up behind him. "This is my friend Lizzie . . ."

I don't hear the rest of what they say, instead burying myself in the work of eating an undercooked steak and praying that I haven't done anything tonight that can't be undone.

"Your phone," I mumble into my pillow. "Make it stop going off."

"You do it!" James calls from the other bed.

I came back to the room and went to bed right after dinner last night, after trying and failing to talk to Cara one last time. I wanted to be absolutely clear that the hype session in the bathroom about a hypothetical asshole was in no way meant to be a condemnation of *the actual groom*. But she just shushed me and said I'd "given her a lot to think about." When I insisted that no,

I definitely had not, she barricaded herself behind a wall of happy guests eager to congratulate her, and that was that.

James, however, had spent the night raging with his new soon-to-be brother-in-law. He crawled into the room around 2, maybe 3 A.M., so he's definitely going to be hurting today.

"Why do you even have the ringer on?" I groan and pull my pillow over my head.

"In case of emergency," he mumbles. "I told Max to come in here if he needed to puke, since he was splitting a room with my dad."

Okay, so Max can come puke in our bathroom, but I can't get spit on the mirror? Talk about double standards. And then I realize what he just said . . .

"Why is he splitting a room with your dad?"

"I don't know," he whines, reaching for his phone and managing to knock it off the nightstand and under my bed. "Mom wanted to do a 'girls only' night last night. She kicked my dad out, which just left Max's room."

"Weird," I say. The phone finally stops ringing and we both sigh and nestle into our pillows like *glad that's over.*

"Probably wanted to talk about extending my car's warranty," he mumbles, burying his face in his pillow.

We both drift off, trying to sleep through our respective hangovers since we don't need to actually be up or moving around until closer to 4 P.M. for this 7 P.M. wedding. But then, barely an hour later, his phone starts ringing again, and this time it doesn't stop.

"James. James!" I yell and throw a pillow at him for good measure. His phone is still under my bed, making it echo even more. "Answer your damn phone!"

"What time's it," he slurs.

I glance at my phone just as his stops ringing, only to start back up again. "Ten-thirty."

"Too early."

I flip my blankets back with a huff and grab his phone. "It's your dad," I say, staring at the screen just as the ringing stops again.

"Probably just wants to yell at me for getting Max trashed. Don't answer it."

"Doesn't this defeat the purpose of keeping your ringer on for emergencies?" I punch his code in the phone, a four-digit combination of his favorite football players' numbers, and go to missed calls. "Holy shit. James, you have like thirty missed calls here from your parents. Oh, wait, that first one this morning was Cara."

"Cara?" He bolts up in bed. "Why would she call?" He grabs his phone out of my hands and tries to call her, but his dad calls at the same time and James accidentally answers that instead.

"Hey, Dad," he says, stretching the words out in a semi-apologetic way. "If this is about me keeping Max out too late—

"What? When? Okay, I'll—yeah, just let me throw on some pants and I'll be right down."

He hangs up and scrolls back over to call his sister, before throwing the phone onto the bed in frustration. "Her phone's off!"

"What's going on? What did your dad want?"

"What is she even thinking right now? What could possibly be going through her head?" James gets up and starts frantically clawing through his sheets, hopping into his pants from yesterday before rushing into the bathroom and slamming the door.

And okayyyyy. I'm about to knock and ask again what's up. But then I hear what sounds like a growl coming from the other side, followed by the sound of him slamming his hand on the sink. A beat later his electric toothbrush flicks on.

I perch myself on the chair across from the bathroom door instead and run through various scenarios. He said "what is *she* thinking," so I can only imagine what Stella did now. Insult the caterer until they quit? Screamed so loud all the flowers wilted?

But when James pulls the bathroom door open a minute later, he doesn't look mad, he looks sad, and maybe even a little scared. I jump up, not used to seeing him like this. James is the funny one, the lighthearted one.

"What happened?" I ask softly.

He slumps against the doorframe. "Cara's gone. The one time she reaches out to me, and I didn't even pick up the phone."

"What?" I ask, my stomach dropping to my toes. "What do you mean, gone?"

"She left! She's gone! The wedding's off! My parents are fucking losing it. *Max* is fucking losing it."

"Why would she leave?" I ask, terrified that I already know.

"I don't know." James runs his hands through his hair and then shakes his head. "I called her a few months back, to ask a question for Mom, and Cara was so not into the wedding . . . It was weird, but I chalked it up to just nerves. Normal shit. She was fine. She was *fine*," he says again, and I don't know if he's trying to convince me or himself. "When you talked to her about makeup or whatever, she was good, right?"

"Yeah," I lie, not sure if now is the right time to come clean. "Totally."

And okay, call me selfish, but the relief of knowing I wasn't the cause of this washes over me. If she was already getting cold feet two months ago, I can hardly be blamed for our convo last night. This is great news. Well, not great news but better than the worst it could be.

"She left a note."

"What'd it say?"

"It said a lot of things were put in perspective for her last night, and she was sorry, but she couldn't go through with the wedding." James looks up at me with the saddest face. It feels like a weight, no, like an entire grand piano, was just dropped on my head.

"Last night?" I ask, even though I really *really* don't want that confirmed.

"Oh shit, do you think she cheated on him? Is that why my mom kicked my dad out? Was she covering for her?"

"What? No. No!" I say, because at least I know that much to be true. Even if a part of me wanted to give her that level of . . . um . . . *perspective* before I knew who she was, I definitely didn't. I may have been roaring drunk, but I'd remember *that*.

"Yeah, you're probably right. But how could she do this? This is going to kill Mom! And Max is like *so* chill. He was teaching me all about Bitcoin last night!"

"Maybe he just isn't the one for her?" I say quietly, hoping I'm wrong. But Bitcoin? Seriously? I would have run too.

"He's her person, trust me. Do you know he's like low-key planning to run for office someday? She could have been with the next fucking Obama or some shit. That's like winning at life. And now she blew it all up for what? What the hell is she thinking? Someone must have got to her, bad."

"I don't think political aspirations count as—"

"I swear to god," he cuts me off. "If I find out who messed with her head last night, I'm going to kill them. I will. No questions asked. Even if it's my great-aunt Edna or something."

I swallow hard. "Yeah," I say, "and I'll . . . I'll bail you out." I force the familiar refrain out of my mouth. I'm so fucked.

Chapter Eight

It's taken two weeks for life to regain some semblance of normalcy.

Or at least for Stella to stop wailing every time she comes in about how she's embarrassed and humiliated, that her social status is ruined, that the senator's refusing to show up for their doubles matches, and that Max's family is apparently determined to blacklist hers from . . . I don't actually know what. Something about wine or wineries or something. Given that this winery almost-wedding was the first I had ever heard of there being any sort of familial interest in such a thing, I'm surprised that matters. The way Stella goes on and on about not even being able to show her face at a wine tasting again, you'd think she was a sommelier in training.

I have tried on three separate occasions these last fourteen days to tell James the truth about my conversation with Cara in the bathroom . . . but his constant declarations of wanting to kill whoever ruined his chance of being future brother-in-law to the president—alternating with guilt for not picking up his sister's call—made me squash that notion. Permanently.

Not to mention the fact that he still constantly extolls the virtues of Max to the point where, if he wasn't regularly sneaking away to FaceTime Ramón, I would assume he was preparing to marry Max in Cara's stead. I guess one night of drinking till you puke will bond you like that.

So yeah. Definitely not the right time to tell him.

Besides, Cara took off—rumor is she went on the honeymoon by herself. I'm sure once she comes back to the States, she'll disappear into the ether from whence she came. It's not like she was a factor in my life before this, and she won't be after. She's not even taking her parents' calls and has only texted James once saying she "needed a minute to regroup." I'm sure she'll settle back into her other, more important, big-city life soon, rendering all of this a giant nonissue I shouldn't even waste brain space on.

Telling James, or god forbid his parents, about my little role in this runaway bride fiasco would only pour kerosene on a fire that is finally starting to burn itself out. Besides, it's not like James isn't full-on preening over suddenly going from the family disappointment to the golden child overnight. I don't really get this supercompetitive thing he has with his sister, but overall, this is kind of a win-win. A new, better, hopefully drama-free normal that we're all finally getting used to.

Which is why, when I open James's door to pick him up for an early morning gym session before my workday starts, I'm shocked to find Cara in his kitchen wearing one of his oversize T-shirts like a nightgown.

I manage to drop not one but both of the protein shakes in my hands. One of them pops its lid, sending the chocolatey liquid spilling all over his newly refinished wood floors.

"Oh!" Cara says, spinning around. She's holding a spatula, little bits of eggs stuck to it as she makes some sort of morning scramble. She pulls an AirPod out of her ear with a guilty expression.

"Sorry, I—" I lose my voice at the sight of her wide eyes, her perfectly ruffled bed head. I trail my gaze over the curves of her body, some visible even through the T-shirt, and down the skin of her legs.

Shit, shit, shit.

"Here, let me help! James said you'd be stopping by. Sorry," Cara says, gesturing to the remaining AirPod in her ear. "Got sucked into this podcast and lost track of time. I would have put on more clothes, I swear."

She grabs a roll of paper towels off the counter and crouches in front of me to soak up the spill. The shirt slides up just enough to show a hint of her seafoam-green boy shorts underneath and I resist the urge to lean back, just a little, for a better look. God, I'm going to hell.

"No, hey, let me," I say, crouching down beside her and soaking up all the spots she missed. And then it becomes a battle of towels, both of us trying to out-clean the other from guilt or awkwardness.

"You're here," I say, when she finally stops cleaning. We're both wearing some of the shake now, little splatters on my nylon leggings, a bit of it dappling her toes—I'm trying not to notice her flawlessly painted toenails.

I should be terrified that she's going to tell her brother that it was me who told her to run. I should be worried her mother will put a hit out on me after that, if I somehow survive James's wrath. I should be worrying about a thousand other things, but instead all I can do is wonder what shade of pink her nail polish is. It's probably got some cute name like Kitten Mittens or Everything's Rosy.

"Yeah, I got in late last night. I hope that's okay?" she asks, pulling me from my thoughts.

"Why?"

"Why am I here or why do I hope it's okay?"

"Both, I guess," I say, taking the massive pile of soaked paper towels from her and combining it with my own before heading over to the trash can to toss them.

Cara wipes her hands, leaving faint tan spots on the sides of her shirt. James's shirt, really, from the pile he leaves for people during impromptu sleepovers. I wonder if it's weird having your sister wearing one of your hookup shirts. I wonder if she knows. I decide not to tell her. I wish I didn't know, to be honest.

"I'm here because Max asked for a few more weeks to get his stuff together and move out, and I figured it's the least I could do after, well, you know. I didn't really have anywhere else to go. There was no way I was going to my parents' house, and I couldn't go home, so I decided to capitalize a little on my brother's guilty conscience about missing my call." She smiles. "But don't worry, I won't be in the way. I promise."

"I wasn't worried about that."

"Okay, good. Because I just want you to know up front that I'm not going to insist on third-wheeling it with you guys. James has already filled me in on your sacred *Bachelor* nights and—"

"He did?"

"Shit, my eggs." Cara bolts to the stove as her pan starts to smoke. She dumps the largely charred and utterly unappetizing eggs onto her plate with a frown. Great. First I ruin her life, and now I ruin her eggs.

"You want my shake?" I ask, offering up the one that didn't spill.

She shakes her head. "No, I'm good on that. I hate how chalky they are."

"Oh, this one's not. Trust me, I tried like every single one. This one's actually great. I got your brother hooked on it too." I glance at where the spill was, a sticky spot all that's left. I should probably get some spray and clean it up for him. But also, he could have texted me a heads-up that his sister was going to be here, half naked, making breakfast.

The shower's going—no doubt James trying to wake himself up after another long night of sexting with the hotel manager. I guess at least something good came out of that weekend, even if the rest of it turned into a pit of despair, forever ruining his family's chances of being invited to wine tastings and political events they'd never been invited to in the first place.

"You are so thoughtful," Cara says, scraping her eggs into the garbage disposal and then grabbing a banana out of the bowl. "Seriously, the fact that you'd make him a second shake and then bring it over here all cold and perfect?" She hops up onto the counter, swinging her legs as she peels her banana. I wonder if sitting on counters is her thing, or if this is just the universe torturing me by bunching up her shirt even more.

I force my eyes up to her face and awkwardly mumble, "It's not that nice."

She ignores me.

"Where do I get a best friend like you? Even Max never did stuff like that for me, and we were getting married." She kicks her legs. "You know he would fake it in front of other people, like pretending to order for me at our rehearsal dinner. But this is nice. You coming here with a shake, thinking there's no one else to see it? It's real. That's love. There wasn't anything *real* between me and Max—romantic or otherwise—for a long time. You have a way of making that hit home for me, don't you?" She laughs, honestly laughs, and I want to die.

"Actually, about that—"

"It's okay," she cuts me off. "I'm not upset about the breakup other than, like, the headache of it all, and the money we lost on nonrefundable payments. Max and I had been over for a long time, you know? I just didn't want to admit it."

"Then why did you even say yes to him in the first place?"

"Because there was nothing really wrong, I just didn't . . . love him," she says, taking another bite from her banana. "But it was fine. We had been together for a while, and we mostly worked. His friends and my friends all got along. He looked good on my résumé, I looked good on his. It was easier to stay. And okay, the sex *was* next level."

I choke on my own spit when she says that, covering my mouth as I struggle to breathe. And no, thank you, I do not need to think about her having phenomenal sex while she's sitting here eating a banana and swinging her legs.

"Luckily I have an entire drawer of things that can take care of that for me whenever I want." She winks at me. Actually winks. "You made me realize that I need more from a partner. I want to have a real connection, an emotional connection. I deserve that."

I force my brain to reboot from the thought of her and her . . . drawer. "You do, but are you sure—"

"Oh, hey," James says, cutting me off as he comes around the corner. "I see you found Cara." He's in a towel, using a second one to dry his hair as he walks to his room. "I just need a minute to get dressed."

"Okayyyy," I say, as he shuts his door. "I'll just be out here."

... *praying you don't find out the truth about the mystery person in Cara's note. Fuck.*

The second the door shuts I turn back to her, my voice urgent. "You didn't tell him, right?"

"Tell him what?" she asks, hopping down off the counter to grab more eggs, along with some chopped peppers and onions, out of the fridge.

I glance at James's door and step closer, lowering my voice. "You didn't tell him that I was the one who inspired your runaway bride act, did you?"

She looks confused. "Why? Is it supposed to be a secret?"

"Yes!"

She tilts her head. "You don't want him to know that you helped me when I was in a jam? I would think that would be a plus, not a minus."

And is that what I did? Is that what she calls leaving her fiancé at the altar the morning of their wedding? Being stuck in a jam?

"It's not that I don't want anybody to know that we talked, it's just that I don't want anybody to know what we talked *about*." I scrunch up my face, realizing how that must sound. "Your family is really upset about what happened."

"Don't I know it," she says, sprinkling a handful of vegetables into the pan. "Nothing like your own family siding with your ex in the breakup. James has been pretty cool about it other than accusing me of stealing his Jackie O moment when he picked me up from the airport last night, which doesn't even make sense! He'd be more like one of her evil stepbrothers or something."

I snort, I can't help it.

"My mother's been driving me nuts about it though. I know she's just disappointed but it's too much!"

"You'd think it was her wedding that was ruined or something."

Cara mumbles something under her breath that sounds suspiciously like "it basically was" as she cracks the eggs into a bowl and begins whisking them together.

I lean against the counter. "I'm just worried that if they find out it was me . . . I work for them, you know. I have to—"

"Oh, right, yeah, did you get that promotion?"

"I haven't applied." I cringe. "I've been too mortified after what I did at your *almost* wedding."

She rolls her eyes. "Well, I think I successfully diverted their attention from your shrimp stealing slash attempted kidnapping, so you should be good to go."

"Yeah, thanks for that, I really owe you," I snark. "But seriously, if they knew I had anything to do with this, they might make my job harder, or worse. I downplayed our conversation to James. He thinks it was somebody else who 'got to you' that night. I need everyone to keep thinking that, okay? They can't find out I'm the person in your note."

She raises her eyebrows. "You think my mom would fire you just because we talked about how I deserve more in life? That's ridiculous. She's not like that."

I almost say that Stella is *exactly* like that, but I know Cara probably won't believe me. Even James doesn't. Instead, I try: "I just don't want to be caught in the middle."

Cara stirs her veggies a little harder. "I still can't believe she made you wrap all those almonds."

"I didn't mind," I lie, because it seems like the polite thing to say.

"I'm sure you did, but I don't know you well enough yet to call you out, so I'll just thank you for your service to the wedding that never was. And I'll keep my mouth shut about our bathroom hype session, if it's that important to you." She sets the spatula down, pouring the eggs into the pan, and then turns to look at me. "But I do feel weird about lying about the best thing that ever happened to me."

"It's not lying if it doesn't come up, right?" I say, trying to ignore the fact that, in a super roundabout way, if you squint, she just called me "the best."

"I'm sure it will come up," she huffs. "It *always* comes up. You should tell James though, seriously. If you guys are best friends, you should be able to talk to each other."

"We do talk to each other. Just not about *that*, okay? Can you trust me on this?"

"Fine—answer one question, and I'll keep your secret."

"Anything," I say, instantly relieved and maybe low-key hoping she's about to ask me on a date. I'd say no, probably, but still.

Cara narrows her eyes. "Are you secretly in love with my brother?"

Wow. Not where I thought we were going at all.

"Uh, no. You do remember he's gay, right?"

"Obviously, but that doesn't mean that *you* don't have—"

"He's my best friend, yes, but there's nothing romantic there."

"Okay, I just had to ask."

"Why?" And I mean *why did you have to ask*, but I guess she thinks I mean *why did you think that was a possibility at all* because she answers, "The way you talked about him in the bathroom that night? It felt like love."

Oh. Right. This isn't the first time that people have gotten the wrong idea. "Well, it is, but not the romantic kind."

Cara points the spatula at me. "You're positive? Because I swear I get a little bit of 'meant to be' vibes off of you."

"Like you and Max?" I tease.

She snorts. "Touché."

"Trust me, I couldn't be less of his type if I tried, and he couldn't be less of mine." My mind wanders to the hot hotel manager James is no doubt boinking by now. He says they're getting serious, which means he probably has a month or so before he blurts out "I love you" and the guy bolts, leading us right back to sitting on my couch eating takeout and crying over Queen Cassie again. "I love him to death, but I rarely go for guys, if you catch my drift?"

Cara narrows her eyes and turns back around with a little "hmm."

I'm debating whether to announce it's her that I have the crush on, given that she seems remarkably well-adjusted for someone who just jilted her groom, but then she adds, "Good to know," and turns back to her eggs.

Good to know?

Good to know?!

Before I can press for any more details, James appears in one of his dorky tank tops. This one says "Han Swolo" in that famous yellow Star Wars font. I look at him and shake my head.

"What are we talking about?" He pulls my shake out of my hand and takes a sip.

"Nothing," I say at the same time that Cara says, "How cute you guys are and how people could get the wrong idea."

"Let them." James puts me in a headlock and says in baby talk, "Who's the cutest, we're the cutest," which, thanks for that, I kidney punch him and then stand up to fix the hair that he has definitely just noogied out of its bun.

"Owwwwww," he whines, rubbing his side. "Hitting me before a workout? You're a monster."

"No noogies, no kidney punches." I shrug. "You brought this on yourself."

I glance over at Cara, who is doing a terrible job of hiding the smile on her face. And right, I can see how to an outsider maybe this would look flirty. But there is only one person in this room who I'm interested in, and it's not my beloved himbo to my left.

"See," Cara says, her hands on her hips. "Adorable."

"If only she was a guy," James says wistfully, grabbing my chin. "Then she'd be the perfect package. Unless . . ."

"Definitely still a woman. Definitely not into dudes like you."

James mimes cursing the sky as Cara giggles.

"Maybe next lifetime they'll get your gender right," he says, like it's a given that if one of us were to change, it would be me.

"You know who else was cute?" Cara asks and points her spatula at James. "Jude."

Wait, what? Did she just say Jude? Jude—*Jude*? As in James's ex-boyfriend from hell?

Jude was a Tinder find that should have never been swiped on. A random hookup turned six-month "love affair," if you can even call it that, considering how Jude spent most of it alternating between leaving James on read and love bombing him. It was toxic with a capital *T*.

I flash James a worried look and he shakes his head.

"Shit, I just realized my sneakers are in the car, Lizzie. I'll meet you out there." He rushes toward the door and I guess that's one way to change the subject.

"Be there in a sec," I call after him.

James hesitates on the front step. "You're good today though, Cara? Right?"

"Yeah, go," she says, taking the subject change in stride. "I'm going by Aunt Edna's later."

"Good plan," he says, snapping his hands into finger guns. "She'll love that, and she won't tell Mom. She's been dodging her calls as much as you've been."

"Egg-zactly," Cara says, winking as she shovels her perfectly cooked replacement eggs onto the plate.

And oh my god, that was so, so bad, but also so goddamn cute.

Fuck.

Chapter Nine

"Are you shitting me right now?" James asks, turning his head so fast he nearly loses his balance mid–dead lift. We've been at the gym for about half an hour, most of which he's spent asking me what's wrong over and over again while I try to resist the urge to kick him. Leg day is usually my favorite day—I'm nothing if not the queen of squats—and he's ruining my reps with his real-life drama.

What's wrong is obviously that his sister is here, and might tell him about our little bathroom convo, and then he'll tell his parents, and then his parents will calmly explain that I'm fired for embarrassing them in front of the (state) senator. And then gone will be not only my dreams of a promotion, but also my entire life.

I'm not like James. I don't have a family that doubles as a safety net. I guess I'm *almost* like Cara in a way—took off running and tried not to look back. I just didn't get as far. And if shit hits the fan, there's not going to be anyone there to pick up the pieces but me. I don't have a safety net; I *am* the safety net.

Normally, I'm okay with that. I am. Seriously. I'm not some bitter person sitting around wondering why nobody loves me. Being on my own is a lesson I learned early and harshly, but I'm used to it. I'm good at it. It was actually harder to adjust to letting James in my life than it was to adjust to being alone.

But still, if I lose this job, I'm fucked, and not in any of the fun ways.

Which is why instead of telling him what's really bothering me, I've chosen to distract him with something that is also true . . . which is that I would totally bang his sister.

James sets his bar down, wipes the dust off his hands, and looks at me. "You seriously want to . . ." he says, trying to speak through laughter. "I knew you thought she was hot but—"

"Okay, okay, you don't have to laugh so hard."

"You know it's not that," he says, punching my shoulder gently. "It's just, you're you."

"What's that supposed to mean!"

"I mean, you don't date people. And she wouldn't like—no offense, but you're *really* not her type."

"I didn't say I wanted to date her, I said I would bang her. And I land plenty of women above my pay grade, thank you very much." He's right, and we both know it, but that doesn't mean I won't try to save face.

"'Above your pay grade'? Are you sure you're not a guy?" He punctuates the last sentence with mortifying hip thrusts.

I shove him out of the way and pull a couple plates off his bar before getting into position. "Positive, and even if I were, you wouldn't have a chance." I stand up, bringing the massive weights with me—a new PR—and then let them slam onto the ground. Okay, maybe the slamming part's not strictly necessary, but it just feels good.

"Yeah, because you're hoping to land my sister." He snorts and mimes throwing up.

Awesome.

God, I shouldn't have told him this. I was so panicked over him possibly realizing the real reason I was stressing that I just blurted out the first thing in my head. Okay. Okay, we need to change subjects.

"Speaking of hooking up, what was that shit about Jude? Please tell me you're not talking to that nightmare on legs again."

"God, no." He shudders. "He's probably the only boyfriend of mine she remembers. It's not like she was ever around for any of the nice ones. She's grasping at straws, trying to take her mind off things, I think. Yesterday, she asked me if I would consider going skydiving with her. Last night, she wanted us to start a dating podcast."

"A dating podcast? By the chronic codependent and his runaway bride sister?" I try and fail to stifle my laugh.

"It's not like I agreed! But yeah, this morning she's all about playing matchmaker." James shrugs. "I don't know, man. She's tearing through ideas and flailing hard."

I sigh and finish my reps. "Are you gonna tell her about Ramón? That'd get her off your back about setting you up."

"No way. At least not right now, when she's extra motivated to drop a new family scandal to get out of hers."

"You really think she would do that?"

We trade places, and he adjusts the weights. "No, but I never thought she'd leave Max at the altar either, freeing up that 'good kid' position for the first time in our lives. Mom would have a nervous breakdown if she knew I was dating someone from the hotel. I need to tread carefully on this one."

"That's ridiculous."

"That's my mom. She said my last boyfriend was beneath me and he was a dentist. She complained I didn't 'at least' bring home an oral surgeon!"

"God, what does she want?"

"Someone like Max, obviously. A hot, rich presidential hopeful with the type of connections she's been chasing her whole life. I wouldn't turn that down myself but . . ."

"You're horrible."

"I know." James sighs. "But for the first time, I'm not the screwup in the family. I want to keep it that way for as long as I can. Which means no one can find out about Ramón. At least not yet."

"You know that's fucked-up, right?"

He sets down the weights and I can tell I've struck a nerve. "Can we talk about something else?" James scratches his chin. "Like what about you. You've been going through a dry spell. You got anybody on your radar? Besides my sister, I mean, which is definitely not happening."

"Nope," I say, popping my *p*. "And I like it that way."

I'm lying to my best friend. Again. Because the truth is, I hate it this way. I've hated it ever since Cara stepped out of that bathroom stall and my brain started making heart eyes. But I can't *say* that. Especially not to her brother.

James snorts and looks around the gym. "How about him?" He points to a man in oversize headphones, bopping his head in the leg press.

"No."

"Them?" He points to Presley McGuinness, who is happily

jogging away on the treadmill. They've become a fixture at the gym ever since they moved back from college. They'd be more of a maybe than a no . . . but still.

"Why are you suddenly trying to pawn me off on people?"

"It's for your own good," he points out. "The way she was fishing about the whole Jude thing? And I heard her ask you if you were into me—so cute how much you love me, by the way." I smack his arm but he just grins. "My guess is that both of our single asses are on her matchmaking radar, at least until she decides to take up competitive bungee jumping or whatever ridiculous idea she googles next."

"Okay, but you *aren't* actually single, whether she knows it or not!" I say, doing my best to tamp down my disappointment. She wasn't asking because she was interested in me, she was asking on behalf of her weird little hobby-seeking spiral.

"First of all, Ramón and I are seeing each other. Not dating-dating. I'm taking it slow," he says. "Well, trying to. And second, you're the only one who knows Ramón and I even talk, let alone anything else, so for all intents and purposes, I'm single."

"Okay, but it's not like you're really going to go on dates with other people so you don't have to tell your family about him." I laugh but he doesn't, and my eyebrows shoot up. "James. Really?"

"You don't understand. It's . . . complicated."

I understand complicated family dynamics all too well, I want to remind him.

He shrugs. "It's so new with me and Ramón. What's that say-ing? 'Don't wear your wedding dress to your first date' or whatever."

"Who says that?"

"I don't know. *Cosmo*'s guide to not being clingy?" He shrugs.

"I really like him, I do. But I'm not ready to share him with the world yet. Whatever I've gotta do to protect that, I'm going to do."

"I get that," I say, even though I don't. I don't ever share my hookups with the world because they aren't important, not because they're so special I want to keep them safe.

"Besides, aren't you at least a little curious about who she'd set us up with?"

"No," I say, finishing my reps. "And if she's got Jude on her radar, that should be a double no from you."

"Obviously she's just looking for a distraction from the fact that she blew up her whole life." He stands up a little straighter. "I'd rather have her sending us on dates than jumping out of airplanes and getting herself killed."

"Aww, that's sweet," I tease.

"Yeah well, what's the fun in being the good kid if you're the only kid."

"Wow, that got dark." I snort.

"I'm kidding." He shakes his head. "Seriously though, you got a better idea than letting her set us up?"

My face must betray me because he laughs.

"*Besides* breaking the bro code and fucking my sister?" He drops his head back with a groan. "God, can I just have one friend not into her?"

"What does that mean?"

"Everyone gets a crush on her," he says as we start doing walking lunges side by side down the center of the gym. "Even people like you who never get them. It's actually weird that you didn't until now. You're the longest holdout of any of my friends."

"To be fair, I never met her before that weekend," I point out.

James looks at me, a curious expression on his face. "Well, before you get any ideas, you should know, everybody loves Cara, everybody crushes on Cara, but she's like me. We can't make it stick. I come on too strong, she runs too fast; we're both doomed. You saw what happened to Max, and he got her all the way to the altar before she bailed."

"I have no intention of trying to get your sister to the altar," I say, cheating on the next couple lunges. "I have no intention of doing *anything* with your sister, actually."

James tips his head back, his face scrunched up in thought. I think he's going to say something profound, something important. But he just shakes his head at me. "Dude, knee to the floor. What kind of half-assed lunges are you trying to pull?"

A LOT OF people say "the best part of working out is when it's over" or things along those lines. But that's not true. Not if you're doing it right—and, not to brag, but if you're working out with me, you probably are.

Once I outgrew that knockoff-gym day care my mother used to leave me at, I found excuses to keep coming anyway. I was fascinated by the idea that a person could truly be in control there. They would set the reps, the weights, the routines—all you had to do was stick with it to reach your goals, and everyone's goals were different, just for them. Some people wanted to lose weight, sure, but a lot of people just wanted to feel stronger and fitter, no matter what that looked like.

For the member with MS, it was about keeping her muscles limber and staying active; for the powerlifter, it was about breaking the previous gym record; for the cardio bunny, it was to get in all her steps; for the grandma, it was to get off her high blood pressure medicine. But the beauty of it all is that they came together at the same place—despite different starting points and abilities and limitations. And with consistency, and a little bit of help from me or the actual staff, they could get to where they wanted to be. It was simple and reassuring during a childhood that was anything but. A cause and effect that made sense among the chaos of my life.

By the time I was a teenager, I was swallowing up every fitness book, video, and website that I could find. Once I realized that there wasn't just one path from point A to point B—one-size-fits-all approaches don't work when you're dealing with the diversity of the human body—I wanted to be able to find as many paths as possible, for as many people as possible.

The idea of being a personal trainer, like James is, had crossed my mind more than once in my retail days—gotta love being a Target desperation hire, and I think I'm still traumatized by my time at TJ Maxx—but the courses and tests to get certified were long and expensive. There was no way I could do that and still cover bills for both me and my mom. And besides, if I was a personal trainer, I would be working with only a few types of people: those who could actually afford private training and had the time for it.

But I realized if I could find a way, somehow, to have a gym of my own, I could help everybody. I could offer pay-as-you-go services, elite memberships, sponsorships for those who didn't have it in the budget. I could have a team of trainers and staff on standby to help. A robust day care so parents could work out without worry. It would be my own little miniature utopia . . . if only I had the funds to do it.

Working at The Fitness Place was the next best thing. I may not have been able to set the tone for the whole gym, but by insisting I did all the new guest orientations, I could at least make sure they were getting off on the right foot.

In fact, I'm just heading back to my desk after finishing up my third new guest orientation of the afternoon when James runs over, a bizarrely concerned look on his face.

"She already found someone!" he yelps, holding up his phone.

"What?"

"Cara! She already found someone! She's trying to set me up on a blind date."

"Let me see." I grab his phone to study her most recent message. My forehead crinkles as I take in the words in front of me. "This just asks if you want to get sushi tonight."

"Exactly," James wails.

"Maybe she's just hungry and wants some company."

"She absolutely is *not*." James rolls his eyes at the disbelief on my face. "When we were in high school, she used to always invite me to meet her somewhere and then *boom*, as soon as I arrived, we'd 'run into' someone else that would be just 'perfect' for me. Then she would dip. She's obviously doing that now."

"Or she just wants sushi."

"She hates sushi," James says, looking very serious. "This is a setup."

"O-kay," I say, drawing out the word. "Then tell her no and to ask one of her other friends."

"What other friends?"

"You said everybody had a crush on her so . . ."

"Yeah, in high school. As far as I know she hasn't kept in touch with any of them. Did you not notice it at the wedding? She didn't have anybody there."

"I just figured your mother cut them from the list because they weren't coronated or elected or some kind of *Grey's Anatomy*–esque super-surgeon who was good enough to share air with the state senator."

James laughs. "Yeah, *if* Cara had a bunch of people to invite that probably would have happened. But she didn't. If my mother hadn't packed the wedding with her own friends and some distant family we barely knew, there really wouldn't have been anyone there for our side. Max had a couple people fly in for him, but all Cara's bridesmaids were cousins we don't even talk to. Mom always bragged, 'Cara's so focused on her job! James, you should be more like your sister.' Bet she's eating those words now, isn't she?"

"I guess?" I say, trying to keep up.

"Cara's been here a day and a half and she's already driving me nuts," he says. "She's got nothing else to do . . . unless she decides to go and grovel at the feet of Sherry and Jane, I'm it. I need backup! I need you to—"

"Wait, who are Sherry and Jane?"

"Friends—well, ex-friends of hers. The three of them were inseparable until Sherry and Jane got together and Cara didn't take it well. She said they were all friends, but I think Cara had a thing for one of them."

And that? That makes my ears perk right up. "Oh, Cara's queer, then?"

James smirks. "Wouldn't you like to know."

And okay, note to self, maybe tone down the whole wanting-to-bed-his-sister thing, at least to his face.

"I'm kidding," he says, flicking my forehead. "Of course she is. She's been out forever too. Still doesn't mean I want you banging her though."

"No one is banging anyone in this scenario." I wave him off. "What happened with Sherry and Jane? That was it? Cara just never got over her school crush?"

James frowns. "Not exactly. They managed to loosely remain friends until like a year ago when they refused to go to Cara's engagement party."

"Why not?"

"No idea, but they ran off and got married like a month later and didn't invite Cara. She was really hurt by that. As in, so upset she even called *me* and *our parents*. That was the end of that for good."

"Ouch," I say, logging into my computer to check my personal email . . . speaking of parents.

Mom has taken to forwarding me her online bill requests now, and if I don't acknowledge them as soon as they come in, she'll start calling. Historically, my inbox is nothing but cobwebs and spam, so there's been a learning curve when it comes to remembering to check. But hey, if it helps me avoid having to go to her apartment, and bonus, keeps her from calling me at work, I'm in—even if it does really solidify that our relationship is more business arrangement than mother-daughter anymore.

God, I need coffee if I'm going to survive this day.

And, more important, I need to stop daydreaming about what it would be like to hook up with Cara, bro code be damned. I know it could never *really* happen. We're not even remotely in the same social sphere, which clearly matters to people like Cara

Manderlay. I mean, you don't just *end up* with someone like Max by accident.

James's phone buzzes in his hand. "Jesus," he groans, staring down at it like it's going to bite. "Cara just asked for my Tinder password. I told you, Lizzie! I told you this was a setup."

"Okay." I hold up my hand. "In light of this new information, I am willing to concede that maybe there is more to this sushi date."

"See! And this is where you come in."

"What do I have to do with any of this?"

"You're my best friend," he says slowly, like that clarifies anything.

I wait for him to elaborate, but he doesn't. "And?" I finally ask.

James pinches the bridge of his nose. "And obviously, I need to blow off this supposed sushi date and have you go instead, thus foiling her plan."

"And what do I get out of this?" I ask, ignoring the little rush that comes with the idea of more one-on-one time with Cara.

"Free sushi?" He winces. "Knowing you saved my ass and are the best, best friend in all the universe?"

"No."

"Seriously? How is spending time with someone you admittedly think is hot such a hardship for you?"

I drop my head back. "I knew it was just a matter of time before you exploited my crush on your sister for your own ulterior motives." I check my watch. "But this was efficient, even for you."

"Come on, don't make me beg," he whines. "I need you!"

"Right, because the last favor I did for you went so well." I shake my head. "Even if I did go, then what?"

"I don't know. You have fun? You keep her off my back about boyfriends? You explain that hooking me back up with Jude would be world-endingly bad?"

I sigh. "Shit, keeping you and Jude apart would actually be a good reason to go."

"Exactly, you know I can't control myself around him. One glance at his face and I'll—"

"Please don't finish that sentence."

"I'm just saying! Cara's been here like less than twenty-four hours, and she's already tried to get me to jump out of a plane and re-date the Antichrist. This is not going to end well for me! Please, if you love me at all, distract her! Find a way!"

I bite my lip. I happen to know that I can be an excellent *distraction*. Ask any of my past partners.

"Not like that. Bad, bad Lizzie!" James points a stern finger in my direction. "Take her golfing. Teach her to lift. I don't care, as long as she's out of our love lives and away from parachutes or bungee cords or whatever else she comes up with. But, please, for the love of god, keep your pants on while you do it."

I laugh, walking over to pick up a wet towel someone left on one of our leather seats. "Did it ever occur to you that you're complaining about her setting you up, when you're trying to do the same thing to her?"

"It's not remotely the same. This is a *friend* date for you two. A distraction date."

"Do you hear yourself?" I drop back into my desk chair with an exasperated huff as a fresh wave of guests wanders in, including Mrs. Goldstein, one of my favorites. Even she can't save this day.

"You used to be more fun," James whines. "Where's your whimsy, Elizabeth!"

And god, I hate when people use my full name. Not for the first time, I find myself doubting the whole "every queer woman needs an emotional support himbo" thing. Mine is currently free to home, doesn't even need to be a good one.

"Dead," I answer, scanning in Mrs. Goldstein. James doesn't bother responding.

A steady stream of people pours in the front doors after that, but still, he spends the next hour lingering around my desk anyway, messing with pamphlets for our various programs here or there—obviously waiting for me to, I don't know, agree to his scheme or yell at him to leave.

If I'm being honest, I want to do both. This is a terrible idea, but I can also understand how, in that absolute golden retriever heart of his, it makes sense. He wants somebody looking out for Cara. Just not him.

The worst thing is, a part of me wants to agree. Don't I kind of owe her anyway? Cara wouldn't even be on his couch suggesting death-defying stunts if I hadn't blown up her idea of marriage that night. Keeping her on the straight and narrow is the least I can do.

Well, okay, maybe not *straight* and narrow, but—

Jesus, I need to get a grip.

And then there's that tiny voice inside my head that's saying even if I *am* just a distraction, at least I'll be *something* to her. God, that sounds pathetic. I'm not doing this.

"I'm out, James, seriously." He starts to protest, but I hold up a hand. "Talk to your sister. Tell her you're not interested in being set up and neither am I. Just handle it, okay?"

I can tell he's about to argue. He's probably already working on a revised plan in his head to figure out exactly how to get me to agree. He's sneaky like that, even when he doesn't mean to be. But when I put on my best no-bullshit face, his shoulders slump in resignation.

"Alright, I'll talk to her but—" Before he can finish that sentence the phone buzzes in his hand again. This time a wide smile breaks across his features.

"Ramón?" I ask.

"How did you know?" he asks, without looking up.

"Because you look like all of your blood just turned to oxytocin."

"Are you trying to say I'm high on love?"

I frown. It never ends well when he breaks out the *L* word this early. "What happened to not wearing your wedding dress?" I remind him.

"I don't wear it to our dates." He smiles. "But what's the harm in trying it on a little around the house?"

Chapter Ten

The rest of the week passes blissfully quietly.

I make a habit of waiting outside James's house on days that it's my turn to drive, which means I mostly don't see Cara. It's not that I'm really avoiding her, it's just that . . . okay no, I'm definitely avoiding her.

James says she's doing well, "for the most part," but frustratingly refuses to elaborate beyond that. I tell myself I don't want to know, but I sort of do. I try to convince myself that there's a middle ground here, that maybe we could be friends. Unfortunately, that idea flies out the window the night I walk in on her doing yoga in a sports bra and the tightest workout pants I've ever seen. In that moment, I don't even care that she had those stupid socks on.

That's when I know there's no way I can keep her safely friend-zoned. If she can make socks during yoga cute, it's over. Yoga socks are an *abomination*.

Avoidance is better.

Anything is better. Bro code, bro code, bro code. One does not think dirty thoughts about one's best friend's bendy sister.

Jesus.

And so I sit behind my desk at work. Typing. Avoiding. Like a good, responsible adult.

Forget the new gym location, maybe Stella can transfer me to Mars.

"What's that?" Mina comes up behind me, pulling papers from her class folder. She's in her mid-thirties, Japanese American, and super pregnant. God knows Stella and George like her way more than they like me. She's been a staple at this gym chain since she graduated high school and got certified to teach fitness classes. She mostly does Spin classes at The Fitness Place, along with a few HIIT and Zumba classes thrown in for good measure. She's the closest thing I have to a best girlfriend. I mean, James wins in the overall best friend category, but sometimes it's just nice to talk to another woman.

"It's my résumé," I say, frowning at all the white space.

There's just not much to report. I graduated high school but never went to college. I'm not in any clubs or volunteering or doing community service. I worked at TJ Maxx, and after that I worked at Target, and then I realized that I could at least take baby steps toward my dream of owning a gym, and I got a job here. The last five years of my life have been spent inside these walls.

The white space stares back at me. Do I even *deserve* a promotion?

"Ooooooh, is that for the new gym manager position? You're finally going to do it?"

I flick my eyes to hers and back to my computer screen. "I don't know. I feel like if they were going to give it to me, they just would. And writing all this out . . ."

"You know how Stella is, she makes everybody work for it. I had to interview three times for my transfer here and I was already working at one of their other gyms."

I wish I believed her, but I can't ditch this nagging feeling that maybe I'm just not good enough. Thanks for the complex, Mom.

"Hey, Lizzie." Cara's voice snaps me out of my pity party.

Wait, what?

"Oh heyyyyy, Cara," I say, hoping I sound, if not normal, at least nonchalant. "You looking for James?"

"No." She smiles.

Cara's dressed in a tight Adidas tank top and capri yoga pants. Her long hair is pulled up into a bun on top of her head, and if she's wearing makeup, I can't tell. It should be illegal for someone to look this good without the benefit of contouring and eight pounds of mascara. What the fuck.

"No?" I echo, the only word my brain is capable of pushing out.

Her eyebrows scrunch up and I try to ignore how cute it is. "James said you were the one to see about a tour. Is that not right?"

I choke on my coffee. Of course he did. That dick. Obviously, he's not above torturing me.

I clear my throat. "Right, yeah, I can do that or Mina, Mina! You could?"

Mina looks at me like I've got two heads and I don't blame her. It's not exactly in her job description. "Sorry, but I've got a class in fifteen."

I stare pointedly at Mina, praying she'll, I don't know, psychically understand exactly why I can't do this. Why I *shouldn't* be the one doing it. Why, if I have to demonstrate to Cara how to use the abductor machine, I will literally implode and possibly also explode. There will just be tiny bits of me floating around the gym like lusty Lizzie confetti.

"Are you okay?" Cara asks, her head tilting toward me in the unmistakable gesture of *what is wrong with you?*

"Cara!" I say, spinning away from Mina as if I just now noticed her. Naturally this takes her by surprise because a) I've already greeted her once and b) she's been standing here for well over a minute.

"I'm great! Just great," I grit out. "Of course I can give you a tour! I just need a second. I'll be right back!"

Mina and Cara watch me with wide, confused eyes as I burst into the manager's room—thank god Roger is off today—and slam the door shut. Then I push the chair in front of it for good measure. And then I crouch down behind the half wall so they can't see me in this giant fishbowl office. Half credit for not crawling under the desk, although admittedly I am tempted to.

Okay. Breathe. I can do this. I can totally act normal around this woman. I can pull it together. I am not some lovesick teenager. This is fine. This is my job. I've done this hundreds, if not thousands, of times. I peek up over the wall and accidentally make eye contact with them before shooting back down.

I can't do this.

I slide my phone out of my pocket.

> WTF JAMES!!! You give her the tour!

And what the fuck. What the fuck?!

Shit. SHIT. Okay.

I'm two seconds away from cramming myself into the vent and crawling toward the parking lot when Mina shoves the door open. The chair goes flying across the room with a thump I'm sure Cara heard.

"Oh!" Mina says in a booming voice as she glares at me cowering on the floor. "Yes, I *can* help you find your earring, Lizzie. Why didn't you say so?" She hurries in and awkwardly squats down beside me. "Why the hell are you acting like such a weirdo?"

"That's James's sister!" I urgently whisper.

Mina pops her head out the window. "The runaway bride?"

I drag her back down. "Yes," I say through gritted teeth.

"And why are we hiding from her?"

I stare at Mina, trying to figure out how to explain this whole mess, and a knowing smile breaks out across her face.

"Ohhhhhh, I get it. You think she's hot and your gay little brain is about to explode. You're so cute."

"No. No! This is a totally platonic freakout."

Mina tilts her head, her arms already crossed. She's definitely not buying it.

"Okay, it's not, but it's also not just the hot thing! It's—"

"No, I think I get it now," Mina says in a singsong voice as she taps her chin. And oh, oh no.

"Mina?" I say slowly. "Whatever you're thinking—"

"Oh! Here it is!" she calls loudly, standing up and holding out an imaginary earring. "Well, guess I better get to class, and you have a tour to run! Glad I could help."

She disappears out the door before I can even find a pencil to stab her with. Fuck me, looks like we're doing this. I sigh and stand up, giving Cara a little awkward wave as I pretend to put an earring back in my definitely not pierced ears.

This requires me to take my hair down and keep it there, probably for the rest of my life. It's fine. Given that I am likely to spontaneously combust mid-tour, it won't be that long. I fluff my hair around my shoulders as I walk toward her.

"Ready?" I ask.

"As I'll ever be," she answers.

I AM GOING to hell.

There's really no way around it. Cara is currently in front of me doing cable kickbacks while I check her form, and I don't really know what to say other than I'm going to murder James. And Mina. With my teeth if I have to.

Why is it so hot in here?

James, to his credit, has done his best to hide his laughter as I've stumbled through the tour, but I can tell by the look on his face that he's enjoying watching me make a fool of myself. If this is revenge on me for not helping him, it's working. He's lucky he's got one of his personal training clients on the mat with him, a fact he happily pointed out when I took Cara over to ask if she wouldn't prefer to get the grand tour of her family's facilities from her brother. If he didn't, I—

"This is fun," Cara says, waiting for me to unhook her ankle. "Whoever thought gyms could be fun?"

"Literally everyone," I say, hanging the cuff back up beside the pulley handles. "Who knew the heir to The Fitness Place empire could hate working out?"

"I'm not the heir to anything." She scoffs. "And I don't hate working out, I just don't really see the point in lifting things up and putting them back down again when you could, I don't know, go for a run in a park? Pet some dogs along the way?"

"Pet some . . . you are a menace. And I say that as someone who is willing to concede that cardio *can* be a healthy addition to some people's fitness routines."

Cara rolls her eyes, tapping her fingers on her hip as she looks around. "What are those? I want to try them."

She's pointing to the steel racks lined up in the corner.

"Those are for squats," I say.

Stella had them in the center of the gym when I first started here. It took me a full year to convince her to move them. Sure, a lot of the super-fit dudes like to be front and center when they lift heavy, but not everyone feels comfortable. Especially not with the cardio theater right behind them. Even I was too intimidated by the idea of all the people on ellipticals watching my ass to enjoy them, and squats are my favorite.

I would be lying if I didn't say I wished they were still in the center though, just for today, just for this moment.

Like I said, I'm going to hell.

Cara grins. "Ooh, I do like squats. Will you spot me?"

I die a little in my head.

Be professional. Beeeee professional. Just pretend she's a regular new client and not the biggest fucking crush you've had since Heather Comer in third grade.

"Please?" She smiles. "I want to try."

I pinch the bridge of my nose and lead her over. "Do you want the Smith machine or the free bar?"

"What's the difference?"

"The Smith is self-spotting. It's a little safer. The bar stays on a fixed track, and you can just lean forward to hook it. It's more restrained."

"Oh, hmm. I do love being restrained," she says with a wink. "Smith it is."

I choke on my spit. It's not graceful or elegant, and I rush to load the weights in between gasping breaths.

"Everything okay?" She arches an eyebrow, and is she fucking with me?

No. Definitely not.

I quickly demo one set and switch places with her. Her eyes feel like fire as we move past each other. It's all in my head, I remind myself. There is absolutely no way a woman like her would be flirting with a woman like me.

"Thanks, coach," she says, when she settles into position. "James says that you can deadlift almost as much as him. These weights you set for me must feel like nothing."

And oh. Okay, this is safe. This I can talk about forever.

"Eh, sort of, but when you work with lighter weights you can really focus on form."

Cara's eyes sweep over me and she smiles. "You have really great . . . form."

"I . . ." And nope. No way. "Speaking of form," I say, trying to get us back on track, "you're doing well. Newbies don't usually tackle squat racks and pulley systems on their first visit."

"I don't like the gym, but I've definitely picked up a few things from the family business." She drops the bar onto its pegs and steps back to shake out her legs.

"Then why did you need a tour?"

"To rescue you!" she says. "Obviously."

"What?"

"James mentioned you hated sitting at that desk all day. I thought I could spring you for a while. Besides, he's being a total dick about giving me his Grindr and Tinder passwords. You've got to help me." She lowers her voice then, putting her hand up as she does like we're telling secrets. "We cannot let this man die alone."

I glance at James, but he just shoots me a thumbs-up and goes back to helping his client perfect their Russian twist.

"I think he's good."

"He's not, thus my plan."

"Your plan?"

"Yeah! To set him up. You know more than I do about him. What do you think he'd like for a first date?"

"You should talk to your brother about this, not me."

"I did!"

"And what did he say?"

"Doesn't matter. I *know* I can find him his happily ever after. Just give me a hint where to get started. I only met Jude; what do you think about rekindling that somehow?" She looks at me with a gleam in her eye. "And don't worry, once I'm done with him, you're next on my list."

Whatever James said to her about this setup idea, it doesn't sound like it was a hard no. I'm half tempted to pretend to set him up myself just so I can whisk him away and spend the whole time yelling at him. But then the rest of what she said registers.

"Uh, I'm all set, thanks. So, do you want to see the cardio theater next?" I ask, heading toward it.

When I glance back at Cara, she's frowning.

And if avoiding Cara, or at least keeping things as professional as possible, is so right, then why do I feel like such an asshole about it?

Chapter Eleven

You have to tell her," I say, tracing the lines of the wood table with my pinkie. I hate confrontation and I hate confrontation with James even more. I'm trying to suck it up though, because this is serious.

Somehow Cara got my phone number, and by *somehow*, I mean that James must have given it to her. Just this morning, I woke up to a cheery text from her saying, Good morning! Welcome to the first day of the rest of your life, and no, thank you. First of all, I am not one to appreciate that level of optimism first thing. And second of all, if today is the first day of the rest of my life, it is turning out to be embarrassingly mundane.

"I told you she's an unstoppable force," James says, throwing up his hands.

We're at our favorite coffee shop, surrounded by the strong scent of cookies and coffee beans. And while I generally dislike brunch—it's breakfast or lunch, pick one!—the urge to have late-morning meetups with James, and sometimes Mina too, when our days off overlap, remains high.

To get around that, we meet at Burned Beans Coffee, after James has had a late breakfast and I've had an early lunch, where we gorge ourselves on cookies and caffeine. And yeah, I know that neither of those is especially healthy or good for our "high-performance machines," as James unironically calls his body, but sometimes, you just gotta eat the cookies, dude.

"She'd be significantly more stoppable if you hadn't given her my number."

"I didn't give her your number." James looks confused. "Did she call you?"

"She texted me. I assumed you were behind it."

"Not this time." He sighs and unlocks his phone. "I'm gonna kill her."

"Why?" I ask, popping another bite of their famous Kitchen Sink cookie into my mouth. And it's nice, I think, to have my best friend on *my* side again.

"Look what I woke up to this morning. She must have figured out my password." He squeezes his eyes shut and turns his phone toward me. "I don't even know how to change this back."

And wow, this is a lot. Every app has been changed to some kind of weird Pepto-Bismol pink, each label now in a cheerful, looping font. I laugh despite his scowl, until I notice the background picture. "Is that—"

"Me and Jude on that doom cruise. Yes. And, oh, look, there's you and the *captain* in the back."

"Oh, shut up."

The doom cruise. What a time *that* was. Moments after this picture was taken, Jude dumped him for the hundredth time. Why you would dump someone you're going to be stuck on a boat with for the next ten days is beyond me, but he did.

God, we're so drunk in this picture. They had just gotten in a huge fight—the huge fight before their second-to-last breakup—and I was trying to drink myself into another timeline.

If I recall correctly, and I'm not at all positive that I do, James is referencing how I spent half of that night making out with a woman I thought was the captain but turned out to just be a tourist in a white suit.

James spent the next three days gambling away his tears, until he met a very nice cocktail waiter named Luca who he promptly fell head over heels with. After which he proceeded to spend the last several days of the trip trying to get my fake captain to marry them, by reciting "O Captain! My Captain!" everywhere she went, even though I told him that's not what the poem is about.

Jude, predictably, got jealous and begged James to take him back, which, regrettably, he did. For two terrible weeks that resulted in one keyed car and an entire set of broken dishes.

This cannot happen again.

"Where did she even find that picture? And why did she make it your background?"

He shrugs. "She must have dug through my photos. That's probably when she got your number too. Shit! What if she read my messages? Ramón and I were, uh, *you know*, not that long ago."

"Well, for her sake I hope not."

James pinches the bridge of his nose. "Her sake? What about mine! What if she saw—"

"You've texted half of Grindr your junk. Forgive me if I'm more worried about her eyeballs than your modesty."

"Hey, just because my nether regions are always ready for their close-up doesn't mean that—"

I plug my ears. "Please stop, I swear to god."

"Fine, but as much as I appreciate your concern for my sister's eyeballs, that's not what I'm worried about. If I want to send nudes, I'm not doing it via text, and the odds that she actually got into *those* apps are slim to none."

"Again, I don't wanna know."

"Okay, but don't come to me when you accidentally text your boss nudes," he says, snatching up the last bit of my cookie and popping it into his mouth.

I shudder. "That would be your mom," I point out and James stops chewing.

"That's nasty," he says around a mouthful of my cookie.

"You said it, not me." I snort. "If this isn't about your dick pics though, what exactly are we freaking out about?"

James wipes his mouth with a napkin. "What if she saw Ramón's?"

"Did you not just lecture me about your impenetrable sexting apps?"

He glares.

"Wait," I gasp. "You *save* the pictures? Like to the photo album on your phone? James, what the fuck! Why even bother with encryption, then!"

"That's not the point!" he practically wails.

I want to ask *how is that not the point* but the poor guy looks so stressed I don't bother. I grab his hand and squeeze. "If it's any consolation I really don't think she saw anything."

"No?" he asks, his eyes searching mine. "Why not?"

"She was super cheerful this morning in an 'I definitely still want you to help me set up my brother' kind of way. If she found out you had a current boy toy, don't you think she would have switched gears back to Extreme Sports Cara™? You didn't see her ordering bungee cords or spikes or anything, right? *If* she did see anything, I bet she brushed it off as a random hookup."

"Yeah," he says, visibly relaxing into his chair. "That makes sense. Unless . . ."

"Unless what?"

"Unless she figured it out and is planning on using it to blackmail me to get in good with Mom again." His knee starts to bounce. "Fuck."

"Okay, okay, let's take a beat here," I say. He looks up at me so worried it takes all my willpower not to leap over the table and hug him. "Why do you think she would do that? I know I don't know her that well, but she's seems better than that. I don't think she'd be upset about Ramón."

"Dude, she was basically married to royalty and I'm dating a guy that works at a hotel."

And wow, I see *extra*-dramatic James has made an appearance. Max wasn't the next president or a crowned prince. He was just some dumbass crypto bro with a Wall Street job.

"You work at a gym and she loves you," I point out, which just makes his frown deepen. "Look, if a service job is a deal breaker then fuck her all around. Not literally though," I add quickly, when he gives me a look. I rub soothing circles on the back of his hand. "I know Stella fucked you guys in the head about jobs and appearances and stuff, but that doesn't mean Cara is secretly plotting against you."

"Dude," he says, flopping back in his chair. "I just don't want anything to happen. I . . . I really think I'm falling for him, and I can't stand the thought of my family ruining it. What if he's the one and I'm just—"

"Oh my god, James, you are hopeless."

He rubs his hand over his scruff. "You know, there's an easy way to solve this."

"You're going to finally talk to your sister *like you were supposed to?*"

He sighs. "You know what I'm talking about."

I narrow my eyes. "You better not still be trying to . . ."

"If you would just start hanging out with her, you could do a little recon and see what she did and didn't learn when she went through my phone."

"No. We already put this to bed!" I say, tearing up my napkin so I don't tear up the man across from me. "I can't be dealing with this while I'm worrying about the promotion. You need to get her to stop."

"You don't know her. Once she gets something in her head, she's impossible."

"You just have to tell her no, simple as that. 'No' is a complete sentence. And if you hadn't fed into this in the first place, you wouldn't currently have a Hello Kitty nightmare for a phone!"

"How did I feed into this?" he asks, somehow incredulous, despite the fact that he definitely, 100 percent did.

"Oh, I don't know, having her come in for a tour, even though she doesn't like the gym, which gave her the opportunity to actually start fishing for details about your dating life—that wasn't your prank? Weird, because she said you told her I hate being stuck behind the desk and needed to be rescued, so!"

"Okay, but hear me out," James says, pursing his lips. "You *do* hate being stuck behind the desk!"

"Not the point," I say, just as another text from her dings on my phone. I read it quickly and then shove it in James's face. "Look at this, she's asking me if I think you would want to go rock climbing with Jude." I scoff. "You, Jude, and a cliff? Does that sound like a smart combination to you? Does it?!" James shakes his head rapidly. "Get. Her. To. Chill. Then."

"Dude, come on, she doesn't listen to me! And I can't risk her getting more suspicious about Ramón. She's acting like Stella 2.0 right now—just pushing and pushing and pushing. And you know how it goes when anyone contradicts my mother! I can only imagine how Cara would react. Please, Lizzie, I need your help."

"It's a terrible idea," I say, and cross my arms. "Trust me."

James scrunches up his face. "No, it isn't! If you could just keep an eye on her for me . . ."

"What if she falls madly in love with me and then your poor mother is stuck with *two* service workers for in-laws?" I mock gasp, desperate to cover up the truth, which is that no good could possibly come out of us spending another second together. Not with me feeling the way I feel about her.

James snorts, pulling me from my head. "We definitely won't have to worry about that."

I try to play it off like his utter disbelief doesn't hurt, but it does. Just another confirmation that, no matter how close James and I are as friends, it's not a level playing field with the Manderlays. I'm not one of them, and I never will be.

James flicks a stray crumb off the table and looks up at me with a satisfied smile. "But that's why this plan is perfect. None of the risk, all of the reward."

I roll my eyes. "I am not gonna pretend to be her friend to spy on her just because you're too scared to have an adult conversation!"

His phone pings with a fresh email, a tiny divot appearing between his eyebrows as he reads. "Fine, can you at least do me a different favor, then?" he asks, setting down his phone.

"I'm not doing your laundry again, so don't even ask. I'm still scarred from the last time."

"No, not that." He laughs. "I want to go scope out this yoga class. That's who just emailed me. I'm trying to convince Mom to add it to the gym, but she doesn't want to unless I tell her how it's different from the classes we already offer."

"And?"

"And I need you to go with me, so I don't make an ass out of myself doing 'acrobatic yoga' on my own. I figure I should go at least once before I write up an acquisition plan. We can expense it. No out of pocket. Meet me there tomorrow morning at seven-thirty. Give me something to look forward to, and I'll have the scary talk with Cara."

"I hate yoga nearly as much as I hate waking up early on a Sunday."

"Yeah, that's why it's a favor. If you loved yoga, it would be a reward. And there are no rewards for making me talk back to my very imposing sister."

"I hate you."

"You love me."

I roll my eyes. "Or instead of twisting myself into a pretzel at an ungodly hour, I could just stop replying to *both* of your calls and texts. Problem solved."

"You could, except the 'Women Tell All' episode of *The Bachelor* is next week. If you think Mina will be *half* the company I am for that, I dare you to try it."

I flare my nostrils and groan. He's got me there.

Chapter Twelve

I beat James to the yoga studio, which is unsurprising considering how he's late to virtually everything.

It's stuck in the middle of a strip mall that probably should have been torn down about a decade ago. Crumbling stucco, cracked pavement—I can see why this studio is looking to partner with The Fitness Place and get out of Dodge.

The pandemic hit a lot of the fitness industry hard, and The Fitness Place was one of the few around here that were lucky enough to survive it. I had already added livestreaming to classes for paid members the year before, so we were largely able to keep offering enough clients enough classes even through the shutdowns that we didn't lose much (not that Stella would ever acknowledge that I saved her ass, but still).

Judging by this yoga studio's sticky, cigarette-littered location, I'd guess it didn't fare quite as well.

The instructor greets me with a wide smile when I walk in. "Oh, it's nice to see a new face! Welcome, I'm Jessa, the owner and instructor at Some Like It Hot. Can I ask how you heard of us? We're always trying to figure out what marketing works and what doesn't."

"Oh, I'm with James, I'm meeting him here."

She looks at me, clearly drawing a blank, before saying, "Well, we always love direct referrals."

Weird—shouldn't she know who James is if he's supposedly scouting her classes for a deal? Damn, I hope this wasn't supposed to be some kind of stealth mission or something.

"That's going to be fifteen dollars for the class."

"Oh, James is—" I cut myself off. If this *is* supposed to be undercover, then I definitely shouldn't explain that he's expensing it. I sigh and pull out one of my very last twenties. He'll have to pay me back when he gets here. Maybe I'll even charge interest for getting me up so early.

I find an empty space and roll out my mat, then drop my gym bag into the space next to it and spread out my things. I probably look like an asshole, but this class is filling up and I need to save his spot.

I check my phone. Still no text from him.

> Where are you???? Class is about to start!

No response. I frown and toss it into my gym bag, doing some gentle forward bends while I wait.

"Lizzie!" Her voice rings in my head and I bolt up so fast I almost fall over.

"Cara," I say, looking behind her as the instructor shuts the door. "Is James with you?"

Cara frowns. "He didn't tell you? Mom called him flipping out, something about the build site for the new gym. He told me to cover for him here, I hope you don't mind. I can move over there if it's a thing?"

"Nope," I lie. "I don't mind at all." I move my bag and watch her unroll her mat and stretch out. She looks decidedly happy. Like James-definitely-*didn't*-talk-to-her-last-night level happy.

I'm going to kill him.

Cara smiles at me then glides into downward dog with a wink.

Correction: if I survive this, I'm going to kill him.

I COULD HANDLE cat-cow. I could handle finding my breath. I could even handle the entire first fifteen minutes of class spent sitting beside Cara listening to her little sighs as she stretched out her long lithe muscles beside me.

But then things start to heat up. Literally. The instructor announces with an apology that the AC went out that morning, and while someone is coming to fix it, it won't be anytime soon. Perfect.

Cara doesn't seem bothered by this news and continues to warm up. But her next deep side stretch sends the strap of her flowy tank careening down to her elbow. I go stone still—trying and failing not to notice the swell of her breast over the top of her now half-exposed Nike sports bra.

Cara clears her throat, snapping my eyes back up to hers, but she doesn't look away. No, she *smiles*. She arches that damn eyebrow and she actually smiles.

I don't mean to be a creep, I swear.

God knows I've chased enough men out of the gym for leering at women, and I know women can be sexual harassers too. But the way Cara keeps looking at me. Fuck. It feels deliberate.

I stare at my toes, wiggling them a little, and then at hers—

covered by dumb yoga socks again—to distract myself. But then she forward folds beside me. Almost tipping into me when she loses her balance.

And okay, seriously? I thought this was a one-way street, but now I'm not so sure. I can't go there. I shouldn't go there, but if she sends one more arched eyebrow in my direction I—

No. I decide to play it off, but just barely. Playfully pushing her back to her mat before shifting into cobra pose with the rest of the class. I don't know, man. I might be reading into this too much—I'm *probably* reading too much into this. Maybe Cara's just very friendly, and smiley, and flirty in general and—well, I shifted into sweaty pig mode several minutes ago but somehow, she's just *glowing*.

I glance at her out of the corner of my eye as a bead of sweat trails down from her hair, curving around her neck before hitting her collarbone and dripping to the mat beneath her.

I lick my lips and swallow hard, forcing my eyes forward. How does she make even sweating sexy? How? The room is surrounded by mirrors, and from each and every angle, I look like a disheveled gremlin—a disheveled gremlin with damp skin and *poor flexibility* who shouldn't have even come here in the first place. And Cara's just over there fucking glowing in all her bendy glory and—

"Lizzie?" She nudges me with her toes. I blink hard and realize that everyone else around me has moved to sitting, while I'm still stuck in cobra. I clench my teeth and force out a smile while the rest of the class watches me curiously.

"Sorry, I got lost in the stretch," I grumble.

"Never apologize for that," the instructor says, placing her hand over her heart in a way that's probably supposed to be validating or comforting or something. "Yoga is about more than just stretching. It connects your mind and body and transcends reality. Finding enough peace to wander the spiritual realm is the highest compliment that you could ever give me as your guide."

If by "wander the spiritual realm" she means trying and failing not to think about how bad I want to make out with my best friend's sister right now, then congrats, coach. We made it.

"Suck-up," Cara whispers beside me with a wink.

"Alright, class, time for the moment you've all been waiting for!"

And what? I look around the room trying to figure out what she means. Isn't stretching and sighing what everybody's here for? God, what more can there be?

Which is when I notice everyone around me shifting closer together, some are even sharing a mat now and . . . what the absolute fuck?

"Is there anyone here who doesn't have a partner?"

I start to raise my hand but then Cara grabs it, lacing her fingers through mine. "Partners?" she asks.

I'm still not entirely sure what we even need partners *for*. I look at Cara, who seems strangely settled, gazing at the instructor with an open expression. Almost like she knows what's coming next.

"What's going on?" I whisper.

She gives me a confused look. "Acrobatic yoga, right? That's what James said."

"Sorry, right, I guess I forgot," I say, trying to cover for the fact that I assumed acrobatic yoga was just the extra-stretchy stuff we had already been doing. What *is* it, then? And why does it seem to be a team sport?

She taps my temple. "You gotta stop wandering so far into the spiritual realm."

"Yes, never again," I say, which is true, only because "never again" sums up the next time I intend to take one of these classes.

"My place or yours?" she asks, gesturing toward our mats.

"Uh, mine, I guess," I say, shifting over. She smiles and scoots closer, sitting cross-legged so close our knees touch. I don't look at her collarbone. And I definitely don't look at her face. I don't look anywhere actually, except the wall and the floor and the ceiling.

"Okay, everybody seems to be paired off now!" The instructor smiles. "We're going to start with some simple positions since this is an introductory class. There are ways to modify if you're feeling adventurous, but for those of you who are new . . . ," she looks directly at Cara and me, "I would recommend taking things very slowly. It is possible to get hurt doing this, so we want to make sure there are no mistakes."

And if I believed in signs and higher powers and all that, I would swear the universe was talking directly to me. Go slow. You could get hurt. No mistakes. I glance at Cara and pull my hand away from hers, ignoring the way they fit together so perfectly, even if only for a second. Shit, this is bad. This is so bad. I'm acting like James. I'm wearing my wedding dress to a first date.

NOT that this is a first date. Because it's not. It's not!

Shit. Shit! SHIT!

Cara, to her credit, keeps staring ahead at the instructor, oblivious to the massive meltdown my brain is currently experiencing.

And Jesus, this is not me. At all. I don't think about lingering touches, or hands fitting together, and I especially don't act like a gym perv. What is *wrong* with me?

"Okay, so, Lizzie, right?" the instructor asks, ripping me out of my head.

I nod, a sense of dread already growing in my belly. *Do not ask me to demo. Do not ask me to demo. Do not ask me to demo.*

"I'm going to have you and your partner come up and demonstrate for the class."

"She's not my partner," I blurt out. "She's my best friend's sister."

The instructor looks confused. "Partner for this class," she clarifies.

"Oh, right," I say, my cheeks heating. Cara shifts beside me but I don't dare look at her. Worried that if I do, she'll be able to see right through me. The lady doth protest too much and all that.

"Would you mind coming up?" Cara's on her feet before the instructor even finishes the question.

"I have no idea what I'm doing," I say. There's a small stage up front, carpeted, unlike the cheap linoleum that lines the rest of the room. It's elevated about two feet off the ground so we can all see it well from where we sit on the floor. Behind the stage is a wall of mirrors, and in the center of it is a thick, sturdy yoga mat. I scratch the back of my neck and step onto the platform beside Cara.

"Okay," the instructor says, kneeling down beside the mat. "I know you're probably wondering why you're being asked to demonstrate as the newest members of the class. It's not hazing, it's actually for your safety. I prefer to spot all the newbies for their first time, after which you're free to go practice on each other whenever you want. Okay, Lizzie, I'm going to have you on the bottom, and your partner can top. You don't mind topping, do you, dear?"

And suddenly, I am Jim Halpert staring at the camera. If that was a sign from the gods before, then what is *this*?

"No, I've been known to occasionally enjoy it." She giggles.

I lay back on the mat and take a deep breath, praying that a bolt of lightning comes from above and puts me out of my misery. Instead, the instructor says, "Part your legs a little, dear, and okay, Cara, I want you to come right here between them."

Fuck. FUCK.

I stare at the ceiling. This is fine, this is fine. I think about my grandmother. I think about the time I got food poisoning from bad seafood. I think about anything except the heat of Cara's body between my legs and the word "come."

It barely works. I squeeze my eyes shut and then blink them open fast, trying to ground myself, as the instructor has Cara lean forward over me and guides my hands to her hips.

"Alright now, dear, come up on her legs a bit, there's a good girl," she says, and suddenly Cara is leaning over my legs, her knees pressing into the mat behind us.

"Now that she's balancing against you, Lizzie, I want you to slowly, slowly," the instructor says when I move too fast, "move your hands one at a time to her hands. And Cara, I want you to push back against her so that you're essentially doing a half plank. Equal and opposing forces so that you stay nice and steady. Lizzie seems like a strong one, so don't be afraid. She'll catch you if you fall."

"You're not going to fall," I say, and her eyes shoot to mine, hesitance bleeding into excitement as our hands find their way to each other.

"Excellent." The instructor claps her hands together, but I only have eyes for Cara. "And now, Lizzie, I want you to lift your legs up off the ground, supporting her body. You are Cara's base, you're the foundation to this whole thing, and now, because of you, she gets to fly."

CARA ASKS ME to join her at the juice bar slash salad bowl place on the other side of the plaza after class, despite the fact that we're both covered in sweat. I'm not entirely convinced that I don't smell like shit, despite the industrial-strength deodorant I slathered on this morning in preparation for the class. When I hesitate, she adds, "We can eat outside?" with a little wince that makes me worry she feels like I rejected *her* and not the idea of sitting in public in my sweat-soaked yoga gear. I am, objectively, an idiot.

I notice a picnic table in the way back of the extremely empty restaurant patio—if you can call some gravel nestled into a corner of the parking lot surrounded by a few two-by-fours so it doesn't all spill out a "patio." I personally remain unconvinced.

"Okay," I say. "Over there, though." And she agrees, seemingly satisfied.

We make our way inside—she orders a sweet potato bowl, whatever that is, and I go for the more traditional oatmeal breakfast bowl, topped with peanut butter and bananas. The cashier gives us a little placard with a number on it and tells us to take a seat anywhere.

We make our way outside and sit in the warm sun, the breeze light enough to cool us off but not enough to chill. I try not to think about how I'll be living off ramen and protein shakes this week to make up for this very expensive bowl of oats I have coming. It's fine, it's fine. Stella lets us get the protein powder at cost through her distributer; it's literally the only cool thing about her.

Cara takes her seat across from me, dropping down with way

too much energy for someone who just lost their body weight in sweat at an ungodly hour. A few strands of hair stick to her face that must have escaped from her bun at some point during our group exercises. I want to tuck them behind her ear, but I don't. Whatever happened in that class was intense but now it's over.

She reaches her arms up in a stretch and lets out a little groan. "God, don't you just feel so good after that class?"

"I guess," I say, but not in the way I think she means. At some point, holding her up with my body, the butterflies turned into a tsunami and now I need to get a grip.

"So, my brother," she says, and I have to look at the sun to make sure it's still shining because it feels like a storm just opened up right over my head. James. Right. He wants me to be friends with his sister. *Friends.* A babysitter, really. Not whatever the hell this is that I'm feeling. I should want to kill him right now for blowing me off and sending her. I should. So why don't I?

"Did you look at those links I sent you the other day?" Cara asks, smoothing out her paper napkin. "You never texted me back about rock climbing. I was thinking that I could get tickets for him and Jude."

"Cara, I really don't think he and Jude should . . ." But she looks so crestfallen I can't bear to finish the rest of the sentence. "Go rock climbing," I finish.

"Oh, it doesn't have to be rock climbing. What about, hmmm . . ."

I want to ask her to stop talking about her brother at a time like this. I want to remind her that her body was just pressed against mine; that she just flew. But any thoughts of asking her about it skitter off into the darkness with the realization that he's still her primary concern.

The server comes over and sets our bowls in front of us, topping off our waters before heading back inside. I welcome the interruption from having to hear any more about what a great date she's planning for someone that is not us.

And then it really hits me: I'm just a means to an end. She didn't invite me to breakfast because she wanted to hang out more, she invited me for recon. Just like James wants me to do to *her*. What did I expect, honestly? I'm just the person who works at her parents' gym and knows her brother. This isn't about me, or us. This is the Cara show, and I didn't even make callbacks.

That annoys me.

It annoys me so much that I blurt out, "Why are you so goddamn worried about setting him up with Jude?" before I can stop myself.

God, I suck.

Because what if James is right, and she *needs* this distraction? I shouldn't let it get to me. It's not like Cara and I could really ever be a thing anyway. Bro code aside, if "basically a president" is her type, that's definitely not me. If she now wants to send her life flying right off the rails, that's not my problem. At all. Just because I had one conversation with her at—

"I just want someone in this family to be happy," she says, her eyes piercing mine. "I think James deserves that, don't you?"

She bites her lip and looks away. My head spins with a thousand thoughts like "He *is* happy, but he's too scared to tell you about it" and "You deserve to be happy too" and "Shit, I wish it were *my* teeth biting that lip," but it's not my place to say or even really think any of those. The table goes silent for a minute, both of us becoming suddenly very interested in the bowls of food in front of us.

"Okay, I have it," she says quietly, a meager effort to break the tension. "What about a pottery class?"

"A pottery class?" I ask. "Are you serious?"

"Okay no, you're right, that one's bad."

"Cara," I say, and wait for her to look up. "Stop."

And I know, I know, I shouldn't care, but I do. This has gone on long enough and if James won't be the one to tell her, then maybe I should be.

Her eyes shoot back to mine, and they look so disappointed. Shit.

"I can't," she says. "If I do then I have to start thinking about how I blew up my whole entire life after our bathroom conversation and I just don't have the capacity for that right now, okay? If you don't want to be a part of it then don't, but I need this."

I want to say something helpful, kind, maybe even profound because I like the way "our" sounds coming out of her mouth, even if it is referencing probably the worst day of her life. I hesitate, but I can see the desperation in her eyes. *Just go with this*, they seem to say. *Please. Even if only for today.*

I rub the back of my neck. "Yeah, James mentioned you had been . . . exploring new ideas lately," I say, doing my best to sound happy about it. "Podcasts, eh?"

I must not have quite pulled it off because she frowns. "What do you have against podcasts?"

"Nothing, but what about the rock climbing? Bungee jumping? *Skydiving?*"

She shifts in her seat. "There's nothing wrong with exploring new things."

"Under normal circumstances, I support thrill seeking in all its forms." I lean forward. "But from what James tells me, this isn't you at all. Are you doing okay, Cara? Really? No bullshit."

She picks at the food in her bowl, ignoring my question. "You want to hear something pathetic?"

I raise my eyebrows and wait several long seconds for her to continue.

"I'm pretty sure the first time I ever really felt alive was the night I ran away."

I wait for her to elaborate, but she doesn't. I hesitate, trying to choose my words carefully. "So, what then? You're gonna chase that high, no matter what it takes? Cara, you shouldn't have to light yourself on fire just to feel something."

"Why, you know another way to make me feel alive?" she asks, her gaze drifting to all the places my tank top sticks sweaty to my skin.

I swallow hard and feel my cheeks heat, no doubt fucking blushing like a schoolgirl. *Bro code, bro code, bro code.*

"Cara, you—"

"I don't even know who I am." She cuts me off. "Do you know how surreal that is? I've been so wrapped up in doing what everybody else thought was right, my entire life. So, yeah, maybe I love skydiving and just don't know it yet. Maybe I have a future as a matchmaker instead of a stuffy real estate attorney. Maybe the best orgasm of my life is waiting for me on the other side of a dating app and I just don't know it."

I drop my head back, biting my cheek hard at the thought of

her getting off with someone else, some random person from a dating app.

Bro code, Lizzie. Goddammit.

"I'm a queer woman that has been tied to probably the most straitlaced man on the planet for so long. My entire relationship with being bi has taken a back burner to being intensely palatable. And I'm done. I'm done doing the so-called right things. Now, I want to live. I want to set up my friends, and fall out of planes, and fuck whoever I—"

"So, um, this James and Jude thing," I interrupt, hating myself for steering us back into safer waters. But I have to. I have to. There is only so much restraint in this world, and I have used every drop of it to keep myself from jumping across this table and begging her to come back to my bedroom.

She wants to take a deep dive into her queer side? I am all the fuck about it; god knows I'd love to be at her service, even though I know I shouldn't be. Can't be. But if she doesn't stop talking about it? All bets are gonna be off.

She crosses her arms. "Like I said, if you don't want to help then don't. But I'm not backing down."

Help? I would love to fucking help. I could help her so hard that she would be shaking for days and . . . wait. What were we talking about again? Oh, right. Jude. Jude and James. The same James whose sister I promised not to hook up with.

"Jude really fucked him up," I say, once my mouth catches up to my brain. "He was a total narcissist that treated your brother like shit. James ate it up for a long time. Too long."

"Really?" Cara crinkles her forehead. "I only met him once, but he seemed like a perfect gentleman. I thought they were happy."

"Yeah, that would be all the love bombing. Jude was really good at that when he wanted to be, especially after he did something truly nasty. It was part of why it took James so long to leave." I set my fork in my now empty bowl. "Look, I'm not going to tell you what to do about the rest of it—jump out of an airplane, hack his Tinder, do what you gotta do—but I *am* gonna ask you not to bring Jude back into your brother's life. He barely got out in one piece last time, I don't know if he will again."

"I had no idea any of that was going on. Why wouldn't he tell me?"

"You didn't seem to exactly confide in him about your stuff either," I point out.

She looks away and, shit, is she trying not to cry? I'm such a fucking asshole. "You actually any good at this matchmaking garbage?" I blurt out, desperate to cheer her up. "Since you're two steps away from quitting your job for it and all."

"Three weddings and counting!" she says, her entire body relaxing.

"How many divorces?" What the fuck is wrong with me? "Sorry, I didn't mean—"

"Why would you ask that?" She frowns.

I stare at her. I have no idea. I settle on, "Because I suck."

"I'm tempted to agree," she says, but there's no heat behind it.

I nudge her with my foot. "What can I say, I'm the worst."

"I wouldn't go quite that far. It's nice, the way you look out for James. And your pep talks are pretty decent too." She sighs. "Okay, fine, in the interest of full disclosure, there's been one divorce so far, and one trial separation but they're getting back together so it doesn't count. And I'm determined to find a new match for the first one, so soon that one won't count either. That's almost a one hundred percent success rate."

"That math is mathing." I take a sip of my water. "Why are you so invested in other people's love lives? This doesn't seem to be a new thing, like jumping out of airplanes."

"Honestly?"

"No sense keeping secrets now that I've seen your yoga socks, right?"

"Hey, my yoga *slippers* are cute!" she says. "But yeah, I don't know. I've always just liked making people feel good."

And huh. I can actually relate to that one.

"I get that. It's kind of like me and the gym. I just want to help people."

"Yeah. Everybody's so lost and lonely." She stabs a chunk of sweet potato with her fork.

"Are you?"

"Desperately." She laughs, low and sad. I don't ever want to hear that kind of laugh from her again.

"Oh," I say quietly. "I mean, that's understandable, given what you just went through."

"What I just put Max through, you mean? You can say it. I didn't handle that situation with grace. And yes, my mother is being a nightmare about it, but she's not completely wrong. I screwed him over. He thought things were good! And now I'm suddenly realizing that things hadn't been good for a really long time. It's like we weren't even in the same relationship sometimes. 'Lonely' is kind of an understatement for how I've been feeling this last year or so. I was drowning." She shakes her head. "He didn't even notice."

I shrug. "I think when people are planning a wedding together, they generally assume things are good, right? Otherwise, why would you get married?"

"My parents got married because my mom was pregnant, and my grandparents would have killed her if she didn't."

"I definitely did not know that," I say, leaning back in surprise. I'm not judging Stella getting pregnant or anything. To be fair, I'm not even convinced my mom knows which of her rotating boyfriends even is my father. It's Stella's hypocrisy that I hate. How she prances around like her shit doesn't stink. Like her whole life has just been a pile of never-ending gilded roses.

"It really goes against the image she makes of her perfect life, right?" Cara says. "But yeah, it was a shotgun wedding. It's hilarious because of how much shit she talked about my cousin Becca who got pregnant in college. Mom didn't even *go* to college." And it stings the way she says that, like not going is something shameful and embarrassing.

"I didn't go to college."

"Oh. You're fine. I just meant my mom, because she's so stuckup and . . ." She trails off, shoving some of her food in her mouth and chewing fast like she's trying to outrun her last comment.

Thanks, I hate it.

Just another confirmation that I'm less than. That I'm somehow not as smart for not having wasted money and time on a piece of stupid paper. I work. I pay bills. I even support my mom—not that she deserves it, but I'm glad I can. And granted, my apartment's not the best, but it's mine and I'm proud of that. God knows I spent enough nights sleeping in my car.

But the bitterness still wiggles into the back of my brain where my biggest insecurities hide. I know that's how other people see me too. And I know when and if I apply for that gym manager position, Stella—Stella, who apparently never went to college but constantly flaunts her children's degrees like they're her own—will look down on me too.

"I'm sorry," she says, grabbing my hand. "I made it awkward, didn't I?"

I wave her off. "It's not a big deal."

"I mean, if it makes you feel any better, college or not, I think you got the better life out of the deal."

I stare at her, incredulous. "How do you figure?"

"You seem really happy. Like you have your shit together."

"I don't know what you're basing that on, but I assure you I do *not* have my shit together."

"I'm basing it on the fact that you light up like the sun whenever you talk about the gym or give people tours. Not to mention the way you were there for me when . . . I wish James knew that you were the one behind that pep talk."

"Cara . . ."

She holds up her hand to quiet me. "I know, I know. I'll keep it a secret. But it's not just that stuff. You seem so confident and just settled here. I want that too, you know. I'm over here squatting at my brother's house because I blew up my miserable long-term relationship, on a sabbatical from a job I don't even know if I want to go back to, begging people to jump out of airplanes with me or set them up on dates. I'm doing anything I can to distract myself from spending another second thinking about how screwed up it is that I don't even know who I am anymore." Her voice cracks and I'm startled to find her wiping at her eyes. "You must think I'm so ridiculous."

"No. *No*," I say again, this time more firmly. "You're not."

"I'm driving you nuts trying to figure out these dates for James just so I don't have to think about *my* own mess and it's—"

"It's fine. Really," I hear myself say, desperate to cheer her up. "I won't jump off a cliff or out an airplane, but I'll help you figure out the date for James if you really need me to."

"Oh god, pity doesn't suit you," she says, the tears coming in earnest now.

"No, it's not pity. I want to, I do," I lie. "Just not Jude and not like a big, weird thing," I say, because well, I doubt a date is going to happen in the end.

"You're a terrible liar," she says as I pass her a napkin.

"No, I want to." I wait for her to meet my eyes. "Let me help you."

Finally, finally, she smiles. And this is fine. *It's fine.* I can do this. I can be her distraction. Or rather, I can help her *plan this* as a distraction. It's not really unethical, right? I'm not spying or babysitting or any of that shit James wanted. I'm just . . . lightly supervising at worst. Cheering her up at best. And she did say she wanted to explore her queerness so if . . . *No. Stop it, Lizzie.*

"So, nothing big, then?" Cara asks, saving me from falling any farther down *that* particular rabbit hole in my mind. "Are you sure? I always loved it when Max went the extra mile for me. It was the only time it felt like he cared."

"James isn't Max, and he isn't you. He doesn't like big showy things." I'm lying again. James absolutely loves big showy things. "How about just a home-cooked dinner. Something really great."

I don't mention that it's also something James and I do regularly anyway, so at least it won't be weird when he tells the mystery date to go home immediately and we devour whatever Cara cooks ourselves instead.

"Okay." She smiles, and I feel like I can breathe. "Want to help prep? We can make them an awesome dinner and then leave them to it?"

"Sure," I say, because saying no just feels rude. Especially when I'm expecting to be the one eating it at the end of the day. "We can do it at your place," I add, because no matter what, I never want her to see my little apartment on the wrong side of town, nestled cozily between a liquor store and a pawnshop. She's too good for that place. I try not to think about what else she's too good for.

Chapter Thirteen

"Okay, so you're going to cut these in half," Cara says, handing me some acorn squash and a very sharp knife.

We're in the middle of James's kitchen. He's got a late training session tonight and then will be coming home for a "family dinner" right afterward. What he doesn't know—well, what she thinks he doesn't know—is that this is part of Cara's grand date-night plan for him. After trying, and failing, to hack his phone a second time, she set up a profile of her own on a dating website, labeled "please date my brother." She's spent all week vetting applicants. She finally landed on one, and promptly set up a scheme to surprise James tonight.

Cara's heading out right after we've finished cooking to grab drinks with her friends, Sherry and Jane. I gotta admit, that was super surprising given what I know about how things went down between them. Odds are, she's just using this as an excuse to make herself scarce in case James is mad about the setup . . . but her leaving for the night actually makes things easier, so I'm all for it.

According to her plan, I'm supposed to stay here long enough to make sure the guy she picked isn't an axe murderer and then find an excuse to take off too.

What Cara doesn't know is that a) I already told James the plan. Obviously. And b) I got the guy's info so James could tell him he's actually seeing someone and not interested. The dude—Sam—is still coming over though. It turns out he's new in town and mainly just looking for friends anyway. Unlike Cara's plan, *James's* plan is for the three of us to watch horror movies and split the food and then later they'll both just tell Cara they're better off as friends.

Complicated, I know.

Would it have been easier to just tell Cara the truth? Yes. Is James still 100 percent against that for some reason? Also, yes.

I guess it'll be worth it if the worst thing that comes out of my effort to cheer Cara up is a good meal, a potential new friend, and movie night with James—*Annabelle Comes Home*. I'm guiding his scaredy-cat ass through the *Conjuring* universe as payback for ditching me at the yoga class. (Which he swore was a genuine emergency, and not a setup, but I absolutely do not believe him.)

"What are we making, again?"

"You're making baked eggs in acorn squash topped with feta, roasted peppers, and fresh dill. I guarantee you James is going to love it. Healthy and protein packed and all that. Meanwhile, I'm going to handle the steaks because, no offense, you look like a girl who can't grill."

"What's that supposed to mean!"

"Nothing, no judgment! I'm just saying." She hands me a spoon to scoop the seeds out of the squash. "You seemed marginally terrified when I asked you to start the briquettes."

"I'll have you know that I am an expert griller," I say, and Cara raises an eyebrow. "Okay, fine, maybe not 'expert.'" I dump out some of the seeds from the squash onto the cutting board next to me. "But I know my way around *regular* grills. You know, with kerosene and automatic starters and stuff."

Cara fake shudders. "We are not cooking these gorgeous steaks on a gas grill." She flips through James's cabinets. "I wonder if he has any wood chips." I shrug. Up until an hour ago, I didn't even realize he had two grills. Usually when we whip the gas grill out, it's just to throw on some chicken or fish to go with our veggies when we don't want to stink up his house.

I finish cleaning up the acorn squash, slice the back so that it lies flat, and carry them over to the oven. Cara grabs various spices to sprinkle on them, along with some olive oil and salt. Anything she does to one, I imitate on the other.

We work side by side in relative silence, our arms brushing against each other as we go, each time sending a jolt of electricity through my body. I hate that it reacts like this. I especially hate that it reacts like this when my head is working so hard to keep things casual and platonic between us.

She opens the oven door and slides the tray in. "Okay, those need to bake awhile. What do you want to do while we wait?"

My mind flips through about three thousand options at once, everything ranging from sweeping her into a kiss to a friendly socially distanced game of Uno. It's not that I want to treat her like an infectious disease, it's just that my libido finds her very . . . contagious.

"Twenty questions?" she suggests.

"What?"

"Not the game Twenty Questions, but like a rapid-fire, not-thinking-too-hard, get-to-know-each-other-better type of thing," she says.

"That sounds dangerous."

"No, it sounds fun."

"You have a very, very twisted idea of fun, woman."

She laughs. "Come on, please? You can ask me anything you want too."

"I don't want to ask you anything," I say, and her face falls for a split second before flipping back to neutral.

"Oh, okay." Cara carries what I'm pretty sure is an already clean dish over to the sink.

And I've stepped in it. Again.

Shit.

"I don't mean I don't want to know you. I just don't want to ask you a bunch of invasive questions that you feel like you have to answer because you want me to answer in kind. I don't work like that, I'm sorry. I'm not a big sharer, especially not as like quid pro quo or something. I'm not trying to be an asshole though, I swear. I just don't do deep."

She seems to consider this for a moment and then smiles. "How about easy questions, then? Surface level. Favorite song and all that. Deal?"

I roll my eyes, watching the time ticking down on the stove clock. "Okay," I say, and hope I don't regret it.

"Favorite color?" she asks.

"Green."

"Favorite drink?"

"Vega One Chocolate. I do not vibe with vanilla."

Cara scrunches her forehead. "Seriously?"

"Seriously."

"Boring, but okay."

"What's yours?" I ask.

"Lemonade, specifically the one from the county fair. It reminds me of being a kid and going there with my grandparents."

"Cute."

She taps her chin. "Favorite food?"

"Raw Rev Glo bars, Sea Salt and Peanut Butter specifically."

I'm met with another surprised look, followed immediately by a sad shake of her head.

"What? I like things I can just grab and go. I don't usually have time to cook like this," I say, gesturing around the kitchen.

"Mine's fried dough, for the same reason as the lemonade."

"You really have a thing for fair food, huh?"

"Everything in moderation," she sings. "Isn't that what James tells his clients?"

"Yes, but only to be nice. In real life he practically dies every time I make him eat takeout."

"Well, lucky for him we aren't frying anything, then."

"Yeah, lucky for him," I mumble. Because for a second, I almost, *almost* forgot this was all about James and his pseudo date, Sam. "Where'd you learn to cook like this?" I ask, changing the subject.

"I don't know. I've just always loved it," she says. "Favorite . . . way to cut loose?"

I stare at her, because what does that even mean? "I don't know," I answer slowly. "I pretty much work, go home, work again. You?"

"I don't think I know either anymore. If you asked me a few

weeks ago, I would say a glass of wine and a bubble bath. A leisurely walk around a farmers market. Going out to some of the bars downtown. But if I'm being honest, it always kind of rang empty."

"Why?"

"It just felt like I had to do that stuff. It's expected. After a tough day of making other people a lot of money, you drink wine in the bath, or you go out for champagne to celebrate. That's what they do on TV. In books. I've been so worried about what I was supposed to do, I don't even know what it is that I want. I don't even know what I *like* anymore."

I lean against the counter next to her. "You don't have to know exactly what you want right now."

"Then why does everybody keep asking me what the plan is? Every other text is some variation of: *What's the plan now that you left Max? What's the plan now that you took a sabbatical?* What's the plan, what's the plan, what's the plan. Everybody just wants to be reassured that everything is fine and still on track. Go to college, get a job, get married, drink your fucking wine." She winces. "Do you ever feel like your whole life is something that's happening to you? Like you're just being swept from one point to the next on an ocean of other people's expectations?"

"Yeah," I say softly. Like right now, I think.

If I was really in control of things, I would have turned in my résumé for the gym manager position already. I would have told both James *and* Cara that I didn't want to go along with their schemes and meant it. I wouldn't be standing here talking about bubble baths—we would be in one together, one hand snaking through Cara's hair while the other . . .

I clear my throat and look away, watching the oven timer tick down to the moment she's going to leave. We always duck and dodge like this. If our messages got any more mixed, they'd be tie-dye.

"You probably think I'm pathetic," she says, and that sound drags my eyes back to hers.

I slide a little closer, nudging her with my shoulder. "I absolutely don't. I think you're really brave actually."

"You do?" She tilts her head just slightly, eyes going soft as she licks her lips. I resist the urge to pull her toward me, to close that last couple of inches between us, to show her how perfectly our bodies can fit together.

"Brave, funny, hot," I say, my voice going low. "The total package."

Her lips part a little at the word "hot" as she angles her body toward mine. "You're not so bad yourself," she says, and her voice comes out a little more breathless than it was before. And in moments like these—fuck, why do we keep having so many?—hope blooms in my chest like an ugly weed: persistent, determined, *unwanted*.

I lean impossibly close. "Cara—" But before I can get out another word, the oven buzzer goes off and we both jerk back. Probably for the best. I don't even know where that sentence was going. Nowhere good.

She glances back at the oven and then at me, but I'm gone, already making my way across the kitchen. "Heh, if I were in your shoes, I'd probably be married by now. On a horrible honeymoon with a dumb boy." I crinkle my nose at that last word, and she laughs.

"Or a dumb girl?" she asks, watching me.

"Oh shit," I say, shoving my nose into the handwritten recipe she's pinned to the fridge and pretending I didn't hear her. "It looks like we need feta cheese," I say, hoping that seems like a nice segue.

Judging by the look on her face it wasn't.

"We got some the other day, check in the back." Cara pulls the squash out of the oven and flicks off the timer.

I wonder who "we" is. I wonder if it's her and James, or her and somebody else. I wonder if she's using the dating site for more than just finding people for her brother. I don't know why I thought she wouldn't be. It's clear she's been over Max for some time.

I shut the fridge a little harder than necessary and force my thoughts away. I need to focus on surviving the next hour without blowing James's cover. That's all that matters. This isn't about me, and I need to remember that.

"I'm going to go start the grill," she says, as if she can sense my shift in mood. "Are you good with the peppers and eggs and stuff?"

"Got it," I say.

IT DOESN'T TAKE me long to finish up; the eggs are poured in the little hole in the center of the squash, topped with roasted peppers and some feta. It's sitting on the counter resting on the tray, just waiting for Cara to come back and give me the all-clear to put it in the oven.

James is due home in about a half hour, maybe a little less, so soon she'll be off to the bar with her friends. And I'll be . . . here. This is so stupid.

"You good?" she asks, coming in the patio door. She smells like smoke and looks quite proud of herself.

"All set." I gesture toward the pan. "Can I pop it in?"

"Yep." She grabs the steaks out of the fridge where they've been marinating, and heads toward the back deck. She moves through the kitchen with a confidence I've never experienced, and I add it to the list of things I should definitely not be noticing about her.

I toss the pan in the oven and then follow her back outside, where she takes her spot in front of a short black Weber grill. It seems like it's seen better days.

"Did you know he had leaves in this thing? Literal leaves." Cara shakes her head and drops the meat onto the grill. The flames shoot up with a hiss and we both jump back. "Maybe a little bit too much lighter fluid on this batch, but don't worry, he shouldn't be able to taste it."

"Somehow I doubt lighter fluid would qualify under your brother's strict nutritional requirements."

"Probably not, but oh well." Cara flips the meat thermometer in the air, a little red folding type, and catches it before pointing it at me like a sword. "And we didn't finish our game."

I roll my eyes. "What else could you possibly want to know about me?" I snort. "You already know my favorite drink and food. That about covers it."

She groans, actually groans. "Why are you so difficult?"

"Me?"

"Yes, you! It shouldn't be this hard to have a conversation with someone. Schmoozing is part of my job, I'm good at this! People like talking to me! I have countless closed deals to prove it! But you act like it's torture."

"I don't want you to schmooze me," I say, a little offended. Is this what this is? This flirting, these mixed signals, is she *schmoozing*?

"Don't worry, I'm not, seeing as how I can barely get you to talk to me." She puts her hands on her hips. "You want to tell me why you're so determined for us not to be friends? I'm getting a complex over here," she teases. "I'm starting to think our bathroom convo was a fluke!"

"I was very drunk," I deadpan.

"You wound me."

"Truth hurts, baby," I tease.

"Ohhh, I'm 'baby' now? That's quite the nickname." She steps closer, the dare apparent.

"If it fits . . ."

She pouts. "You're an asshole."

"I never said I wasn't."

She rolls her eyes. "Come on, back to the game."

"Fine."

She raises her eyebrows. "Fine?"

"Fine, but it's my turn to ask."

She meets my eyes. "Go for it."

"Favorite movie?"

"*Reservoir Dogs*," she says, and I arch my eyebrows.

"Okay, fine, *Step Up*," she says, crossing her arms. "I used to dance in high school."

"Favorite color?"

"Blue."

"Best day?"

She scrunches up her face. "How big of an asshole am I if I say 'when I ran from my own wedding'?"

"Biggest red flag?"

"What I consider to be the biggest red flag in people or the biggest red flag about me?"

I cross my arms. "Both, now that you mention it."

"Let's see, the biggest red flag in others would be somebody that talks more than they listen. And in me?" She taps her chin. "When things get messy, I run. I don't do second chances."

"Ever? Not even if they deserve it?"

She shrugs. "I've never dated anyone that deserved it. Your turn. Red flags in other people and yourself. Go."

"When people wear socks at yoga, one hundred percent."

"You are such an ass." She smacks my arm. "But fine, what's the biggest red flag about yourself, then?"

I shake my head. "You don't wanna know."

"Fair is fair," she says, checking the steaks.

I clear my throat. "I don't . . . care."

"You don't care?"

"I just . . . I don't get invested, like romantically." She studies my face and I pray that she's not going to ask me why. I'm not about to spew all my mommy issues all over this night.

Cara narrows her eyes. "You're one of those 'here for a good time, not a long time' kinda people?"

"Something like that," I say, desperate to move the conversation to safer ground. And then because I'm an idiot, I ask, "Biggest fantasy?"

"Someone else taking control." She meets my eyes and heat instantly pools in my belly.

"Have you ever been with a woman?" I shouldn't be pushing this, but I have to know.

"Define 'been with.'"

"You know what I'm asking."

"Not . . . fully."

"But you want to? You said—"

"Why? Are you offering?" she asks, holding eye contact.

I might be.

And it's that exact second that the smell of burning meat hits both of our noses. Fuck, how many moments can one meal ruin?

Cara grabs the tongs and rushes to flip the meat. "Oh god, oh god! I ruined it."

I stare down at the meat, pitch black on one side and mostly raw on the other. "It doesn't look too bad," I lie.

"I've killed it. I took a beautiful cut of meat, and then I killed it."

"To be fair, the butcher beat you to it." I put my hand on her shoulder reassuringly and she leans into it. Some of her hair has flopped into her face in all of the excitement, and I brush it back, tucking it behind her ear.

"Lizzie . . ." She shakes her head, swallowing whatever she was about to say.

The buzz of my phone echoes in the silence that's rapidly spreading between us. Cara glances over and sees the goofy picture of James that flashes whenever he calls me.

"You got this, right?" she asks. "I have to go get ready." Before I can even answer, she's headed inside.

I click accept on the call and breathe deep. Part of me wants to yell at him for being late and part of me wants to thank him. I'm not entirely sure what happened between me and Cara tonight, but it felt like something. Something that I would really like to happen again, even though I shouldn't.

"Don't kill me," James cries in my ear.

"What did you do?"

"It's what I'm not doing that I think you might get mad at me for."

I groan. "Are you bailing on me again?!"

"Ramón just told me he got the weekend off. He wants me to drive up now so we can spend the full day together tomorrow. Don't be mad. I already texted Sam and rain-checked our hangout. He was totally cool with it."

"We were supposed to watch *Annabelle Comes Home!*"

"And now you can watch it with Cara instead. Maybe she'll grab you on all the jump scares and stuff."

"There's not that many. I told you! This one's practically a rom-com," I say, brushing off the rest of what he said. If I start thinking about Cara grabbing me in any scenario, I might explode. Lust confetti, thy name is Lizzie.

"A rom-com with a haunted doll? Sure, I believe you." He snorts.

"Fine, well, what happened to the bro code? Now that it's convenient for you, she's suddenly fair game?"

"Dude, freaking her out with your little movies and fucking her are not the same thing. I said she might grab you, not jump your bones."

The telltale beep-beep of her automatic car starter outside rings through the house. It's a hot one, she's probably got the air conditioner on full blast. And right, yeah, she has plans.

"Come on, she's leaving anyway. She's going out with Sherry and Jane. Can you just get home?"

"Oh," he says, and I can tell by his voice he's not going to. "I'm kind of already on my way to see him. I can call Sam back? Maybe he can still come over at least?"

"You're already on your way?"

"Yeah, my evening lesson canceled so I left a little while ago from the gym. I'm so sorry, Lizzie, even if I turn around now, I'm gonna be super late. I honestly didn't think you'd care."

"What am I supposed to do now? She's going to notice if we don't eat all this food. You're making this a thousand times more complicated, and it was already a shitshow to begin with."

"Bring it home with you, then. I'm really sorry. I didn't think it would be this big of a deal. Now I feel like shit."

"It's fine," I say, even though it isn't. "Have fun. Tell him I said hi." I am happy for him and Ramón, but also . . . this sucks.

"You're the best, Lizzie," he says.

"Yeah, I know," I grumble. "I'll wait for Cara to leave and then lock up. If she asks, you and Sam still met up tonight, okay?"

"Yeah, of course," he says, and I don't miss the relief in his voice, the feeling that all has been forgiven. "Love you," he adds, with a hopeful lilt.

I know he feels bad, and I know he didn't do it intentionally. He just didn't think it through. Not thinking things through is kind of his thing.

"Love you too," I say, and click my phone off.

I stare down at the steaks, now fully burned on both sides, and then drag them onto the plate that Cara left sitting on the table beside the grill. The oven timer goes off right as I get back inside, so I slide the tray out—feeling numb and lonelier than I have any right to. It's not like this night was for me. It's not like *any* of this was for me.

Cara comes flying out of the guest room a few minutes later. I'm still messing around in the kitchen trying to make myself busy, hoping she leaves soon so I can get on with my night.

"Alright, well, I'm off," she says. She doesn't even look at me.

"See ya," I call to the already closing front door.

I wait for her to back out of the driveway, and then I fish around in James's cabinets to find some Tupperware big enough to fit all the food. This is way too much for just me, but if I leave it then she'll definitely know something was up.

I shouldn't even care, honestly. This should be James's problem to deal with, not mine. But I do. I don't want her to know tonight was all for nothing.

I do a quick once-over of the kitchen and am just about to walk out the door, the little plastic containers bundled in my arms, when Cara comes bursting back in.

"Sorry, I forgot my wallet. I'll only be a—Wait, what are you doing?"

I have no answer that makes me sound cool. "Um . . ."

"Where are you going with all the food?"

I slump my shoulders down. No use in lying now. "Your brother's not coming. He called to tell me."

"Oh," she says, a heavy frown pulling at her features. "What happened?"

"He . . . uh . . . got hung up."

She blinks at me.

"With a client or something, I don't know. I let Sam know we had to reschedule," I add in a last-ditch effort to cover James's tracks.

She glances at the Tupperware in my arms. "You're taking all the food?"

"I didn't want it to go to waste. I can leave you half if you want." I hold out one of the containers.

"No, that's okay, you can take them."

"Thanks," I mumble. Just a few more steps to the door, and then to my car, and then I can drive far, far away from this confusing, embarrassing night and never look back. I wonder how long it would take me to drive across the entire United States but then realize that doesn't feel far enough. Maybe a cargo ship could—

"Hey, Lizzie, wait," she says, as my hand touches the doorknob.

"Yeah?"

"I'm kinda hungry."

I turn back and look at her, not sure what to say. It feels like an invitation, but I don't know why. We both know she's got plans.

"I'm okay eating alone," I say, because I can't tell if this is pity or not, and if it is, I don't want it.

"Oh," she says, and I both love and hate those two little letters and the perfect curve of her mouth as she says them.

"If you're worried about me or something. It's fine, I'm used to it."

"I wasn't," she says, and sounds sincere, "but if you'd rather—"

"No!" I say, too quickly. "I mean, if you're hungry, there's plenty of food and I wouldn't mind the company. But don't feel obligated."

"I don't." She smiles.

"What about your friends?"

"They can wait," she says. "Actually . . ." She bites her lip, letting the words trail off.

"Actually what?"

"Actually, I'm kind of nervous to see them. Would you want to . . . forget it."

I tilt my head. "Would I want to what?"

"I was going to ask, would you want to come, but I'm sure you have way better things to do than that."

"Where are you meeting?"

"Johnny's."

I raise my eyebrows. Johnny's is an Irish pub in the center of town. It's nice enough, but kind of rowdy. A lot of college kids playing pool, getting wasted, and stuff like that. I know the bartender there; he works out at the gym. I'm kind of surprised. I pegged her as more dance club than dive bar.

"You don't have to," she adds when I take too long to answer.

"I could get a drink," I say, trying to sound nonchalant even though my heart is hammering a hundred miles an hour at the thought.

"Excellent," she says, with a grin that hits me square in the chest.

Chapter Fourteen

We make quick work of dinner, each of us gnawing comically on the charred steak—hey, free food is free food—while trying to pretend it tastes good. It brings back memories of the turkey scene from *National Lampoon's Christmas Vacation*, and I spend a good ten minutes ragging on her for not knowing what "I don't *know*, Margo" means as a result.

She says she's seen it once, she thinks, but it "could have been *Home Alone*," and I almost fall off my chair. This needs to be remedied. Immediately.

"I hardly think it's like the pinnacle of cinema. It's no *Citizen Kane*."

"Have you even seen *Citizen Kane*?" I snort.

"No, but . . ."

"Exactly. You only said that because you think you're supposed to. Because for some reason people put that kind of pretentious bullshit on a pedestal. Art should exist to affect us and a dumb movie that makes us laugh isn't any less worthy than one that leaves us yawning and confused in some art house that's two matinees away from going bankrupt. In fact, I would argue that it's more valid than something you think is important just because someone told you it is."

"Wow." She giggles, clearing my plate. "You're extremely passionate about an old Christmas movie."

"It's the best Christmas movie of all time." I snort. "Show some respect."

"Noted," she says, carrying our dirty dishes to the sink.

"Here, I'll do those," I say, coming up to the sink behind her. But she shakes her head.

"No, James can wash the dishes whenever he gets home. He deserves it for ruining our devious plan."

I smile when she grabs my hand and tugs me out the door behind her. And yeah, I could definitely get used to this.

JOHNNY'S IS A loud, dimly lit bar, complete with sticky floors and straw wrappers littering the tables. It's comfortable, though, with large, overstuffed booths and heavy wood chairs. The bartender is named Mickey, with a bulky build and a bright red beard to match. His grandfather owns the place, and while I don't frequent bars really—drinking isn't my thing, weddings aside, apparently—he does frequent the gym. In fact, we've spotted for each other more than once.

"Lizzie," he calls, coming around the bar to wrap me in a big bear hug that nearly knocks the wind out of me. "You finally came!"

"Here I am!" I say awkwardly, not sure what else to say.

"'Bout time. What'll you have? It's on me." He tosses his bar rag over his shoulder, crossing his bulging arms as he waits.

"Um . . ." I stare at the wall, totally out of my element. *Not three Dark 'N' Stormys, that's for sure.*

"I'll surprise ya," he says with a wink. "Go find a seat."

Cara and I head toward the only empty booth left in the back, but just as she's taking off her coat, a couple of rowdy college kids cut in front of us and drop into it themselves. I try to get their attention, but they just laugh and ignore us. And cool, cool, cool.

Fuck that.

"Hey," I say again, stepping closer to the table. Cara tries to pull me back, but I shake her off. "We were sitting there."

"I didn't see you." One of the boys snorts, and the annoyance rises up inside me.

"Yes, you did. Now get up."

"What are you gonna do about it?" he asks. I look him up and down, sizing him up. He's maybe 153 on a good day, scrawny by anybody's standards, and it's clear that most of his confidence comes from his beanie, which sits perfectly askew, and his big round glasses that would give off a "Hi, I'm an asshole" vibe even if he wasn't currently making me look bad in front of someone I'm trying to impress . . . *not* that I'm trying to impress her.

I shove up my sleeves and tilt my head, watching it slowly dawn on him that I'm not intimidated.

"You really want to find out? Because I'm sure that me and my friend over there would love to show you." I wave to Mickey behind the bar, who's watching with rapt attention, a scowl on his normally jovial face as he slowly dries a glass.

The table goes quiet. "No, ma'am," one of the other boys says, sliding out of the booth. "Sorry, ma'am." Beanie asshole slides out too, refusing to meet my eyes as he does. I grin when I realize they aren't just vacating the booth, but the place in general. I'm sure the fact that Mickey continues to glare at them from his spot behind the bar had something to do with it, but I'm gonna count this as a W for me too.

"That was *awesome*," Cara practically squeals as we slide onto opposite sides of the giant U-shaped booth.

"It was nothing, they were being rude," I say, like my body isn't literally shaking from adrenaline. "Besides, Mickey and his glare really did all the work. All I did was wave."

"I would have just given them the table. That took a lot of guts. I'm impressed."

"I guess so," I say, trying not to let her compliment go to my head. She checks her phone. "Ooh! Jane and Sherry should be here in a second, they texted they're parking."

"I figured they would have beat us here since we're an hour late."

"I told them they should probably grab something to eat first since we were running behind and this place isn't exactly known for its food."

"Makes sense."

She keeps fiddling with her phone, chewing on her lip like she does whenever she's nervous. Another thing I shouldn't be noticing, because her tells aren't mine to notice. They belonged to Max and whoever comes after Max. To her real friends. To other people who aren't me.

"Don't be nervous," I say. "I'm sure this is going to be great."

"I haven't seen them in so long."

"Yeah, James mentioned something happened?"

"Long story," she says. "But it's been awhile. We've been texting a little since I've been back, but this is the first time I'm going to see them and I just . . . I miss them, you know? But what if they're just coming to tell me they hate me or something and to stop texting them?"

"They're not." She looks at me with an expression that says she isn't totally convinced. "And if they are, then Mickey will just get us really drunk and I'll call an Uber and we'll have a good night either way."

She tilts her head. "How do you do that?"

"Do what?" I scrunch up my forehead.

"Always make me feel better so fast?"

Before I can answer, Sherry and Jane arrive, standing beside our table. Cara handles the introductions while I take them both in. Sherry is a white woman, in her late twenties, I'm guessing. She has straight blond hair that hangs like sheets around her angular face, and her ears, which peek out between her flat strands, are adorned with countless piercings and cuffs running up the sides. She has distrustful eyes and a wide toothy smile bordering on menacing, and when she shakes my hand, she squeezes a little too hard.

Jane, on the other hand, seems like sunshine personified, a Black woman with curly hair and big brown eyes. Her smile feels genuine, and instead of a handshake she pulls me into a hug.

I slide back into my side of the booth at the same time as Cara slides into hers, and we end up bumping into each other in the middle with a laugh that sounds a little too nervous. We quickly scoot away to give each other space, but Sherry and Jane have already sat opposite each other on the open ends of our U-shaped booth, effectively trapping us. Mickey comes over with a round of shots and a mystery mixed drink for me, all on the house, and then takes everyone's actual drink orders. A woman perched at a high-top tries to flag him down when he leaves, but he just shrugs and says he doesn't do table service despite the fact that he's clearly doing it for us.

Johnny's is not the sort of place that employs waiters and waitresses—it's an "every man for himself" fight to place your order at the bar, so I sincerely appreciate him taking care of us.

"The bartender seems really into you," Cara mutters, and I glance at her, half thinking she sounds jealous. But no, I'm definitely reading into this. As usual.

"Sorry we had to push back the time," I say, when the table goes unexpectedly quiet. I can tell that everyone is nervous, not really sure what to say. It's only fair that breaking the tension should fall on me, given that I'm the only one without any sort of backstory or history that needs unpacking. "But we—"

"They didn't mind," Cara says, glancing at the women on either side of us. "Did you?"

"No, we didn't mind at all," Jane says.

Sherry is still watching me closely, like she's trying to figure me out, or like she recognizes me but can't place it. "So, you're Lizzie," she says finally, knocking back a shot. I had assumed that we were going to make a toast, but I guess that's out the window.

Cara gives my hand a squeeze under the table but makes no outward motion to acknowledge it.

"I'm Lizzie!" I smile and hope it looks friendly instead of pained. "And you're Sherry. Good to meet you." Honestly, with the way that Sherry is looking at me, I think maybe I *would* rather be home eating sad acorn squash out of Tupperware and watching *Annabelle* by myself.

"I didn't realize that we were going to have extra company," Sherry says, and this time Jane cuts in.

"But how nice it is to meet another one of Cara's friends!"

Sherry frowns and looks away. I don't know what her deal is, but clearly she has a problem with me. I guess I *am* third-wheeling it. Or fourth-wheeling it, which I didn't even know was a thing. But Cara asked me to come, to help her be brave, and as much as I want to go hide at the bar and chat with Mickey until it's time to go, I know I should stay. I didn't fight this hard for the booth just to get run out of it by an overzealous lesbian with mismatched earrings. Even if they *are* great earrings.

"Cara says you work at her parents' gym," Jane offers, probably not realizing that she's landed on another equally awkward conversation topic.

"I do, yeah. I'm the front desk manager for now but I'm hoping to one day own my own."

"Cara, didn't you have that job in high school? You used to complain about being stuck scanning in all the little gym rats," Sherry says, looking at me in a way that isn't exactly kind, and oh, okay. I get it. I know that look well. It's the look of somebody who thinks they're better than me. I don't really know why this has turned into a pissing match, but clearly it has.

"Really?" I snap and she looks taken aback.

"I'm just making conversation," Sherry says. "I personally think it's nice that Mommy Dearest has moved on to hiring adults in that role."

"Right, right, my job's a joke to you. Too bad I like my shitty job, and I like being a gym rat, and I love helping our guests, so I don't really care whether you think that's beneath you or not."

"That's not what she meant." Jane smiles, trying to smooth things over, but it's too late.

"Can you let me out?" I ask, suddenly claustrophobic. "I need to use the restroom."

Cara shimmies out with a frown, clearly not liking how this is going down. Still, the sinking feeling in my stomach, that familiar feeling of not being good enough, threatens to drown me. I wonder if Sherry and Jane are both lawyers or in real estate or finance or something like that, people with big expensive futures who I apparently shouldn't even be sitting near. People like Cara.

I push open the bathroom door, to find a gaggle of girls reapplying their makeup and generally looking like they're having the time of their lives. I ignore them and opt for a stall instead, barging in and locking the door, content to hide out for a while.

Finally, there's the swing of the door and the bathroom goes quiet. I know I've been in here too long already, but I don't want to leave. I don't want to go back to that table. Maybe Mickey will let me live in here if I ask really nice.

The unmistakable creak of the door swinging open again fills the silence of the bathroom, and I pull my legs up, so it looks like the stall is empty. I don't hear a stall door click or water run or any other sound for that matter. It's not long before I start to think I imagined someone else coming in. After an unreasonably long time, I unlock the door and step out . . . only to see Cara quietly leaning against the wall. She offers me a sad smile and pushes off.

"I thought maybe you could use a bathroom pep talk this time." She shrugs.

"I'm fine," I say, trying to brush her off. I wash my hands, fully trying to keep up the charade that I just had to pee, nothing worse than that. That nobody hurt me or poked their well-manicured fingers in all my fragile wounds.

"Okay, then in that case, can I have one?" Cara asks, and my eyes shoot to hers. "Sherry's being horrible to you and now Jane is pissed at her, and it's all so awkward and awful. Maybe you're fine with it but I'm not. I'll give you five bucks if we can sneak out that window over there and pretend none of this happened. We'll go home and watch a movie. I'll even let you pick."

I'm tempted to. Even more tempted because she said "we" instead of "I." I wonder for a second if I can get her to watch *Christmas Vacation*, then wonder if I should start with *Annabelle* instead.

And then I realize we shouldn't do either.

"Cara," I say softly. "You'll regret it if you leave. You miss them, right? That's what you said? Which means if you leave now, you're going to have to do this all over again later. It's awkward, yeah, but just get it over with instead of having to start fresh a second time."

"But she's being a jerk to you."

"Yeah, she is," I say. "But who cares? She's not here for me, she's here for you and your friendship. I don't matter at all to any of this. I'm just getting in your way."

"You're not," she says firmly.

I sigh. She's lying and we both know it. "Look, I'm going to go hang out with Mickey at the bar for a little while. You go have fun with your friends, and I'll have fun with mine. Talk shit out. Do what you gotta do. I'm here if you need me, and to be your designated driver, but I don't need to be involved in the nitty-gritty. Me being there is just making it worse."

"Are you sure?"

"Positive," I say, but I'd be lying if I said part of me wasn't hoping that she would choose staying with me instead. But deep down, I know I'm not the person she jumps to protect. I'm just a bathroom Yoda that happened to be in the right place at the right time, or the wrong place at the wrong time, depending on who you ask. I'm not the person you stay and fight for, never have been.

Cara sighs. "I don't know."

"Go, seriously. You're going to regret it if you don't."

"Okay," she says, studying my face for any signs of deception, and if she thinks I'm going to crack in front of her, she's got another think coming.

Chapter Fifteen

Mickey and I are about a half hour into debating the merits of powerlifting versus Olympic lifting when I feel a tap on my shoulder. I'm expecting it to be Cara, and turn around with a smile, only to find myself face-to-face with Sherry. Perfect. I glance at her and then go back to shuffling the coasters in front of me.

"You need another drink?" Mickey asks her, unimpressed. And okay, I may have told him why I was hiding out at the bar. My bad. Or not, because Sherry *was* technically being a huge dick to me. Whatever stink eye he's giving her, she's earned.

"No, actually . . ." She trails off and if I didn't know any better, I would think she sounded almost shy. "Do you wanna go have a smoke?" she asks, holding up her vape in front of me.

"I don't smoke," I say. "Professional gym rat, remember?" I watch wistfully as Mickey gets pulled away to take some more orders—*Bring me with you! Don't leave me alone with this woman who—*

"Okay, yes, that makes sense," Sherry says, leaning against the bar to place herself directly in my line of sight.

I wait for her to say something else. She doesn't. "Is there something you needed?" I finally ask.

"I'm trying to choose my words carefully," she answers.

"It shouldn't be this hard to be polite to someone."

"I'm not trying to be polite."

I snort. "Believe it or not, I kind of picked up on that."

"I apologize for my earlier rudeness." She sighs and rubs her arm like it physically hurts her to say sorry. "I didn't mean to scare you off."

"You didn't," I say, turning to fully meet her eyes. "You just made me not want to hang out with *you*. I have other friends here that are actually worth my time." I gesture toward where Mickey stands, peeking at me out of the corner of his eye as he makes a row of Sex on the Beach drinks for the rowdy girls from earlier. "Besides, whatever's going on is between the three of you, not me."

"I'm trying to say sorry here," Sherry says, clearly frustrated by my unwillingness to find her intimidating.

"And I'm telling you it's fine. We'll hopefully never see each again, so let's just forget we ever met."

She looks at me, confused. "Why wouldn't we see each other again?"

"Because we aren't friends?" I say, and now it's my turn to be confused. "I don't generally make a habit out of hanging out with rude strangers."

Sherry gives me another puzzled look and then gestures over to the corner, to where Jane and Cara are playing a game of darts— very badly, I might add. I watch them cackle as a dart misses the board entirely and ends up next to the pinball machine.

"She's a menace." I smile as Cara struggles to pull her dart out of the wood-paneled wall.

"She's great," Sherry says fondly, and my stomach twists again— jealousy kicking up a notch. I'm not entirely clear which one of these two women Cara dated, but my money's on the one standing in front of me, which would make Jane the best friend who betrayed her. "Look, I don't care if we get along, and I don't care if Cara wants to hate me just as much as you do, but that," she gestures toward Cara and Jane again, "that's important. Jane has been lost without her. I don't know what she's told you, but they were the epitome of best friends forever until I came along and ruined it. I'm not going to be the one that makes them fall apart again. If there's any way that you and I can tolerate each other for our partners' sakes . . ."

And then it clicks. She thinks Cara and I are together.

"Oh," I say, ignoring the warm feeling blooming in my chest at the thought. "You definitely have the wrong idea about where I fall in all of this. I'm not . . . we're not even remotely together. You do know that, right? We're nothing."

"But . . ." She trails off, looking between me and Cara like somehow the answer will be painted on the floor between us. "What?"

"Yeah, I'm nobody in this little quartet of drama we've found ourselves in tonight. So, you don't have to worry about it. Your speech was nice and all but—actually, it wasn't even that nice, now that I think about it. Tolerate me? You want to be able to tolerate me." I snort. "I might be a professional gym rat, but you're a professional asshole. Has anybody ever told you that?"

She laughs. "Many, many times, much to Jane's chagrin. What can I say? I'm inherently suspicious when it comes to people surrounding Cara."

"Jealous?" I suggest.

"No. Protective. I'm very, very happy with Jane. But historically, Cara hasn't dated the best people. She dated me and I think we've pretty much established my faults. And don't get me started on Max." Sherry rolls her eyes.

I laugh, I can't help it. Maybe Sherry's growing on me, just a little.

She flashes me a mischievous look. "What do you think? Should we go crash their game?"

"You go ahead, I'll catch up in a minute."

I can tell she doesn't quite believe me. "Are you gonna make me grovel?" she asks. "Jane will put me on the couch if you don't come over there and prove that we made nice."

"So coming over here was all in your own self-interest, then?"

She clicks her tongue. "Professional asshole, remember? I can rarely be persuaded to do anything that isn't."

I laugh again. "Alright, just let me say bye to Mickey first."

"Deal," she says and takes a step away before turning back to me.

"Lizzie?"

"Yeah?"

"You're not nothing," she says. "You're definitely not nothing."

"You don't have to butter me up," I say. "I already said I would come over and play nice."

"That's not how I meant it," she says, walking away.

CARA IS DRUNK. Like very extremely drunk. And it's very extremely cute.

After approximately 97,000 rounds of darts, during which half the bar's patrons nearly lost an eye, and one final round where a dart ended up skidding to a stop under one of the barstools, Micky gently suggested that it might be time for me to take her home. I was good to drive by then. I'd only had that one drink ages ago.

Cara's car is incredible—even the worst roads feel like driving on fresh pavement, and it corners like it's on rails. I don't want it to end. I want to ask her how she settled on this car, and how much it cost, and if she'll let me drive it forever in exchange for handing over the keys to my eight-year-old certified-pre-owned Kia, but she's too busy singing along to the radio to notice.

There's no sign of James when we pull in—not that I was expecting him to be home—but somehow bringing Cara into his quiet, empty place feels different, more charged. I walk her to the door, grabbing her arm when she's a little unsteady on her feet, and she responds by planting a big theatrical kiss on my cheek.

"You're it!" she shouts, before racing around the side of the house and into the backyard, her heels flying off behind her.

"Cara, no!" I whisper as loud as I can, afraid the neighbors will hear, but she's already gone.

She's fast for a drunk girl.

I walk around the back of the property, searching for her in the dark. "Cara?" I whisper again. "Cara!"

No answer.

"Cara, come on, this isn't funny, we have to go inside! It's one A.M.!"

No answer.

I can't decide if it's awful or endearing as I sort through the bushes surrounding James's patio. A spine from one of the plants digs into my palm, a thin trickle of blood visible in the moonlight, and shit, that's definitely going to hurt when I lift tomorrow.

A loud splash behind me breaks the stillness of the night, and panic replaces any annoyance in my head. James's pool. It isn't very big, more for hanging out in than swimming, but still deep enough to get yourself into trouble when you're drunk and it's dark.

"Cara!" I yell, neighbors be damned, and rush over to the side. I scan the surface, but she's underwater, swimming. She breaks the surface a few moments later with a gasp and a tinkling laugh and suddenly we can both breathe again.

"You found me," she says, with a fake pout. "Guess that means it's my turn to be It."

"It's your turn to go inside and go to bed," I say, while she swims over. She's stripped down to her bra and panties, purple lacy things that stand out against her perfectly tanned skin.

"You're no fun." She flicks water at me. "You have to come in, it's so warm tonight!"

"It's always warm. He heats it," I point out, not that it matters. I just needed a minute for my brain to come back online after the sight of a bra strap finally losing its grip on the delicate curve of her shoulder. I try not to stare. I definitely try not to imagine what it would be like to dig my fingers into her skin, her side, her hips . . . other places, every place. I swallow hard and look away.

Right. Think of James. James and his pool. His warm, wet . . . shit. This isn't working.

"Come on," Cara whines. "Swim with me."

My body moves of its own accord, tearing off my tank top and kicking off my jeans. And then I'm standing there in the middle of James's backyard, where any of his neighbors could see, in a sports bra and boy shorts. A sly look breaks across Cara's face.

"See, Lizzie, I knew you had balls, you just had to find them."

"I don't actually, but I appreciate the sentiment," I say, as I slip into the water. It isn't quite as warm as she led me to believe, and I squeeze my eyes shut and suck in a sharp breath as the water laps at my skin. But then Cara's in front of me, all body heat and wet skin, her hands on my arms, pulling me farther out. Suddenly, I'm drowning and being born all at once.

She stops right before I lose my footing in the deep end, her hands still on me, the water brushing against our chins.

"Hi," she says, her face so close to mine. I could kiss her right now, and I bet I would barely have to move.

"Hi," I say back, my heart pounding in my ears.

"Tonight was fun, right?"

"Yeah," I say, ignoring the sting of chlorine on my cut, knowing that I'd ignore it a thousand more times to have this moment with her.

She moves even closer toward me, impossibly close now, her eyelids heavy, lips parting. I slide my hand against her side, debating if I should pull her in or push her away. Both. Neither. I tighten my grip, a war raging in my head, a thrill coursing down my spine.

She lets out a tiny sigh as she shuts her eyes and leans in and—

No. Not like this. I don't want it like this, with her drunk and me taking advantage.

I hold her still with my hands and take a half stroke back. Her eyes shoot open, confusion and then embarrassment flashing across her face.

"I don't—" I say, but before I can say the rest, which is *I don't want to be your drunken mistake. I don't want there to be any deniability. I want you to mean it. I want you to want it . . .* she splashes me, hard.

"I'm so drunk," she says and forces out a laugh, but I can see the hurt in her eyes, the rejection I don't want her to feel.

"Cara, wait," I say, but she's already swum back over to the ladder, the water sliding off her as she climbs out.

"Cara," I say again, as she scoops her clothes up off the patio and heads to the door.

"You should go," she says, her back still toward me. "You got your keys, right?"

"Yeah," I say quietly. "I have 'em."

"Good. Thanks for the ride home."

"Cara, hang on a sec," I say, this time more firmly as I rush to climb out after her.

"Good night, Lizzie," she says, not even looking back before entering the code to the French doors and disappearing inside.

I don't miss the click of the lock behind her.

Chapter Sixteen

She what?" James asks. We're at the gym, he's back from his long weekend with Ramón, which he has just told me about in way too much detail, while I sit trying to inventory the paper towels and decide whether we need to order more.

Normally, that would fall to one of the custodians to decide, but Harmony's out sick, and god knows Chuck doesn't give a shit. If he can't find a paper towel, he'll just take the nice white terry-cloth ones from the sauna and make my life a thousand times harder.

"She tried to kiss me," I repeat, even though I'm positive he heard me.

"Holy shit, that's hilarious."

"No, it wasn't. I stopped her."

"A true gentleman," he teases.

"She was too drunk. I didn't want to take advantage of her," I say a little too harshly, thinking of all the times my mom came home drunk and crying because of some loser she went out with. James studies my face like he knows what I'm thinking. He might; I've told him enough stories over the years.

His face goes serious. "Thanks for getting her home safe."

"Yeah, I think I hurt her feelings though."

James narrows his eyes. "That explains it, then."

"Explains what?"

"Why she's been so weird. I thought she was just mad I bailed on Sam."

"Oh, wonderful." I groan. First, I ruin her marriage, then I humiliate her. I'm really batting a thousand here.

"Relax, I'm sure it'll blow over in a day or two. It's not like there's real feelings involved."

"Right, no," I say, which smarts even though I know it's true.

"She's probably just embarrassed she got that sloppy. Little Miss Prim and Proper trying to shack up with her brother's bestie in a drunken stupor?" He shudders. "Yikes."

"Yeah." And it does make sense for her to feel that way. *It does.* So why does it feel so shitty?

"But hey, it looks like she took down the 'date my brother' profile too, so I'll take it. Your methods may be unorthodox, but they work!"

I roll my eyes. "One, gross. And two, I'm pretty sure she hates me now, so."

"If you're that worried about it just text her. Ask her to meet you for lunch. Pretend like it never happened. It always works for me."

"I texted her this morning just to check in. And I texted yesterday and even offered to bring her my guaranteed hangover cure."

"Not the fried eggs from Marta's Diner?"

"Yes."

James mock gasps and leans forward. "Oh my god!"

"What?"

"Marta's Diner is a big deal. You didn't even take me there

until we'd known each other a year! One drunken come-on from Cara and you're practically dropping to one knee? How long *has* it been since you got laid?"

I glare at him.

"Don't tell me it was Michonne? That was like nine months ago!"

I glare harder.

"We seriously need to get you over that dry spell." He ruffles my hair then, actually ruffles it, and I want to die. "Maybe we should set up a profile for *you*."

"Shut up," I say, shoving his face back.

"Nine months?" He fakes a shudder. "Dude."

"You're such an asshole," I say, locking the paper towel cabinet.

You wouldn't think that would be something we had to keep locked up, but you'd be surprised. One time the boys' swim team got into it after practice and started a paper towel war. We were fishing them out of our pool filter for days. Stella wouldn't even charge them for damages because the "senator's son is on the team." God forbid a rich kid gets held accountable for something.

"I am." He smiles, like he's proud of that. "It's part of my charm."

I shake my head and walk away, but of course he follows.

"Hey, 'drunk mouth, sober thoughts' or whatever; isn't that how the saying goes?"

"Something like that," I say, plopping myself back behind the desk.

"Okay, well, consider her trying to make out with you a bonus, then. If she's busy with you, she won't have any time to worry about my dating life and she definitely won't be trying to set you up with other people either. It would get her off our backs about that permanently. I vote you flirt back a little." He shrugs.

"Okay, so I guess bro code is just fully out the window now? It was one thing to hang out with her, but I'm not banging your sister to get her off your back. Try again."

"Again, I didn't say you should bang," he says slowly, patiently, like I'm ridiculous. "I said flirt back *a little*. And you know this is about more than the dating thing. It'll stop *all* of her bad ideas. Besides, you owe her."

I freeze and my heart plummets to the floor. "Wh . . . what do you mean?" I ask, trying to play it off. Did she tell him the truth about her wedding?

James gives me a weird look. "Because you said you embarrassed her in the pool. Why? What else would you owe her for?"

"Nothing!" I say, trying not to let my relief show. "Nothing."

He crinkles his forehead. "What's going on with you?"

"Nothing! Like I said!" I grab the scanner and check in a guest who's happily eavesdropping on us, before spinning back to James. "Sorry." I sigh. "I don't think it's a good idea for me to keep getting involved, okay? Especially after she tried to kiss me and—"

"I'm gonna be real with you, Lizzie. I don't love the idea of you two boning, but if it comes down to it, I'd rather have her with somebody safe than some random from Hinge. I mean, you're both consenting adults, so . . ."

"Are we though? When you've got us scheming behind her back? It feels manipulative."

James crouches down in front of where I'm sitting. "It's not manipulative to want to keep her safe. She's flailing right now, and you know it. Come on, you think she's hot, you said so yourself, and clearly, she wants to kiss you! I'm not asking you to marry her. Just keep hanging out!"

"Are you forgetting that she *fucking hates me now*! Even if I did decide to humor you, it's not like she'd even show."

He flashes me the biggest shit-eating grin I've ever seen. "Don't worry about that part. I've got it covered. You tell me when and where, and I'll give her a little taste of her own medicine," he says, adding in finger guns for good measure.

And oh, oh god.

I'm taking dating advice from someone who makes finger guns?

Chapter Seventeen

I stare at the buzzing phone in my hand, the word "MOM" splashed across the screen, as a pile of dread builds up in my stomach. She rarely ever calls me—only when something is very, very wrong. I debate sending her to voicemail but decide that having to call her back when I inevitably cave will just make my anxiety a thousand times worse.

"Hi, Mom," I say, as cheerfully as I can muster when I hit accept.

"Glad you could be bothered to pick up for once, Lizzie," she says, as if I don't usually. I was literally just at her apartment, for god's sake, it's not like I've abandoned her.

And I do answer, every time I do, even when I'm at work and busy with a guest. My occasional online therapist calls it code-pendency, but I prefer to think of it as being helpful. Maybe if I could afford more than one session every month or two—thanks, cheap-ass insurance plan—I could actually be able to untangle that particular knot.

"Everything okay?" I ask, pacing around my apartment.

I know it's not or she wouldn't be calling.

"Can't I just want to say hi to my only daughter? You act like I only call when I need something. 's rude."

She's drunk. Great. And it's not my fault that's the truth of the situation. Just like it's not my fault that she was less of a mom and more of a screwed-up sibling who I had to look after while simultaneously trying to raise myself.

Yeah.

"You can. Of course, you can," I say. "Sorry," I add, because I will always feel guilty about . . . well, everything. I had to move out when I did. *Needed* to, even if she'll never forgive me for it. If I hadn't, worst case we would have killed each other, best case I would have ended up a raging alcoholic like her.

Instead, I turned my addictive personality to fitness and nutrition and being at the gym. Healthier at least, usually. It's gotta be better than being drunk at noon on a Tuesday, right?

"I'm not the worst mother out there, you know?" she says, followed by the unmistakable sound of her taking a drag off a cigarette.

"I'm sorry," I say again, forever apologizing. "I didn't mean to make you feel like you were."

"Well, you did."

And then the line goes quiet. She wants me to grovel, but I'm too tired. Too worn out from the gym and from the James and Cara stuff.

"Things good?" she asks finally.

"Yeah, they're good," I say. "I actually might be applying for a new job."

I don't know why I tell her this. I don't have the faintest idea. It's not something we talk about. But she asked, sort of, and maybe there's a part of me that still wishes I had a real mom, one who called to check in on me because they wanted to know how I was doing and not just as a segue to pad whatever bad news they were bringing me that day.

And with Mom it was always bad news.

The list was endless: her new boyfriend beat her up, she got into a bar fight and needed money for court, she fell when she was wasted and broke her wrist and couldn't afford the follow-up co-pays, she nodded off and drove off the road, she swerved to "avoid hitting a deer," never mind her BAC was through the roof. Bad luck. It was all bad luck, if you asked her. Just a long string of fated bad luck that she had no free will to address or avoid.

And it certainly, certainly never had anything to do with her drinking.

"You going back to retail?"

Because those are the only choices for me, in her eyes. If I leave the gym, I must be going back to scanning scented candles at Target.

I think about Cara again, who's finding herself, running from a cushy real estate lawyer job making more money than I can probably imagine and debating leaving it anyway. Like, yes, Cara's also trying to jump out of airplanes and her methods are more hostage taking than matchmaking, but I guarantee you her mother isn't currently asking her if she's going to work retail.

There's an assumption about some people and where they belong on the grand scale of poverty to billionaire, and while Cara and I aren't quite at opposite ends of the spectrum, there's definitely a wide gap between where she falls on it and where I do.

"Lizzie?"

"No. A promotion at the gym, I hope, if I get it. I could be the gym manager."

"I thought you were the gym manager."

"I'm the front desk manager, it's different. If I get this new job, I'd be in charge of the entire gym. It would basically be mine."

"Sounds fancy," she says. "It come with a nice raise?"

And my stomach falls because I already know where this is going.

"It might, some," I say, because I've never been able to lie to her, even when I was a teenager trying to sneak out to see my girlfriend ... not that my mom really cared about that. I think she was just happy she didn't have to worry about me getting pregnant.

"Well, that could be a good thing."

"Yeah," I say, kind of confused. I thought she was going to ask me for money. I was *sure* she was going to ask me for money. But she didn't? A tentative smile breaks across my face; maybe she did just want to say hi.

But then I hear her take a drag off her cigarette and she adds, "Bills are really piling up around here, you know, even with what you give. Maybe you could send some of that new extra money my way too."

Right.

"I didn't get the job yet," I remind her.

"But you will. Maybe they could even give you a little pay advance if you explain it's an emergency."

Is it an emergency? How? I *just* got her current on cable and electric. How can it possibly be dire already? I haven't even had a chance to save up for her next catastrophe.

"Mom, I don't have any money to spare right now, rent's due next week and—"

"Don't they give you a ten-day grace period up there?" she asks, her voice stern and demanding.

"I . . ." I fall back in my chair and look around my apartment. It could be so much nicer if I wasn't stuck blowing all my spare money for emergencies—hers or mine.

And hers seem to hit with an uncanny regularity.

"They're gonna cut off my water, pumpkin," she says, as if that somehow justifies me paying my rent late. *Maybe you should have told me about that instead of the cable bill, Mom.*

"I'll see what I can do," I say quietly. "I might be able to scrape up a little, but not as much as last time."

"You see what you can do," she says, her voice sounding bitter. "You and your fancy job and your big old apartment, you see what you can do to help your mama, who you left sitting here all alone holding the bag."

"I didn't . . ." I say, because how can someone ever leave their parent "holding the bag" simply by moving out and moving on with their lives? Yeah, I paid half the rent from when I was sixteen on, but that's because my mother never learned to budget properly, and I got sick of us being evicted. When I left, she tried to tell me I was breaking the lease, as if I was a roommate, not her child.

I gave her the money though. I gave her my half for the whole rest of the year. I had to. The guilt would have killed me. I had scrimped and saved and taken on a second and third job, barely graduating high school on time. And then she got evicted anyway, even with my money.

"They gotta wanna help themselves," my grandma had said once. And oh, I wish she was still here. At least then I'd have someone to share the responsibility of raising my mom and keeping her safe and fed.

"Mom . . ." I say again, like somehow that will mean something to her. But she just shushes me.

"Yeah, you see what you can do," she mutters again. "I'm gonna go. I have a friend over."

"Okay, have fun," I say, trying to be cheerful even though she doesn't deserve it.

"Love you," she says, each word landing like lead in my belly.

"Love you too."

DETERMINED NOT TO let my mother derail my day, I spend the rest of it alternating between looking up new lifting routines and letting myself daydream about making things right between me and Cara. Somehow this turns into full-on fantasizing about what the perfect date for her would be *if* I were ever going to do such a thing. I can't decide if this makes me awesome or an asshole.

It probably wouldn't be so bad if James's brilliant plan to get Cara and me talking again wasn't just inviting her someplace I'm at and ditching her. I don't know what I was thinking, trusting old Finger Guns to actually come up with something both clever *and* ethical.

This is the equivalent of him ding-dong ditching his way toward a resolution between us.

But still, would it be the worst thing? Making things right? Being her distraction, her safe place to hang? Her safe place to explore her queerness? Like James said, we're both adults. And she's leaving soon, I'm sure. Back to her old life and her old friends. What's the real harm? Unless spending time with me just ruins her life in other ways I haven't even thought of yet. It's not exactly like we have the best track record.

Shit. I'm spinning out over this.

As much as I want to be this, like, honorable woman type, there's a part of me that just wants to see her again. And I know it's probably the only chance I have. A distraction is better than being nothing, right?

God, this is pathetic. I don't do crushes and I certainly don't do deep. What the fuck is wrong with me?

Just as I'm about to fully give in to my existential crisis, James texts me a picture of her with the caption, mope city, population: Cara. To be fair, it looks like she's just watching TV and minding her own business. I bet she'd kill him if she knew.

When that doesn't get a reaction, he resorts to begging me to go along with things. I don't reply. I can't.

I spend the next few days pretending I'm anything but 100 percent into the idea of hanging with her one-on-one. I also pretend I'm not ridiculously curious about what she's up to every day. But any hope I had of being subtle about it flies out the window when I finally cave and ask James if she's mentioned anything about me, or rather about trying to kiss me. She hasn't, he says, not a peep. I'm disappointed, I'm not going to lie.

But then again, he hasn't told her about Ramón yet, so I guess maybe they're still just keeping each other in the dark.

Seriously, James doesn't seem to know much more about Cara than what she posts on her very public Instagram—which I definitely haven't checked. Okay, fine, I did, but only one time. Or five. Or eleven . . . but only because she kept updating her stories when she was out and I wanted to make sure she wasn't going to get kidnapped by a cliff diver named Brennan and forced to live out her life chained to his carabiner. (She wasn't, she was out with Sherry and Jane, but still.) See, I was just looking out.

But anyway, true or not, it's still gotta suck for James to feel this way about his own family. I sort of get it. My mom is consistently terrible too, just in other ways, and I'm practically as desperate for her approval as he is for Stella's. I don't know what I would do if, like James with his mom, I suddenly had it.

Fuck, maybe I *should* have his back on this thing. Children of toxic parents unite! It's not like flirting with Cara would exactly be a hardship, and she did seem into me that night. Plus, I'd *also* be helping my best friend in a roundabout, extremely dysfunctional way that I'm definitely not going to unpack right now.

Oh god, I can't believe I'm even considering this.

Okay.

Okay, think this through, Lizzie. Start with the facts: James is a flake anyway. Even if he did set something up with her, there's a fifty-fifty chance he wouldn't show and she'd be stuck there alone anyway. I would just happen to have a slight heads-up that it was a 100 percent chance this time.

Plus, it's not like I would try to jump her bones or make it weird the second I saw her. At worst, it would just give us a chance to talk. She could leave if she wanted. Free will is a thing of beauty and all that. And if she *did* stay . . .

Goddammit. I'm really considering this, aren't I?

Alright, but what would we do?

I scroll through my phone, remembering how Cara told me that fear can really bond you to someone. It makes sense—James and I have certainly spent many a Tuesday night witnessing tons of skydiving, cliff jumping, and rappelling dates while watching *The Bachelor*.

And I read once that some plants bloom and go to seed when they're stressed about dying and want to make sure that their species lives on. Beauty from the fear of doom. It's not a stretch to think we're wired the same way. Love, fear, it's all just bullshit brain chemicals, isn't it?

I open Google and start typing. I just have to figure out how to manufacture doom in a way that won't make me lose my lunch, because god knows that puking on a first date is less than ideal. Not that it's a first date. It's not. It'll barely even constitute a hangout.

And that's IF I'm doing this. Big if.

(Except I'm totally doing this.)

I immediately veto any form of extreme sports. I know the "new Cara" is into the stuff, but no, thank you. I scribble out "rappelling?" on a sticky note next to me. It's a maybe. A low maybe. At least this one involves ropes and harnesses, and your feet are always touching something even if it isn't quite the ground.

Let's see, what else . . . spooky corn maze? No, I don't want to be surrounded by screaming kids. That also knocks out roller-skating, which, while not quite death-defying, definitely constitutes scary.

I also want it to be somewhere we can actually talk, so that rules out movies, as much as I'd love to rewatch *The Conjuring 3*—plus, I know that she hasn't watched *1* and *2*. Or the *Anna-*

belles. Or *The Nun*. Or *La Llorona*, which, while a terrible movie, unfortunately is still *Conjuring*-adjacent enough that I consider it required viewing for completionism's sake.

But I digress.

I take a quick break from searching to scroll social media. I'm not on much, and other than creeping Cara's Insta, I haven't been for a while, but I figure now is as good a time as any. Why not replace my "Is attempting to manipulate the hottest woman I've ever met to talk to me again unethical?" dread with some good old-fashioned doom scrolling?

I'm halfway to jumping out the window from the horrors of the world, coupled with all the dad joke tweets, when a targeted ad pops up on my screen.

It's red and white, with scrawling yellow letters that read, "Have a good ole time at the county fair!"

There's a list of things beneath the headline: pig races, rides, games, tractor pulls, and a demolition derby, each punctuated by a different brightly colored exclamation point. I'm about to scroll past when I get to the bottom and freeze. "Food Trucks! Lemonade! Fried Dough!"

All of Cara's favorite things.

She'd be in a good mood just from that, or hopefully predisposed not to kill me at least. Is doing this with her—to her, really—that awful if it's also, on some level, thoughtful?

God, what am I even saying? Of course it is. But . . .

Okay. I pull out my Notes app and set to work on a noncomprehensive list of reasons why I should allow James to secretly set me up on a date with his sister (despite the fact that it's definitely not a date . . . Oh, and that she isn't currently speaking to me).

<u>PROS:</u>

One: She's really beautiful and smart and fun.

Two: She's probably a great kisser and I really want to find out for sure.

Three: The wet bra and panties thing was really working for her and I—

Four: Clearly, I am a perv. Oh my god, pull it together, Lizzie.

Five: James seems really sure she needs someone right now. A distraction. A friend. And for whatever reason he doesn't want it to be him. Meanwhile, I've been told by many girls in the past that I'm very good at being distracting. (Very, very good.) (Jesus, what is wrong with me?)

Six: I can't stop thinking about her and not just in a "hope I get to make out with her" way but also a little in an "I hope she's having a good day" way and a lot of "I want to buy her fried dough and lemonade to show her I was listening" way.

   <u>(But we are **NOT** going to be thinking about that. At all. Period.)</u>
   <u>(Short-term distraction. Short-term distraction. Short-term distraction.)</u>

Seven: If it backfires, I can just keep pretending that James really did flake on us and then she'll be mad at him, not me. Which he deserves for this.

Eight: What if it doesn't backfire though?

Nine: I like her. Fuck. I might even like-like her.

Wait, is that a pro or a con? I flick away the tenth text from James begging me to agree. And then close all my apps and flop back against my chair.

Okay, now to think about the cons.

<u>CONS:</u>
One: It's sketchy, no matter how much James says it isn't.

Two: Trying to hook up with my best friend's sister at a county fair when she's not even talking to me sounds like the plot of a cheesy romance movie and my disaster ass could never pull it off.

Three: Right now, I'm only an asshole. Going through with this could elevate me to full dick status.

Four: She's not even talking to me.

Five: <u>She's not even talking to me.</u>

Six: I think I like this fucking girl. I cannot like this fucking girl and I definitely <u>should not</u> like this fucking girl.

Seven: Maybe she sucks at kissing, and I dodged a bullet in that pool. (unlikely)

Eight: What if hanging out with her just makes me more into her instead of scratches the itch?

Nine: SHE'S NOT EVEN TALKING TO ME RIGHT NOW.

That settles it. I pick up my phone and fire off a text to James.

> She's not even talking to me. This is a horrible idea.

> for the thousandth time, no it isn't.

> it is though! And now you've got me sitting here thinking about taking her to a fair when I should be over here RESPECTING HER BOUNDARIES INSTEAD.

> 👀

> Taking? Her? To? The? Fair?

😍 omg you are the cutest goddamn dork I've ever met.

you realize you're supposed to be leaning into the crush, right? Not going on a play date.

No wonder you're single.

NO. I'M TELLING YOU NO.

uh huh. Sure, sure. But just hypothetically, why the fair?

she told me that fair food reminds her of your grandma, good memories!

Do you really want her thinking about OUR GRANDMA when you're trying to make out? 🙈

Okay, so, I hadn't thought of that.

GOOD THING IT DOESN'T MATTER BECAUSE I'M NOT GOING.

she does really like fair food though now that you mention it.

I'm going to kill you. I'm literally going to kill you. The next time you need me to spot you, my hand just might slip. ☠ Oops.

I wait for his retort, but none comes. Shit, did I just cross a line? Is he pissed? My anxious brain starts spinning out again.

I wouldn't ever do that. You know that right? It was a bad joke.

I'm sorry.

that was in super poor taste.

wow, your anxious attachment style is really shining today. Calm down, dude. I was just texting Cara.

Oh good.

Wait. Why?

I invited her to the fair. Friday afternoon. 😬

Bro.

😬😬😬

WHAT THE FUCK JAMES. I'M NOT GOING.

oh wow, so you're going to just leave her there all alone with the scent of fried dough and memories of our dead grandma. That's cold, even for you.

JAMES

What the hell is demolition derby football? Guess you'll find out that night!

I'M NOT GOING.

Grandma? Grandma, is that you? 😦

I groan and hit the call button, but he immediately sends me to voicemail. Three times.

> ANSWER YOUR PHONE
> JAMES I SWEAR TO GOD.

After what feels like an eternity, my phone finally lights up with a response from him.

> Sorry, had to wait for her to text back. Apparently, she was "getting ready" and I'm "bothering her." Psssht. Friday afternoon. Demolition derby football. You and Cara will meet at the gates. BE THERE OR BE SQUARE BUD.

I'm so distracted by the first thing he said that the rest hardly registers. What's she getting ready for? A date? Is it a date for real this time? I know there's a chance she's getting ready to hang out with Sherry and Jane again. Or maybe she's getting ready to who knows? Go to a guest lecture on astrophysics at the local college or something, it's not like I really know her. It could be any number of things, but my stomach twists in a knot anyway.

I try to resist texting back. I make it about three minutes.

> getting ready for what?

The second I send it, I wish I could hit unsend. I *know* it's what he wants.

> not that I care. I don't.

it's just getting late.

Not that she can't be out late.
I just mean idk

nevermind

to bed, Lizzie. She's getting ready to
go to bed. Don't worry you're still the
only girl she's trying to kiss 😉

that's not what I meant!

sure it's not. Don't forget, Friday at
430. Front gates. 💕

Chapter Eighteen

I'm an asshole.

Or maybe I'm a really good person who simply couldn't let Cara venture to the county fair alone with only the ghost of Grandma to keep her company.

I haven't decided yet.

Either way, I'm perched on a bench by the carnival entrance, watching like a hawk for any sign of her. It's a hot sticky evening, the sun still fighting against the moon for control of the sky. I went back and forth on what to wear, not wanting to be underdressed like that night at the bar, but also not wanting to seem like I'm trying too hard, given the fact that this is, you know, a fairground.

And that we're both supposed to be shocked that we're stood up.

I settled for some flats and shorts, and while I'm still in my standard tank top, at least it's not dry fit. This one is nicer, ribbed, with a little maroon pattern against the navy background. It is, as I like to call it, my fancy tank top. James, however, loves to argue that there is no such thing as a fancy tank top. But what does he know? He has only two modes: gym rat and GQ, with nothing in between. It's not exactly like he's in touch with my Target clearance rack wardrobe.

I smack a stray mosquito off my leg and fidget, my feet on the bench seat, my butt perched up on the back. It's not that I don't know how to properly sit on a bench, it's that I want to be sure I don't miss her. That and I'm deathly afraid of having to face her with back sweat if I did press against the slats of the bench. I wore dark colors specifically to avoid this.

I check the time. She's already late. Only by three minutes, but still.

I start to panic that maybe she won't come, that she's figured out that James isn't coming and she's bailed already. Maybe I'll sit here all night. Maybe I'll be the creepy woman sitting outside of a fair alone with her head hung low. People will describe me as suspicious. If any crimes happen tonight, it's my face that will be sketched, along with the adjectives "lurking" and "weird."

I'm about to hop off the bench and bolt—I'm not going down for these imaginary crimes—when I see Cara. She's looking around awkwardly, clearly searching for her brother. She's dressed in tight khaki shorts rolled up on the ends, and a T-shirt covered in pineapples that says "Newport Rhode Island," the words stretched taut across her chest. A pineapple scarf is tied around her head like a headband, trailing down her back. And I get lost imagining the softness of its fabric, the softness of her skin, the—

I shake my head hard to clear it and watch her move through the crowd, my ability to speak dried up and gone like the spit in my suddenly desert dry mouth.

I hop off the bench and head toward her, not sure how to start or what to say. Her eyes widen when she notices me. For a second, I think she's going to turn and run, but then her shoulders sag and she stomps toward me.

"Lizzie?" she says, confusion pulling her voice up.

"Cara?" I say, trying to smile warmly at her. "Hi. Hey, hi."

She looks around again like she's being pranked. It's possible I'm reading into this and she's just trying to find her brother, but the frown on her face does not instill confidence.

"What are you doing here? Are you meeting someone?" she asks.

I attempt to look confused. "You, I thought? You and James? He told me to meet you here."

"He did?"

"Yeahhhhh," I say. "Did you not know I was coming?" I'm skirting the edge of lying, but I haven't crossed it yet. I try to keep my face open and earnest, to let this play out however is best. However I can.

Yep, I am definitely going to hell. Do not pass Go. Do not collect $200.

Cara crosses her arms. "James asked me to meet him here too. I didn't know *you* were coming though." And I hate the way she says that last part. Accusatory. Annoyed. "It's okay, I guess. The more the merrier, right?" she adds weakly, but I suspect it's mostly to kill the awkward silence that has settled in between us.

"Are you sure, because I can go home. I don't even know what demolition derby football is, so." My heart thuds in my chest and I pray she asks me to stay. But I'll leave if she doesn't. That was part of the deal that I made with myself. We don't do non-con over here.

"No, no," she says, the second no coming a little more firmly, a little more decided. "Stay, it'll be fun."

She spies the now empty bench and heads over to it, plopping down with a sigh. I resume my position perched on the back, but when she cranes her neck up to look at me, trying to block her eyes from the sun, I slide down beside her. Back sweat be damned. Maybe I can just walk behind her the whole time. It wouldn't be the weirdest part of this evening.

I start to ask her why we're sitting out here instead of buying tickets like the rest of the crowd, but then I remember that we're supposed to be waiting for James. Right, that. He should already be texting us both to cancel—his idea not mine—but I guess he's giving us a little leeway to find each other before bailing. As the moments continue to tick by though, I realize that it's entirely possible he forgot, busy as he probably is on his date with Ramón. Mini golf, he said, so he can teach Ramón how to swing a club.

Shit. He definitely forgot.

"Where is he?" Cara asks a passing cloud, clearly getting frustrated.

"I'll call him." Before she can object or offer to do it herself, I slide my phone out and hit *James*. His picture pops up on my phone as it rings, and she purses her lips when she sees it. I turn my back to her, trying to get some privacy.

"James?" I say, the second he picks up. "Where are you?"

"With Ramón?" he says, obviously confused. "You knew I was—"

"I'm here with your sister," I say, cutting him off. "Wasn't tonight that demolition derby thing you wanted to see or did we somehow both fuck up the dates? Are you spacing on us again?"

"You know I wasn't—ohhhhh. Shit. I was supposed to text. I'm sorry, Lizzie, I just—"

"Yeah, oh shit," I whisper-shout, glancing back at Cara. "Um, do you want to talk to your sister? She seems pretty pissed."

"What am I supposed to say?"

"Yeah, sure, you can talk to her," I answer extra loudly, adding a quiet "figure it out" to him through gritted teeth. I give Cara the phone. "He wants to talk to you."

"What the hell, James?" she says, and she sounds furious.

Perhaps this wasn't the best idea after all.

"You've got to be kidding me." Cara groans into the phone. "Yeah, okay. Thanks for nothing." She ends the call and shoves my phone into her pocket. Realizing her mistake, she sheepishly pulls it out and passes it back to me.

"Apparently one of his buddies convinced him to go golfing up near the Finger Lakes." She groans again. "He completely forgot we had plans."

"Yeah, I gathered that. I'm sorry." Because seeing how pissed she is right now, I really am. And I'm almost sorry for James too, for having to deal with her wrath when he does decide to show his face back in town . . . but not quite.

"Well, nice to see you," Cara says with an expression that suggests that maybe it isn't very nice at all. And then she turns back toward the parking lot.

"Cara, wait," I say, rushing after her.

"What do you want, Lizzie?" she asks, and I feel like I could die, right here in front of her, just melt right into the ground when she levels me with her stare.

"We could still go in without him, since we drove all this way." I scratch the back of my neck. "I figure I owe you at least a lemon-ade after what happened last week."

"I don't know . . ."

"I'm not gonna beg, but I saw a kid come out with a cup the size of his head. There were fresh lemons in it, Cara. Fresh. Lemons."

She rolls her eyes and looks away, letting out a deep sigh. "If you throw in a fried dough, I could be persuaded. Maybe."

"Oh. Well, yeah, the fried dough is a given. Even if you don't come inside with me, I'll probably still get two of them."

She laughs, a real one, and maybe this isn't going to be an unmitigated disaster. A girl can dream, can't she?

Cara looks at the parking lot and then back at me, deciding what to do. "You know, I *am* curious what 'demolition derby football' means," she says.

WE'VE BEEN WALKING around for about an hour, mostly in awkward silence, punctuated only when we interrupt each other, trying to break it at the same time by saying things like "so" and "yup." I eventually ask about Sherry and Jane, and she says she's been talking to them a lot more since that night at the bar. But then I ask if she's given any more thought to her career path, and she puts a finger gun to her head and then sips her lemonade without answering.

Okay, message received. I'm officially out of polite small talk anyway.

We are both *definitely* avoiding the elephant in the room, but it's fine, it's fine.

We fill up another half hour eating fried dough and getting covered in powdered sugar every time the breeze whips up a little. I don't miss the way she watches me lick my fingers clean. And if I linger, taking a little longer than is strictly necessary, nobody has to know.

"I don't know why I thought he would show," Cara says out of the blue as we walk around.

"James? Why not?" I ask.

"I don't know. Forget it."

I look at her as I slow my walk. "I can, but I don't have to. If you want to talk about it, I'm all ears."

"He's your best friend."

"He is. But he's also kinda flighty, and a little bit selfish. Just because I love him and know he's got a heart of gold underneath it all doesn't mean he doesn't annoy the shit out of me on the regular. If you want to vent, vent away. What happens at the fair, stays at the fair, right? But if you'd rather not, I can tell you about the time I had to stop people from having sex on a weight bench instead. Anything but this awkward silence, I'm begging you."

Cara laughs. "Seriously?"

I fake wince. "It was silver sneakers hour too. So they were like late seventies? Somewhere around there."

Cara shakes her head. "No thank you, I'm good on that story."

She takes a few more steps before the smile on her face starts to fade. "I don't know. There's been a disconnect between my brother and me for a long time. We were close when we were little. But by the time I got to high school, and definitely in college, he started to make jokes about me being Mom's favorite. It turned into this competition almost, just a constant comparison. My mom fed into it but a lot of it came from him too."

"I bet," I say, before I can stop myself, but she barely seems to hear me.

"Take my job, for example. Whenever I used to try to ask him for advice or confide in him about some work drama, he'd get all self-deprecating that he was 'just' a personal trainer or whatever and I'm the smart one so I should be able to figure it out. He'd laugh but it didn't seem like a joke. Eventually, I just stopped calling him unless it was a holiday or birthday or something."

"Damn," I say, because I know how their story goes, but never from her perspective.

"Right? I always made sure to tell him that I don't care what he does, I just want him to be happy—in case he just needed reassurance or something. If I'm being honest, I was hoping staying with him would make us closer, but it really hasn't. I think I got whiplash from how fast he went from being pissed that I broke up with Max to kind of—this is gonna sound crazy—but it's almost like he's reveling in my life falling apart."

"I don't think that's true," I say softly. "He worries about you a lot."

She shrugs. "Fine, maybe 'reveling' is too strong of a word. But he likes that he's suddenly the good one or whatever to Mom. It's his favorite new 'joke,'" she says, making air quotes.

I bite my lip. I want to tell her it's all an act. I want to tell her how scared he is about Ramón. I want to tell her that he didn't blow her off tonight because he didn't care, but rather because he cared a lot. But I can't. He's still my best friend, and some things are meant to stay between us.

"Sorry," I say, even though it probably doesn't make sense. But I am sorry. I'm sorry she feels this way, I'm sorry he's not here, and I'm sorry I played a role in tricking her into coming here alone with me.

"Forget about it," she says. "Tell me about the weight bench thing."

"Seriously?"

She looks at me sternly. "You said if I didn't want to—"

"Okay, okay, but you brought this on yourself."

She laughs, her mood lightening for the first time today. "Tell me."

And so I do. And we laugh. And then we talk about nothing at all for as long as we can. We even manage to stretch out the "look at that" and "oh my gods" over cute kids in face paint until it's time to go sit down in the bleachers, underneath a giant DE-MOLITION DERBY FOOTBALL sign. We wedge in between a group of men in shiny cowboy boots eating corn dogs, and a couple of harried moms trying to wrangle dusty toddlers into sitting down. A massive flat dirt pit stretches out before us and in its center sits the biggest tractor tire I've ever seen.

What are we doing?

Why am I sitting next to this woman, my heart fluttering so hard I feel it in my brain, staring at a dirt pit instead of, I don't know, actually talking? Actually clearing things up? Or maybe, if I was real brave, asking her if this *could* be a first date maybe, if she was feeling it.

God, I need to woman up.

"Cara," I say, at the exact time she says, "Lizzie," and then we both laugh nervously.

"You go ahead," I say, but she shakes her head.

"No, you."

"I just wanted to say, about last week, in the pool—"

"Oh, we don't have to—"

But before she can finish her sentence, a parade of beat-up cars with numbers spray-painted on their sides and sporting either neon-green or neon-orange tags tied to their antennae begins streaming into the "arena," if we can really call it that. The roar from people around us indicates they seem to consider it one.

An announcer comes over the speakers, drowning out my would-be confession by announcing team names like the Junk-yard Vipers and Don't Tread on Us, which . . . okay. The crowd cheers and stomps on the bleachers and any hope I had of actually talking to her gets lost in their exuberance.

The place fills with the smell of exhaust. I cough impolitely and look at Cara, who is staring very, very hard at the cars in front of us. It's as if she's built an invisible wall between us from the mere mention of the pool. She's sparing herself from ever having to confront what I'm terrified she's still interpreting as a rejection, when it was just bad timing. I desperately want her to know the truth of it though, which is that I wouldn't reject her. Not for real.

If she hadn't been drunk . . .

I just . . . I didn't want to be something she regretted. I'm tired of being something people regret.

"Cara," I say again. She looks at me quickly and points at the cars, which are now smashing into the tractor tire, and each other, while trying to push it to either end. Ah, now I get it. The tire must be the ball, and the crude squares spray-painted on the dirt must be the goals. They're going to disappear in about two seconds once the cars start driving over them and messing up the paint, but nobody seems to care. Maybe that's part of the fun.

I try to watch. I swear. I try to respect the fact that Cara clearly does not want to talk to me about this now, or maybe ever. But the longer she sits next to me, our legs brushing as she crosses and uncrosses her legs like she's just as tense as I am . . . I can't take it anymore.

I don't care if she doesn't ever want to see me again after this, but let it be for a real reason and not because of a misunderstanding. I try to catch her attention, but she's still glued to the chaos in front of us: mirrors spinning off in every direction, pieces of cars going flying. The people around us start laughing and whooping, the announcer speeding up his play-by-plays so it sounds more like he's working at an auction than a game, the tension building and building as one lone smoking car starts to shove the tire closer and closer to the other team's goal.

The driver's going for it, despite the anarchy around him, and it's suddenly as if my whole fate rests on his ability to get it across that line. I jump up as he inches the tire forward, smoke billowing from his engine, which whines and roars as he accelerates once, twice, three times, and then finally it's through.

The entire crowd erupts in cheers. Even Cara jumps up beside me. She looks at me, smiling, and it feels like it's the first time she's seen me all day.

"Cara!" I shout, high off the adrenaline and joy in the crowd. Or maybe it's the exhaust fumes but either way, I don't care. "Cara!" I shout again.

She turns and looks at me, the smile still on her face even as a confused divot forms between her eyebrows.

"I do want to kiss you," I blurt out, my heart pounding in my ears. It's not exactly the most elegant of statements, but I've never been accused of being showy. I don't care if it's blunt and to the point. I just want her to know. If she takes nothing else out of the evening, let her take this.

"What?" she asks, pointing to her ear. One of the cars, or probably more like all of them, has knocked its tailpipe off attempting to rebound the tire to the other end.

"I do want to kiss you!" I say again, this time a little bit louder.

She points to her ear again, leaning a little closer. "You want what?"

The announcer starts calling plays again, and I know it's now or never, so I yell, at the top of my lungs, "I DO WANT TO KISS YOU!"

At the . . .

exact moment . . .

the crowd falls silent.

Cara's mouth pops open in a little O, as it hits me that the roaring quiet isn't just in my head. One of the cars has caught fire and a hush has fallen over the crowd while they wait for the driver to be evacuated safely.

My cheeks and neck blaze to match the inferno in front of us as I realize people are staring at us. A lot of people. And fuck, I'm at a demolition derby in upstate New York, where one of the teams is called Don't Tread on Us. Being a woman screaming she wants to kiss another woman is less than ideal.

But then everyone turns their attention back to the scruffy man being pulled out of the car, erupting into cheers as I stand there, pinned in place, my eyes glued to Cara's.

"Oh," she says finally. "Thank you."

Thank you? Thank you?!

I wait for more, but she runs her hands over her face and sits back down.

We watch the rest of the game in silence while I die quietly beside her.

Chapter Nineteen

In any other scenario I would have gotten up and left.

But I was worried about leaving her alone in this rowdy crowd. A part of me knew she would be fine, and truthfully, that I wouldn't be much help if she wasn't. I think she probably *wanted* me to leave, even, given her stoic stance ever since my confession, but something's keeping me rooted in place.

Maybe it's me being a masochist, or maybe it's my stupid hoping heart. But if there's any chance she's going to say more than "thanks" when we aren't in dusty, sweaty, exhaust-filled bleachers surrounded by a thousand other people, I'm willing to wait for it.

Finally, Junkyard Vipers are declared the winners, not because they got the most goals (the game remained tied one to one), but because the final car in Don't Tread on Us blew out its engine, leaving the two remaining Junkyard Vipers to push it off the field with cars of their own.

It would maybe have been fun if I didn't feel like I was going to throw up the whole time.

"Good game," Cara says, rushing to climb over me and exit the arena with the throngs of other people. She says it the way one might say it to the opposing team after a particularly tough loss, and is that how she feels? Is that what she thinks of me, like we're on opposite sides of the field, crashing together like the Junks and the Treads?

I follow behind her, but not with any real intent. I've done my part. I didn't want it to end over a misunderstanding, and it isn't anymore. She can run, she can never talk to me again, but at least she knows how I feel.

Besides, my car is parked this way too, and I have no interest in staying here now. The rides have lost their luster and the fair food is already churning in my stomach.

Cara looks over her shoulder, making eye contact with me and picking up the pace. And shit, am I making her nervous? Is this crossing into creepy stalker mode or something? I hadn't factored that in.

"I'm not following you," I call out to her, which sounds exactly like what someone following you would say, even though in this case it's true.

"Okay," she says, just loud enough for me to hear, "good to know!"

And god, I don't even know what to do with that. I stop walking. This is stupid. This. Is. So. Stupid. I'm speed walking behind a woman who just told me "thanks" when I said I wanted to kiss her, who probably thinks I'm stalking her now, who almost definitely wants me to go away.

I scrape what little dignity I have left off the trampled-down grass beneath me and take a sharp turn to cut down the parking aisle. She's going straight, so I go to the right. I'm a few rows from her now, but I still can't get the sound of her awkwardly saying "thanks" out of my head.

I took James's advice. I did what he wanted. I went for it, but it didn't work out. What more can I do?

The entire parking area is just a loose grass field punctuated with random cones and strings of nylon rope to try to keep people in some semblance of order. I cross three more rows, until I get to where I think my car is and start cutting up the aisle. I don't know where Cara is anymore, but hopefully she's already in her car and gone. Because it feels like I can't breathe, like I probably won't be able to until I'm back safely in the driver's seat with the doors locked and the stereo pounding. Where I can forget all about Cara.

I pick up the pace, watching the ground more carefully to be sure that there's nothing to trip over, no more boulders or chunks of grass or embarrassing declarations of wanting to make out with my best friend's sister. No, no, thank you. I did not sign up for a side of misery with my fried dough.

I knew this was a mistake. I *knew* it.

"Lizzie?" Cara's voice cuts into my head and I startle, my eyes flying up to meet hers. She's leaning against her car and god-dammit, we practically parked next to each other without even knowing it. Even here, even coming from different directions, the world just keeps throwing her in my face. Get wrecked, universe.

"I'm not following you," I say again, my cheeks heating. "I'm not being a creeper." I don't know why it feels so important for her to know this, but it does.

"No, I know," she says, coming to stand in front of me, and I tilt my head. "It's kind of hard to miss your car." She gestures to the giant pink bobbleheaded leopard that James put on my dash-board. She's all muscley and holding giant weights over her head.

He said that she reminded him of me, and he said it sincerely, which was so stupid and funny and nice that I had to shove his face out of my face before I laughed for a solid minute (fifteen seconds from pure delight, the rest from anxiety).

"Right, yeah," I say.

"I noticed it when I went to get in mine. We parked right near each other." She pats the hood of the car beside her, because of course the universe would do this to me, would take away the tiny little haven that I thought was waiting for me by putting Cara right in front of it. Like I said, get wrecked.

"Did you need something?" I ask, utterly unsure what I should be doing right now. Do I get in my car? Do I stand and talk?

"Maybe," she says, and then looks away.

"Okay," I say, letting the word fall out of my mouth slowly, because I don't know what this is, or what she's doing, but after "thanks" I would very much like to vault myself into the sun.

"It's been fun, yeah?" she says crossing the aisle to where I stand. She looks . . . nervous? I just stare at her, not sure what she's getting at.

"The demolition derby?"

She takes another step closer, until she's standing right in front of me, her eyes shining in the moonlight. And is she . . . ? I mean it kinda seems like . . . ? No. I swallow hard, bracing myself for whatever comes next, because I've read this so wrong so many times, and I refuse to do it again.

"You know that's not what I'm talking about," she says.

"I don't, though," I answer quietly because it's true. Her face softens, and I'm not sure if it's because she's realizing how much she's been messing with my head or because she's thinks she's the only one who feels it, again. And I hate this, how we're always a half step away from each other, just slightly out of sync.

"You said you wanted to kiss me?"

I look away, a little bit sad. "I don't know what you want me to say right now."

"You don't have to say anything."

I glance back at her. "What do you want, Cara? One second you're all 'thanks' and then the next you're hanging around my car like you've been waiting for me when *you're the one* who ran away!"

"I tried to show you!" she says. "In the pool that night, remember?"

"You were very drunk," I say, studying the grass.

"I knew what I was doing."

"I wasn't sure, and I didn't want to do something you'd regret."

"Is that why you stopped me?" she asks, tilting her head with the tiniest smile.

"Yeah, that's . . . of course that's why. But you didn't even give me a chance to explain." I run my hands through my hair. "I didn't want our first time to be when you were wasted."

"Our *first* time? That's a bit presumptuous, isn't it?"

"I didn't mean . . ." I trail off, blushing down to my toes.

"Hey, Lizzie," she says, her hand gently tipping my face to look at her. "I'm not drunk now."

Before her words can even register, her lips crash into mine and she tangles her hands around my neck and into my hair. Fierce and hungry, her tongue slides against mine and everything disappears except us.

I meet her intensity, a shiver running down my arms as I grab her hips, hard, and she lets out a featherlight gasp. I swallow it down greedily, walking her backward until she's pinned against my car. My arms trap her while I look at her flushed face.

"You sure about this?" I ask.

She nods so fast that I laugh, high on her enthusiasm. She tries to pull my head back down, kissing my collarbone, my neck, anything she can reach as her fingers snake up beneath my tank top.

I grab her hands and lace our fingers together, pushing them over her head as I slot my leg between hers and leave a trail of kisses across her skin. I grin when her body relaxes under mine.

"Lizzie," she says, breathlessly searching for friction that I've kept just barely out of reach. "Please." She wriggles one hand free and quickly drops it to my shorts, trying to unhook the button with one hand.

I stop and wait for her to look up. Her eyes are already blissed out and unfocused, her lips parted in the most devious of smiles. And oh, this is gonna be fun.

"Let me guess," she pants, lifting her chin defiantly, "you don't want our first time here either?"

"Now who's being presumptuous?" I smile, faltering when she presses a finger along the seam between my legs. "Shit."

"Take me home," she says, repeating the motion. "You live alone, right? I don't want us to get interrupted. We can get my car tomorrow."

"Cara," I say, remembering my apartment. But I don't have much time to worry because she kisses me again and I'm sold. In this moment, I'd do anything for her. Go anywhere.

She grins when I hit the unlock button.

"Fucking finally," she says, running around the car to the passenger seat.

Chapter Twenty

I t's not really a great place. You probably have a really great place," I say, as we step inside.

Cara lets go of my hand, which she grabbed the second we got out the car. I had been . . . well, my hand had been quite busy before that.

It was easy, nice, even, us in our own little bubble in my car.

Nice is the exact opposite of how I feel as she steps farther into my living room, no doubt inventorying my entire shitty life. The weight of this moment hits me in the chest, instantly turning my blood to sludge, and I lean back against the wall, watching her take it all in.

The stained carpet (that was like that when I moved in). The walls (that have been painted sloppily three too many times, with hard bubbles and cracks formed along the seams). The pile of gym polos and sports bras waiting by the door (for me to take to the Laundromat). Even the air conditioner is buzzing loudly in the window beside me. (I've been meaning to replace it but could never justify the money.) All the stray weights and workout gear just strewn everywhere. It's—

"It's perfect," Cara says, turning back to me. And before I can say anything else she's back, her body warm against mine even in the stale, cold air of my apartment.

She's lying and I know it.

I turn my head away, staring at the laptop on my coffee table that doubles as a TV and only works on the neighbor's Wi-Fi. Shame creeps up my spine, as she kisses her way up my neck.

"Lizzie." Cara tips my head back toward hers and leans forward, sucking my ear into her mouth, hot and wet and welcoming. "Please," she whispers again, and all my insecurities are gone. Because this, I know.

This, I'm good at.

I spin her around against the wall, shoving down the neck of her shirt so I can nip at her collarbone. She squirms against me, palming my hips, chasing that delicious friction. Cara whimpers and presses harder against me, sliding down the wall in her haste. I catch her, lifting her arms around my neck, and carry her across the apartment and to my bed.

Thank you, deadlifts. Thank you, studio apartment.

Maybe it is perfect after all.

Her laughter turns into something else entirely when I grab her hips and pull her to the edge of the bed. Her back hits the mattress, legs dangling to the floor as I cage her again between my arms. Her eyes flick to mine, and I can tell she likes that.

"You're sure about this?" I ask, because I need to hear the words. "You said you haven't ever fully—"

"Yes, god, yes," she says. "You don't have to keep asking that."

"I do, actually," I say, tracing her lips with my own. "But also,"

I kiss her again, "I love the way you say yes." My hand drifts lower, beneath the waistband of her shorts, and settles between her legs. "I wonder if I can make you shout it."

Her eyes widen as she rolls her hips and, god, she's so fucking wet. I can't. It's too much. I bury my head in her shoulder, taking a second to calm down. I want this to be good for her. I want to make this memorable. And none of that's going to happen if I rush.

I pull my hand back and grab the edge of her shirt to yank it off.

I'm met with the sight of a faded pink bra, one tiny bleach spot on the fabric, just to the left of her nipple. Who knew a bleach spot could be so fucking sexy? I lean forward, but she flushes and tries to cover her chest. "I wasn't . . ." She blushes. "I wasn't expecting to—this isn't even a *nice* bra. Let alone a *hot* bra. It's like a frayed piece of—" She gasps as I tug it down with my teeth.

"It's perfect," I say, echoing her words from earlier as I finally unhook her bra and slide it off. I nip at her, teasing her tender skin, before trailing kisses along her ribs. "You're perfect," I whisper.

She drags me back up, ripping my tank and sports bra over my head and then it's *on*.

We roll around, tangling our bodies as we kick off all of our clothes until finally, finally, we're just skin under palms, heartbeats against chests, kissing and touching, sighing and smiling.

I shove a pillow under her hips and throw one to the floor, slipping down between her dangling legs. She lets out a gasp as I drop to my knees in front of her and settle onto the pillow.

Now it's my turn to beg. "Please."

She nods with a shaky breath and her legs fall open.

If I thought I had seen perfection before . . .

I meet her eyes as I trace my fingers around her center before slowly dipping them inside. She lets out a surprised laugh, her thighs snapping shut, when I curl them just right. But no, not yet. I press her down with my free hand, parting her even wider to suck and nip at her most sensitive spot. My mouth and hand work in unison, and I can feel her getting close. She cries out, her back arching as she comes for the first of what I hope will be many, many times tonight.

"Don't stop, please don't stop," she whispers.

And I won't. I won't. Because I know I could die happy, right here, with the taste of her on my tongue.

"I don't know how you can possibly be hungry after how much we just ate," she says when I suggest ordering a pizza.

"Ha-ha," I deadpan. "But now that you mention it . . ." Her eyes widen comically as I suck on one of my fingers and pull it out of my mouth with a pop.

She's in my bed, wrapped in my sheets, and I'd be lying if I didn't say that I love the sight of her like that. Her hair is adorably messed up, tangles and knots making it stand in every direction but down. We should probably shower, but I'm too sleepy and warm to want to do anything other than curl up next to her.

Unfortunately, my stomach has other ideas.

"Thai?" I try again, and this time she says, "Yum."

Thai it is.

"What do you want?"

"Surprise me."

I dart into my kitchen and pull out the menu, making quick work of ordering and paying. I ask them to leave it outside my door and then climb back into bed with my laptop, which Cara eyes warily.

"You're not going to make me watch *Annabelle* now, are you?"

"No, even better," I say, cueing up the opening credits of *National Lampoon's Christmas Vacation*. I set my laptop on the dresser where we can both see it and settle down next to her, pulling her close. She rests her head against my chest, and trails lazy circles on my hip with her fingers. Her laughter vibrates through both our bodies as we watch, and I smooth her hair, feeling warmer and more content than I have any right to.

Chapter Twenty-One

I can't stop smiling at work the next day. In fact, I'm pretty sure that I don't stop smiling for the next week.

James knows something is up, but he doesn't press. When I hint about it, he sticks his fingers in his ears and sings "la, la, la, that's my sister, bro." Okay, no details, then.

But he seems relieved that she's not trying to marry him off like she's a younger, hotter (way hotter) Mrs. Bennet anymore, or begging him to start a podcast with her.

He says whatever I'm doing is working.

Good.

Because what I'm doing is providing his sister with a steady diet of mind-blowing orgasms, terrible horror movies, and great takeout. Win-win-win.

Cara slides into my life so seamlessly, it's almost like she's meant to be here. We have standing dinner dates most nights and she texts me stupid cat TikToks all day. I show up on her doorstep with her favorite smoothies from the juice bar around the corner on nights James works late. There are no labels, no deep conversations about what we are, just a steady colliding and combining of our lives.

I can almost let myself forget that this all started as a favor to James, a favor to Cara, even if she doesn't know it. That I'm just supposed to be a safe "distraction" on her way to something better. A babysitter to keep her life on track, or at least from getting too far off it. I can almost forget that none of this is real when you get down to it.

Almost.

Because as much as I want to shove that away, pretend this could be lasting, I know it won't be. People like Cara don't end up with people like me. Besides, last time I let myself fall hard for a girl, I woke up a year later next to an empty bottle of wine and my phone still open to the Google result page for "how to conjure a demon to eat your ex." Never again.

I know what this is for her, what I *am*: a vacation from real life. I'm the fun story she'll tell her girlfriends in the city. The one she'll think about when she's old and married and stuck babysitting grandkids. The women in my family don't get happily ever afters—just ask my mom—and I'm not about to start expecting one now.

So, I try to just live in the moment, to let it happen. To not get attached.

But she makes that easy to forget sometimes, like right now . . . when she's making sure I'm watching her at the squat rack. And, oh, I'm definitely watching.

The fun we could have in here if I could ever get her alone . . .

"Lizzie," Mina says, snapping me out of it with a look that suggests she's already called my name a few times.

"Oh, hey," I say, shoving the spray bottle I just refilled back into the rack like I wasn't ogling the owners' daughter. Off to my side, Cara sets down the bar and turns around looking pleased with herself. "What can I do for you?" I ask, and if my voice is a little strained it's hardly my fault.

"Stella is looking for you. She's losing her shit that you're not up front. I told her I was covering for you while you filled the paper towels."

"Well, you were," I say.

"Right, but I think the weight room probably has enough spray and paper towels now, right? Unless you think Cara is going to get so wet that she—"

"Okay," I say, shoving the rest of the supplies into Mina's arms, which are now shaking with laughter. "I'll go see what Stella wants; thanks for the heads-up."

"Anytime," she calls, already heading to the utility closet.

I push open the heavy double doors separating the weights from reception to find Stella sitting behind my desk, clicking through my private emails, which are somehow still up on my computer. I must have forgotten to log out.

"What are you doing?" I ask, and she spins toward me slowly in my chair.

"Reading," she says, with a smile that reminds me of a lizard.

"That's private."

"Oh, is it?" she says, closing the browser. "That explains it, then. I couldn't figure out what it had to do with your job, but I guess the answer to that is nothing at all."

"No, it was just . . ." But I stop talking when Stella purses her lips.

"Just what?"

As much as I want to tell her to get fucked, that occasionally checking my email in my downtime is hardly worthy of a lecture, I know on some asshole level she's right. And I'm not about to go toe to toe with her when the promotion still hangs in the balance—even if I haven't technically applied yet.

And I'm definitely, definitely not about to admit that the reason I'm frantically refreshing my inbox is to see if the low-income energy assistance application I filed for my mom last week got accepted. I'm semi-panicking that what's left of my savings isn't going to cover whatever crisis Mom thinks up next. There are only three zeroes left in my bank account, and the single number in front of them is embarrassingly low.

I paste on my best customer service smile. "You're right. It was a slow morning and I thought it would be all right to check quick. I apologize, it won't happen again."

"Thank you," Stella says, standing up with a frown. And wait, is that it? Seriously?

"Is there something else? Mina said you were looking for me." I ask, because even now, in the midst of getting yelled at about checking my email, a part of me hopes maybe she's here to offer me the job, or at least schedule the interview.

"Isn't that enough?" she asks.

"I . . ."

She waves me off. "But actually, yes, there is more. I'll be needing you to pick up some extra shifts for Roger."

"Is he okay?"

"Yes," she says, "but I'm going to be using him as my assistant for the next few weeks. Unfortunately, that means he won't be here to keep an eye on things."

"I'm sure we can manage."

"Yes, just be sure to limit your internet time and we should be all set." She walks away, assuming I will follow her. And I do, of course I do. "I'm going to need you to cover his closing management shifts. Mina can help you up front when needed," she says, sweeping into the office, where Roger is noticeably absent.

"I close on my own a lot, it's fine," I say.

"Good, then we shouldn't have any problems."

"May I ask why you're pulling him out of here?"

"Roger will be helping me on-site at the build, sort of a long interview process. Since we'll be very hands off with this location, I'm going to need someone I can really rely on. We're handling this hiring almost as if it's a franchise opportunity. It's important we find just the right person for the job. A real motivated self-starter."

"And you think that's Roger?" I ask, before I can catch myself. I once found three coffee filters stacked in the pot—grounds included—because he was too lazy to change them out and just kept layering them up. "Self-starter" he is not.

"Potentially," Stella says. "I'm meeting with a few other candidates before making my decision."

"I actually wanted to talk to you about that."

"Yes, I assumed as much from Cara's rehearsal dinner."

"Right," I say, because clearly it was too much to hope she had forgotten all about that. "I was hoping we could sit down and discuss it in a more appropriate setting this time."

"Send in an application," she says, "and we'll see what happens."

"But—"

"I'll email you with your updated schedule and closing shifts," she says, brushing past me. "Should I send it to your work email or your personal one? Which one do you check more while you're here?"

"Work is fine," I say, my shoulders dropping in defeat.

"Enjoy the rest of your day," she says, heading out the door like a witch disappearing into a puff of fog and evil.

"Everything okay?" Mina asks me a few moments later, studying my face as she comes to sit beside me.

"Just great," I say, slumping into my chair.

"Where did you go today?" Cara asks, nipping at my thigh. "You left before I even got to my hip thrusts."

We're on my couch, and she's lying in my lap, letting me play with her hair as we watch Johnny and June bicker their way through *Walk the Line*. My hand freezes as I try to find the right words. It's not like I can shit talk her *mom*. I decide to keep it vague.

"Your mom stopped in and wanted to talk."

"Oh, really? About what?"

I glance down to see her looking up at me, her attention pulled from the movie entirely. "Is she offering you the new gym? I may have mentioned you were interested the other day."

"You did?" I ask her and I can't decide if this makes me happy or mad. I don't want her going to her mom. I want to do this the right way.

"Yeah, is that okay?" she asks, studying my face a little harder. I pull my hand back as she sits up.

"I guess. What did you say to her?"

"Just that you seemed like a great candidate. She was talking about how she was going to be deciding soon, so I thought I'd plant a seed."

"I don't need you to 'plant a seed,' that's not what this is. I don't need you or James trying to pull strings for me. I want the job because I deserve it. Not because I'm—"

"I was just trying to help," Cara says, clearly confused. "I wasn't pulling strings."

"Does your mom know about us?" I ask. "She doesn't, right?" And I don't even know why I'm pushing or what I'm trying to prove. I just want to be back in our safe little bubble, watching movies and eating takeout. I hate that the real world is already bursting in.

"It hasn't come up. Believe it or not, I don't usually talk to my mom about who I'm hooking up with. Would it be the worst thing if I did? Are we supposed to be a secret?"

I run my hand over my face, my brain finally catching up to my mouth. Stella knowing about us would be the worst thing, probably. "Well, we're not *not* a secret," I finally say.

"Oh," she says, and my stomach sinks.

The dreaded "oh."

"It's just, your mom isn't my biggest fan," I say, desperate to salvage the night. "I don't think knowing about us would move me to the top of her perfect candidate list and I really need this job. So can we just not rock the boat right now?"

"I wasn't rocking the boat. I was just telling her that I thought you should be considered. She didn't even have you on the list!"

I frown. "She didn't?"

"I mean, she could have, I don't know," Cara backpedals, but I can tell she's lying. "What did she say about it when you brought it up today?"

"She told me to apply and see what happens."

"You didn't even apply yet? See! There you go, that's why you weren't on her radar."

"No, Cara, your mom didn't say it like 'oh, please apply,' she said it like 'apply so we can end this conversation and I can have the pleasure of setting your résumé on fire the moment it comes through.'"

"Say what you will, but my mom's a great businesswoman. She wouldn't do that. Especially not to another woman."

"I guess we've just had really different experiences with her," I say—but, like, why is Cara defending her mom now when all she's done is complain about Stella since she moved here? I guess family loyalty runs deeper than I thought.

"Not that different. Trust me, she wouldn't do something like that. She's a pain in the ass but she's not *evil*."

"Cara, you have to understand. I really can't give her any more ammo against me, so if we can keep this between us like—"

"Like the rehearsal dinner bathroom talk that you still won't let me tell James about even though it was exactly what I needed to hear?"

"Yeah. Just like that," I say, because we're way past the time I could tell James, even if I wanted to. We've kept it a secret too long.

"Fine. I'm not going to be obnoxious about it because I can see that you're freaking out, but you'd be surprised. I really don't think Mom would ever fire you or hinder your promotion prospects because of us. Max and I were a mismatch from the jump; anybody who was paying attention should have seen that. Even *Max* agrees now."

"Oh, yeah?" I ask, because I can't imagine anybody agreeing that jilting them at the altar was a good call.

"Yeah." She smiles. "My timing could have been better but . . . he's ready to move on too. He'll be out of my place in a few weeks, and he's already been talking to some girl at his firm. Ending the engagement was best for everybody. We really don't have to keep sneaking around and pretending we're not dating."

Wait, dating? Is that what we're doing?

The burst of butterflies in my stomach dies off as fast as they appear when I remember my conversation with James. He said "fun," he said "a distraction." He definitely *didn't* say "dating." In fact, he made it extremely clear that Cara and I had no real future, and if I'm being honest, I don't think he's wrong about that.

Cara boops me on the nose, seemingly sensing my mental turmoil, and then grabs my laptop off the coffee table. She mutes Reese Witherspoon mid-song and opens up a Word doc in the corner of the screen. "You okay?"

"Yeah." I lean forward and kiss her, trying really hard not to think about the word "dating" or what it means that she'll have her apartment in the city back in weeks instead of months. I trail my hand lower. I can do physical, I'm good at physical. This is a distraction, just a distraction.

She takes my hands and laces her fingers through them, effectively stopping their descent. "Let's finish your résumé and send it in," she says, soft and warm.

I lean back, caught off guard but trying to cover for it. "Why would you want to do that when we could be doing something much more fun?"

Cara is unpersuaded. "Because it's your dream and you're good at it. I see how you help all those little old ladies lift weights at the gym, and how you calm the nerves of every newbie on the tour. Hell, you got *me* back into lifting, something I thought my parents had ruined for me forever. Face it, you're a gift to the fitness community, Lizzie," she says. "Besides, helping you sort your life out is the least I can do after you've done an epic job saving mine."

"I didn't save your life."

"Fine." She leans into me. "You just saved me from making the biggest mistake of it."

"I think you're giving a little too much credit to the random drunk girl hiding in a bathroom."

"And I think you're selling yourself short, but here we are."

"Here we are."

"Come on, seriously, let me help," Cara says, flashing her big brown eyes at me. "I'm good at résumés."

"Oh, like you're good at matchmaking and podcasting and—?" I tease and she hits me with a pillow.

"I am good at matchmaking! Sam and James would have been perfect together if they'd bothered to show." She laughs. "It doesn't matter anyway though. James seems almost happy that I'm not trying to get him to do anything anymore."

"I bet." She doesn't know the half of it.

"Seriously, Lizzie. Trust me, I know what my mom is looking for in this position. And before you say it, this isn't pulling strings. You deserve this job. You've worked hard for it. I'm just trying to stand next to you and cheer you on. Will you let me do that? Please?"

"Cara . . ."

"I'm here for a few more weeks," she says, studying my face. "Let me help."

"Only a few weeks, huh?" I say, the words slipping out as she turns her attention back to formatting the Word doc. I don't mean for them to sound as sad as they do.

"Yep." She looks at me, sitting up a little straighter. "Unless there's a reason you think I should stay longer?"

The air surrounding us feels suddenly charged and I don't know what to do. I want to say *yes, there* is *a reason to stay*, but I can't. I won't. I'm not going to humiliate myself by begging her not to leave. She always had another life to get back to. She can say we're "dating" all she wants, but we both know what this is: a stopgap. A Band-Aid . . . a *distraction*. It's not right for me to ask her for more. It's not right to want it.

"No, god, get out of here," I lie, trying not to feel nauseated at the idea of her five hours away in her fancy life while I sit scanning key cards at her mother's gym. I hope I sound teasing, playful. I hope she can't hear the firestorm in my belly begging me to take it back.

"Right," she says, biting her lip.

"Right."

"Actually," Cara adds, not looking up from the screen. "While we're on the subject. My bosses have been begging me to come in. We need to discuss a couple clients. They have some paperwork for me to sign too. I was thinking about heading down quick tomorrow."

"Down to the city?"

"Yeah, I'll just take the train. I might need to stay a night or two."

"With Max?"

"Not like *with* Max," Cara says, watching me. "But probably in the guest room. It's silly to pay for a hotel when I live there. I'm sure Max will be fine with it."

"Right, yeah, no," I say, the jealousy I should *not* be feeling simmering just beneath my skin. I'm waiting, hoping, crossing everything, for her to say it's a joke. She doesn't.

"Does that bother you?" She searches my face.

"No, why would it?" I manage to choke out. I'm just full of lies tonight, I guess.

Cara's quiet for too long and I start to panic she's figured me out. But then she shrugs.

"Okay, let's get this résumé done, then. You can drop it off tomorrow on the way to taking me to the station."

Fuck.

Chapter Twenty-Two

I turn in my application and résumé on Monday, right after dropping Cara off. She barely packs anything for her overnight trip, and I tell myself it doesn't bother me that she has a whole other life there. A whole other bathroom there. A toothbrush lined up next to Max's, just like old times. That this is good. That it's fine.

She's only here for a few more weeks, Lizzie. Pull it together. Keeping her on track was the point. The point! I should be happy; god knows James is. Speaking of, now it's time for *him* to distract *me*. Fair is fair.

I meet him for yoga, for real this time, on Tuesday and afterward make him buy me a grilled cheese sandwich from the awesome food truck in the center of town. Cara texts that she's decided to go out with some friends while she's in town and is going to stay an extra night. I play it off like it's no big deal because it isn't. It *can't* be. James is fucking elated. Especially when my sudden loss in appetite means he gets to eat my grilled cheese too.

Wednesday, I work a double at the gym. Almost no one comes

in during the night shift, and I furiously sketch gym designs, desperately trying to stay focused on what matters. Because sometimes, it feels like Cara is *all* that matters. And that's bad for both of us in so many ways.

Cara texts me her entire train ride home and I'm slow to respond. I need to get used to not talking to her all the time, even if it kills me. She's just another habit I need to break, like clicking my pen when I'm impatient or biting my nails. I've got this. I attempt to drown the butterflies in my stomach with various fruit smoothies and do my best to ignore them, ignore her, because the truth is that every hour that ticks closer to her coming back is also an hour that ticks closer to her leaving for real.

The next time she goes to the city, she'll stay.

But no matter how much I tell myself I have to pull back—that I'm going to end this as soon as she gets home—it all flies out the window at the sight of her rushing to my car. She's carrying a giant teddy bear with a rose bow tie, and I melt.

"Hi," she says, practically throwing herself in my passenger seat. "I got this for you."

"I love it." I tear it out of her hands and shove myself into them. So much for restraint. So much for ending things.

THURSDAY NIGHT, JAMES calls and says we need to catch up on some *Bachelor* episodes we missed. I make Cara meet Jane and Sherry out for drinks. She's hesitant to leave me after just getting back, but I insist. Last night, and the six orgasms we split between us, was a mistake.

We have to stop before I get in any deeper. I was wrong: she's not a bad habit, she's a full-blown addiction. "Here for a good time, not a long time," right? I'd do well to remember it.

Just as I hit peak existential spiraling, James walks in with a bag from The Bowl and pulls me back. I roll my eyes at his choice of meals. Of course he would get protein salads for our family takeout night.

I grab a couple plates and we settle into the couch, *Bachelor* already cued up on my laptop before either of us speaks. He ruins it just as I'm starting to relax.

"So Cara was here last night?" James asks, eyeing the hoodie she left hanging over my side of the couch.

"Yeah." I shrug, wanting to move the conversation along to one that doesn't make me feel simultaneously heartsick and like an asshole. Cara's not the only one who can't know I'm close to catching feelings.

He hands me what looks like a chicken Cobb salad and some low-fat vinaigrette, and I frown. I lean over to see he's gotten himself the same thing. At least we're both suffering tonight.

"How thrilled are you that she'll be out of your hair soon?" he asks.

And "thrilled" is *not* the word I would use.

"It's awesome that she decided not to resign, right?" He scratches his eyebrow. "That really came down to the wire. Mom was flipping out, it was hilarious. But yeah, looks like we did it. She's finally getting her shit together again."

And that stops me, mid bite.

"Wait, Cara was going to resign? I thought she just took a sabbatical."

James crinkles his forehead. "She never mentioned it to you? Wild. She would not fucking shut up about it to me. I was like 'Dude, what are you doing? There is nothing for you here. Run back while you still can.'"

He laughs, actually laughs, as my brain tries to catch up with what he's saying. *Cara was going to stay? And now she's not?*

"Could you imagine picking this place over the city?" James asks. "Thank god you got her to head back down. I owe you a massive thank-you."

"Me? What did I do?" I ask numbly.

"That's what I'm dying to know. How'd you convince her?"

"All she did was help me with my résumé. I don't—"

"Maybe all that white space and retail work freaked her out." He nudges me with his elbow. It's a joke I've made a hundred times, but it hits differently, painfully, hearing someone else say it.

James is still talking, and I shake my head, trying to focus.

". . . the next thing I know, she's signing back on at her firm and asking her boss about the process of transitioning clients back to her. It sounds like he wants her back sooner than later too. Mission accomplished, bud. I cannot *wait* to have my house back." He laughs.

"Yeah," I say, feeling like I'm going to puke. "I bet." The clock ticks louder in my ear. Because was it my résumé that scared her—did it hit home exactly how different we were—or shit, was it when she asked me if she had a reason to stay? *Was she really asking?*

No.

That's ridiculous. She—

"And now you can stop throwing away your gains. Win-win."

"Huh?" I ask, still lost in my own head.

"Don't act like you haven't been slacking on your workouts. You used to hang around the gym for hours after your shift and now you keep getting dragged around by my sister." He punches my arm. "It's a good thing she's been hanging out with Jane and Sherry again too. I bet you would have lost your shit if you had to be that social with her all the time."

"Right, yeah," I say. Because he is right, mostly, I have been slacking—fewer reps, less weight, in a rush to get back to her. Most days, I can't wait to find out what we're doing after my shifts— making an elaborate dinner, trying out a no-mess s'mores kit she'd seen on Insta, reading, watching *Dateline* for the five-hundredth time, I don't fucking care. Whatever she wants. It's all great to me. *Was* all great to me. I rub my eyes.

"We really pulled it off," James says, oblivious. "Operation 'distract my sister' is in the books, and I thank you for your service." He grabs my hand and high-fives it himself. "I couldn't have done it without the assist."

My head spins as the full extent of the lies surrounding Cara's and my relationship (if you can even call it that) hits me.

Like James doesn't have any idea that pretty much any time she says she's with Sherry and Jane, she's actually with me. In fact, most of the time she says she's anywhere else, she's here, in my bed or on my couch or in my shower or my . . .

And it's not just the steady stream of orgasms that's nice, I realize.

We've been doing *all* the gross couple shit: snuggling, fighting over the last crab rangoon, laughing and wrestling over what to watch, alternating my horror movies with her romances. Her hair is mixed in my hairbrush. Her new toothbrush is a steady presence beside mine. And it never once occurred to me to mind it like I normally would. Cara never felt like something I wanted to get away from. Ever.

I was excited to get home for the first time in my life.

And now it's all going away. Everything is going away. She's taking it with her to her old, better life. And I knew this was coming. I knew it. Falling for Cara is like robbing a bank—dangerous, stupid, ill advised. A situation where the consequences will always, always outweigh the reward.

But it's okay, I remind myself. I'm okay. This is why we don't care, McCarthy. Let it go. And I will. I will. Cara will leave and I will be just fine, because home is not a person. Home has never been a person.

It's good that she's leaving. It's good.

You can't rely on people; that's something my mom taught me a hundred times whether she meant to or not. Cara's just reinforcing it. She is not my home.

My home, my real one, is the gym.

No, the *idea* of a gym is my home. It doesn't matter if I'm four or fourteen or twenty-four, it's been the one constant in my life. Gyms make sense. Their machines, their weights, their cause and effect—if you lift heavy, you will get stronger. If you go to Zumba, you will learn the routines—it's predictable. Steady. You can count on the squat racks and the ellipticals and the weights being there day after day. Reliable in a way that no person could ever be. This is fine. I *am* fine. I—

"Lizzie?" James asks, as my phone buzzes in my hand. I bet

it's going to be Cara, and I can't handle that right now. Her kissy emojis, her ridiculous gifs, all those goofy TikToks that make her laugh so hard she snorts. I'm gonna lose it all, yes, but it's not like I ever really had it anyway. How could I when it was all based on lies—a lie to her, a lie to James . . .

Why did I go along with any of this?

I finally force my eyes down, relieved to see that it's not Cara texting, it's my mother. Ironic, because usually Mom makes me feel nauseous in an entirely different way—I never wished I had a mom I could actually run to as much as I do right now. I let myself pretend, just for a second, that I do, that her text will be nice, maybe even loving, but then I shake my head. Pretending I have something better than what I do is what got me into this mess in the first place.

I click open her message and brace myself for whatever is coming next.

> You didn't write back.

I stare down at her text, at a loss, until I decide to just go with a nice neutral question mark reply.

> ???

> I emailed you! You too good to check your email now, high roller?

> I don't know what you're talking about.

Sent again. Jesus. Try not to lose
it this time. It's the heat assistance
application since you're crying poor
about paying it yourself.

Lose it? How can one lose an email?

"Lizzie, is everything okay?" James's voice cuts through my confusion.

I slide my phone in my pocket. "Yeah, just my mom acting up again."

James sighs. "You know nothing good comes from talking to your mom, right?" And okay, pot meet kettle. "If you—"

"How's Ramón?" I ask, desperate for a subject change before I spiral out for real. "I've been meaning to ask. Things still going okay?"

"Amazing, incredible, too good for this world." He sighs. "I really think he's the one."

"You say that about everyone," I remind him, and he laughs, shoveling more food into his mouth with a thoughtful look.

"I know, but this time it feels different. It feels like fate."

"You really believe in that?"

"What are the odds? I meet him at my sister's disaster of a wedding. Everything is awful, right? And then there he is, a perfect bright spot, helping us deal with all the vendors and to calm down the guests. I still want to know who pushed that first domino down to make my sister run"—I shift in my seat, but he doesn't seem to notice—"but I wouldn't have gotten to spend so much time with Ramón if they hadn't. Fate." He smiles. "Bringing people together since the dinosaurs."

Fate.

The word echoes in my head. Fate is for pretty, privileged rich people with time to waste. Fate is for fairy tales and rustic weddings, and my favorite Taylor Swift songs. It's not for me.

I'm not stupid. I know I won't be able to stay away from Cara as long as she's here. But I *can* do my best to keep things casual. Rein myself in. Stop caring.

I just need to keep my feet on the ground and my hands on the weight bar. Because that's what matters. That's what's home.

Chapter Twenty-Three

We have a problem," Cara says as she walks up to my desk. At first, I think she's going to yell at me for blowing off her good-night text last night—I was still reeling too much from my conversation with James to reply—until I realize she's not even in workout clothes.

"What's up?" I ask, trying and failing to sound aloof.

The gym is my home. The gym is my home. The gym is my—

"Two things; do you want the bad or the less bad first?"

"I guess the bad," I say, setting down my pencil. Cara isn't very dramatic, so now she's really got my attention, new mantra be damned.

"I visited my mom this morning."

I crack a smile. "You're right, that is horrible news."

"Stop." She laughs. "But yeah, while that was bad enough, the most important thing is that she was going over the applications with Dad while I was there. She was talking through all the candidates and, Lizzie, she didn't mention you. She's talking about bringing in two new people now. One for here and one for there."

Heh, I guess Roger's working interview was a flop . . . but then the rest of what she said registers.

"Oh," I say. "Shit." I knew Stella didn't take me seriously, but I assumed she would at least let me interview. At least pretend to give me a chance.

"Mom said they need to make a final decision by the end of next week."

"It kinda sounds like they already made it, right? It's just a formality at this point." I blow out a breath. "Oh fucking well."

"No, not 'oh fucking well.' That's the only good news. You still have time. *We* still have time! But we only have a few days to do it, so you need to be aggressive."

I think back to when I trapped her parents during her wedding. I don't know that it's possible to get more aggressive than that. More professional? Probably. But not more aggressive. And that tactic definitely didn't work. Time to default to my usual don't-even-bother-hoping approach. Seems safer.

"I don't know what you want me to do here." I shrug. "I'm obviously not getting the job."

Cara pinches the bridge of her nose and lets out a frustrated huff. "I want you to stand up for what you want! I want you to talk to them, seriously. Don't give up on yourself. Do you think I would be where I am today if I gave up all the time?"

"You live in your brother's spare room," I point out.

"Okay, I'm not talking about right this second, I'm talking about in general! Nobody used to take me seriously either; they'd see some spoiled girl from upstate and think I didn't have what I needed to hack it in New York City real estate. I had to go to bat for myself every day if I—"

"This isn't the same." And maybe I should just let her give me the pep talk. Maybe I should let her gas me up and pretend I have a shot. But I can't. I can't sit here for another second and act like we're on the same page. That our stories are even from the same book.

"How?" she asks, and her tone is just indignant enough to really piss me off.

"Because the same rules don't apply to me! I don't have a fancy degree on my wall. I don't have rich parents to fall back on. I don't have any of that. And if I push too hard, I could push myself out of a job entirely. You take a sabbatical, and nothing changes except maybe you eat up a little of your trust fund interest. If I get fired, I'm fucked."

"That's not fair."

"Life isn't fair. I don't have a plan B. If they didn't pick me, they didn't pick me. Maybe another job will open up someday. And I know it looks like nothing to you, but this front desk position is the best job I've ever had. The most money I've ever made. I'm not going to go piss your mother off and risk losing it!"

"You're content to sit here and scan key cards for the rest of your life?" She shoves her finger at the crude gym sketch I was working on before she walked up. "You sure about that?"

Before she says another word, I crumple it up and toss it into the trash beside my desk. "And what if I am?"

"God, have some ambition for once!" she shouts.

"Why do you even care? You'll be back at your old job soon anyway and this little vacation you're on will be over."

"What?"

"James told me you're going back to your job soon. And you already said Max will be out of your place. What do you care if I'm still scanning key cards and refilling paper towels two weeks from now? My life won't be your problem anymore, and you know what? It never was. This whole idea was ridiculous, even applying was just some silly pipe dream. I let you and your brother talk me into this fantasy like it was something I could actually have. It's not . . . we're not the same. And you know it! You couldn't even be bothered to tell me that you were thinking of staying or that you changed your mind. I had to hear it from James."

Her face falls. "I was going to tell you, I promise."

"When? Right before you left?"

"No, soon. I . . . I'm still figuring things out."

"Maybe I am too. Did you ever think about that? And maybe I don't need you putting ideas in my head about big promotions and owning my own gym and how fucking happy I make you when it's all bullshit!"

Guests are staring now, but I don't care. Let them.

"I wasn't trying to do that," she says. "I'm sorry if I made you feel—"

"It's fine," I say, waving her off. I shove back from my desk, needing to be anywhere but here, when I remember what else she said. There were two bad things. "You never said, what's the less bad thing?"

"Oh," she says, wiping at her eyes. "Don't worry about it."

"Just tell me, Cara," I grumble.

"I let it slip today in front of my parents that I was seeing someone. I told them it wasn't serious," she adds before I can get another word out, and right. Not serious. So fucking not serious she didn't even tell me she was thinking of staying here until she'd already decided not to. "But they wanted to meet them anyway."

"Nope, not doing that." I scoff, turning to leave, but she tugs at my arm. "Didn't you hear anything I just said?"

She slides her hand down to mine and squeezes. "Listen, if you came to dinner, you could talk to them about the job opportunity in a more relaxed setting—it's not a pipe dream, it isn't."

"I didn't think it was possible for there to be a worse idea than James dragging me to your wedding, but congrats. You found one."

"Lizzie, come on! You deserve this promotion—and if you came with me to dinner, they would see, I don't know . . . maybe if they saw how much I care about you then it'll make them look at you differently."

How much she cares about me? I desperately try not to dwell on that, to focus on the "it's not serious" part instead, but the traitor butterflies in my brain have other ideas.

"Yes, now instead of hating me they'll also want to kill me for defiling their daughter," I say, still trying to keep it light. *Not that serious.* "No."

She offers me a sad smile. "Hey, their daughter really likes when you defile her, if it's any consolation."

"Cara," I say, more of a plea than a warning. When she says stuff like that, I want to . . . I want to give her anything she wants. Everything. But—

Cara clears her throat and rubs the unshed tears out of her eyes. "Will you come? Please? It would mean a lot to me. I know I don't deserve it after not telling you about my job stuff, but please?"

I look at her, hating that she's on the verge of crying because of me. "What did they do when you told them who it was?"

She laces her fingers in mine. "I didn't. I wanted to talk to you first."

"Okay," I say. "Okay, then just have Sherry or Jane go and pretend. Or some random guy you find on those dating apps you still have on your phone," I force myself to say, even though the thought pisses me off.

But I can't go to her family dinner. I can't keep having sleepovers. She said it herself: It's not that serious. It's. Not. That. Serious. I need to tattoo that across my forehead and never forget it. I have to. But I'd be lying if I didn't say a part of me wishes I could, *we* could, be family dinner–worthy.

"I don't want them to come, I want you to come." She squeezes my hand.

"Why?" I ask and when our eyes meet, everything else just falls away.

It's just me and her in this room. None of the people who are walking by matter; nobody trying to check in or out, or asking for towels, or complaining that the pool deck is wet because I guess we're somehow supposed to be able to keep it dry despite a dozen preschoolers cannonballing into it every five minutes. Everything's on hold, the entire universe waiting for her answer.

"Because you're the person I'm seeing?" she says, confused.

"But why?"

"Why am I seeing you or why do I want to take you to family dinner?"

And that question, the way she phrases it, takes me back to standing in James's kitchen that first day, she and I splattered in shake, having no idea what our future held. And I can't resist, I answer the same way I did then. "Both, I guess."

She gives me a soft smile. Does she remember too? Is it burned in her head like it's burned in mine?

"Because we have fun together? I like hanging out with you?" She answers me like it's a question, and it shouldn't feel like a vise in my throat, it shouldn't feel like licking a battery on a dare—bitter and hard and final—because she's right, isn't she?

Having fun and hanging out is exactly what we signed up for, *exactly*. It's on me that I ever pretended it could be anything more.

I drag my hand through my hair. "Right, of course," I say, walking back to my desk. I pretend like I'm refilling the printer paper, hanging my head as I regroup. I don't even notice her come up behind me.

"Penny for your thoughts," she says, once she's right beside me.

I open my mouth and shut it. I don't know what to say.

I settle on, "I'm thinking I need to order more paper," as I twist away from her.

"Are you okay?"

"Yeah," I lie. "I'm great, why wouldn't I be?"

"I don't know, because we've been arguing since I got here?"

"We haven't been," I say, because arguing implies a level of commitment that I know fully now that we don't have, haven't had, and will never have. "You gave me some information. We had a difference of opinion, but it doesn't really matter because like I said, you're leaving soon. There's no point to having dinner with your parents or anything else. Let it go."

"I don't get it. Why won't you fight for this promotion?"

"You don't have to get it," I remind her. "It's not that serious."

Cara crosses her arms. "Are we talking about the job right now, or us?"

I shake my head. "What do you want from me? Like you said,

I'm someone you have fun with. I'm just someone you met in a bathroom that happens to be really good with her tongue."

"Don't say it like that. You're not just—"

"Stop," I say, pulling the last ream of paper off the shelf. It bangs against the desk a little louder than I mean it to and she jumps.

She leans closer. "None of that means you're not also important to me. I don't even—"

"Cara," I say, looking at her. "It's fine. We both knew what this was. I'm not the person you take to dinner with your parents." I stare at her, breathing heavy, and hope she drops it. I need her to drop it.

She shakes her head, her eyes staying closed an extra beat on her next blink. She opens them and smiles. "Fair enough," she says in a perfectly cordial tone.

To anyone passing by right now, it would look like a totally normal end to our conversation. Like everything was fine, better than fine, even, like everything was *good*. But there's something about the way her muscles stiffen, the way her eyes go from soft and warm to pinched in the corners.

I hate it.

I run through my options in my head. There's no forever, I get that, but what if we don't have to fizzle? At least not yet. I'm no stranger to hard stops, and she's not gone yet.

I grab her arm hard and pull her into the storage closet, kicking the door shut behind us. I walk her backward as I kiss her, long and hard. I trail my finger down the side of her arm, leaving those little goose bumps that I love, and kiss her again in her favorite spot, where her jaw meets her neck.

"Are you trying to distract me?" she whispers as I press her back against an old desk.

"I'm trying to relax you," I murmur, falling to my knees in front of her and tugging down her leggings. "Is it working?"

"Yes," she breathes. "I'm on my way to feeling very, *very* relaxed."

WE'RE TANGLED UP in my sheets the next afternoon, enveloped in a happy post-orgasmic haze after a long night of *relaxing*, when she brings it up again.

"It would mean a lot to me if you came to dinner."

"It would mean a lot to me if you stopped asking." I sigh and tuck my arm beneath my head. It seems like my plan of fucking that idea out of her head has failed spectacularly.

Cara smacks my side and then snuggles in, one arm draped lazily across my torso, one of her long legs fitted between mine. "You're so stubborn."

I lift my head to see her better. "Wait, did you just get me off to butter me up?"

"Depends, have you been screwing me to make me forget?"

I smirk and look away.

"I guess we both suck, then." She grins and falls back onto her own pillow.

"Come 'ere." I tug her back against me. "I don't like it when you're so far away."

I don't mean to say it, even if it's true. It's going to hurt, a lot, when she leaves. My experiment of being aloof until she left is an obvious failure, and my attempt to ignore the inevitable last night just served to remind me why I really, *really* wish it wasn't. She's got me so twisted up inside that I don't know if I want to chase her out of my bed or chain her to it.

Both, maybe.

"I'm right here." Cara smiles but snuggles in closer anyway.

Not for long, I think. Not for long.

"It *would* mean a lot to me though," she says, nuzzling against me. I can feel her smile against my skin when we lie like this; it's one of my favorite things. "You don't have to, but if you wanted to be cool about it . . . I would appreciate it."

Her *appreciation* goes a long way toward tempting me. She did an excellent job of demonstrating it last night after I . . . focus, Lizzie.

I glance down at her, resisting the urge to kiss her head, and instead ask, "Why does it matter so much to you if I go or not?"

"Honestly?"

"Yeah."

"I kind of feel like a disappointment to them."

"Well, hanging around with me isn't going to help with that," I snark.

She rolls over onto me and pins me with her gaze. "I hate when you say stuff like that."

"It's true."

She sits up. "It is *not*."

I look away, as much as it kills me when she's showing this much skin, but this isn't an argument worth having.

She tips my head back toward her. "You're great, and I'm not leaving here until you admit that."

"Then you'd better start paying half of the rent."

She huffs but there's a smile attached to it, before her face gets all serious again.

I sit up to run my hands over her bare back and lean in for a kiss, but she pushes me back down. "We can't just make out every time I try to talk to you."

"Why not?"

"Lizzie, come on." She wraps the sheet around her.

Dammit.

"Alright, I'll bite. Why do you feel like a disappointment?"

"Glad you asked. Let's see." She starts counting on her fingers. "I left my fiancé at the altar, lost my parents a bunch of money, can't currently pay them back because I basically quit and then unquit my job. I have no idea what I'm doing with my life. I have no idea what I *want* to be doing with my life, and my brother, who I wanted to get closer with, is just absolutely eating up this golden-child shit instead. They're in the process of acquiring that yoga studio he dragged us to, by the way, and now they think he's brilliant. Then they went on and on about how I was a disaster, and my life was a disaster, and how I ruined the only good relationship I ever had, and I should take a note from James's book and—"

"So?"

"So? So?!"

"Why do you care what they think? Stella's awful and George is one hundred percent checked out." Okay, that was a little harsh, but she needed to hear it.

"They're my parents! Of course I care. And yeah, that's when I blurted out that I was seeing someone really great, because if there's one thing that will make my mom happy, it's knowing future grandbabies are still on the table."

I choke on my spit, coughing so hard my face turns red. "Babies?"

Apparently, we have very different ideas of what "not that serious" means.

"Not right this second or anything! But still, if I show up to dinner alone, instead of with that 'really great person' I told them about, I'm going to look like I made it all up. I'm going to seem like an even bigger screwup than I already do."

"Wait, back up, you think I'm really great?" I tease. I run my tongue along the inside of my cheek and do the math on if she's going to let me kiss that look off her face. Probably not, given how she readjusts her sheet to cover more of her skin, like she can read my mind. Ugh, fine.

"You *are* really great," she huffs.

"My point remains that showing up with me isn't going to prove you're not a total fuckup," I say. "In fact, it kind of proves their point."

"I told you to stop that." She grabs a pillow and smacks me in the face. "I will beat this low self-esteem out of you if that's what it takes."

"I don't think that's how it works," I tease, fighting her off. "My mom already tested that theory."

"Lizzie—" Her face falls, and ugh, god, subject change, please.

"I'm just saying, if they don't think I'm good enough for their gym, they're definitely not going to think I'm good enough for their daughter," I cut her off. "You're better off hiring someone for the night."

She stares at me, a mock horrified expression on her face. "Great, so I've reached the 'paying an escort to hang out with me' stage of my life's downfall. Awesome."

"I didn't mean it like that." I laugh and dodge a pillow she throws at my face.

But before I can return the favor, she crawls up my body and leans in for a kiss. "I know how you meant it. But I honestly think if they see how crazy I am about you, it'll help on the job front too. Nothing is set in stone with the promotion, not until next week."

And god, I want to believe her. I do. "What if I do and we find out it's a lost cause?"

"It's not over till it's over, Lizzie."

I arch my eyebrows when the rest of what she just said hits me. "Hang on, back up. Did you just say you're crazy about me?"

"That depends. Are you always going to make me repeat every compliment I give you?" she teases.

"Hey, a little confirmation never hurt anybody."

"How about this for confirmation, then? I wouldn't be going down on you on the daily if I wasn't." She blushes like maybe she said too much but I love it.

"Hmm. When you put it like that, it sounds like maybe you're just crazy about my va—" She covers my mouth with her hand, cutting me off.

"Do not ruin this moment. I will kill you," she says, making the fiercest face I've ever seen. Unfortunately for her, it's also so adorable that I laugh.

She pulls her hand back with a little pout. "I was trying for sexy, not funny."

"You can be both," I say, wagging my eyebrows at her like a perv. "Maybe you should show me again how crazy you are about . . . me."

"Will you go to dinner at my parents' if I do?"

"That's blackmail," I pout, even though I already know I'm going to go. It seems I can never say no to Cara, not really.

"No, it's bribery," she says, sliding down my body and peeking up at me from under the sheet. Her hand drifts down, right to where I want it most. "What do you say?"

"Anything," I say, already squirming. "Anything you want, just please, don't stop."

Chapter Twenty-Four

I'm not going! I can't."

James is sitting on the couch, watching me pace around his living room with concern, while Cara finishes getting ready in the other room.

"I can't believe you said yes to this." He starts to laugh, but swallows it down, doing his best to look supportive in the midst of my meltdown. "Mom is going to *love* this. It's practically guaranteed to cement my golden-child status." He motions for me to sit down and drops his head on my shoulder for a second. "You're the best friend a guy could ever have," he teases.

"Oh my god, shut up. I was under duress. She was being very persuasive."

"Thanks, I don't wanna know," he says, covering his ears.

I let out a huff. "This is all your fault, you know."

"How is this my fault? You're the one who agreed to go!"

"You're the one who got us talking again in the first place! And now I have to go eat dinner with your parents. Who. Hate. Me."

"In fairness, I told you to distract her, not make it family-dinner official," he whispers, glancing toward his bathroom door. "What the hell are you two even doing anymore? It's not like you really—"

"You know what?" I say, standing up. "You're right. I'm gonna tell her that. Right now. I'm gonna tell her everything—including you skipping the fair on purpose. Because if I do, she's not gonna want me at dinner and I'm not going to feel like an asshole for lying anymore. Win-win."

James pulls me back down. "If you tell her everything, she'll kill both of us. Is that what you want?"

"What are you guys whispering about?" Cara walks into the living room, and wow, she looks gorgeous. Her silky pink blouse tapers into tight black pants that cling to her like a second skin. She smiles at me, sliding delicate gold hoops into her ears, and I'm speechless.

"Nothing," James says, finding his voice before I do. "Lizzie's just freaking out as usual, over *nothing*." He glares at me with that last word.

Cara winks at me and I melt. "You're going to be great," she says. "Plus, I'm definitely, definitely making this up to you later."

"Welp, I'm going to go bleach my brain," James says, dramatically rolling over the back of the couch and then sprinting to the bathroom.

Cara takes his place and grabs my hand. "Are you really freaking out?"

I nod.

"Why?"

"Because they hate me. Because you're going to get me fired for this. Because—"

"They aren't going to fire you because I brought you to dinner."

I stare at Cara, and she stares back.

"I won't make you go," she says, after a long beat. "But you look incredible, you *are* incredible, and I think together we can get them on your side tonight."

"Your optimism is adorable, but severely misguided."

"Look, I know I've had my issues with my mother, but deep down I'm sure she just wants me to be happy. Right now, *you* are the thing that makes me happy. How could she not love you for that?"

"I do?"

"Yeah, obviously!" She smiles, tugging me against her. "But I want to make you happy too. If this is seriously too much, we'll both skip. She'll be pissed at me, but you'll be off the hook. They don't even know you're my mystery date yet."

And when she says things like that, things like I make her happy and she wants me to be happy too, I can almost believe this is a real kind of thing.

"I'll come to dinner with you," I say, before I can stop myself.

A tiny glimmer of hope blooms in my chest, flowering all the way up to my brain. Because what if she's right. What if this wins me brownie points? What if she likes having me on her arm? What if, for once, things go my way?

"Are you sure?" Cara asks with a gentle nudge.

"Positive, but I'm still going to hold you to that whole 'making it up to me' thing."

She gives me a quick kiss and then rubs her lipstick off my cheek with her thumb. "I wouldn't have it any other way." Before we can get too carried away, she pulls a folder from the side table and sets it in my hand. "Don't get mad, but I wrote you up a business plan."

"A business plan?"

"Just in case you didn't panic-ditch me, I thought you could slip this to them tonight. I know it'll come up, and this way you can show how prepared you are."

I stare at the green folder in her hand, my eyebrows bunched up. "But I didn't make this."

"I know, but . . . just look." She opens the file and sets it in my lap.

The first thing I notice is my sketches, all of them, from balled up napkins to the one I tossed in the trash. She must have been collecting them without me knowing, pulling out my crumpled dreams and smoothing them out flat again. I flip through the pages and find her drawings, cleaner and better than mine, but everything exactly in their place, everything exactly as I drew them.

Like home.

I swallow hard, my eyes welling up as I get to the last part: a five-year plan to take over the gym, to be brought on not just as a manager, but, by a step program, to become a franchisee, and to let me work my way up, building interest in the company. To make a little piece of it mine from the jump.

This is so nice.

This is too much. I blink hard and look away.

"Do you really think they would go for this?" I ask when my chin stops wobbling.

"I think there's a chance. It's the same plan they were talking about with the other candidates, just at a slightly accelerated rate. They didn't think about how far away the new property was. They don't want to constantly be there or be worrying about it the way they are with the ones in town. If they turn it into a franchise, they'll still get paid, and you'll still get your own gym. Plus, this way you don't need to come up with a huge buy-in right away. You'd work it off in exchange for a lower salary. I don't know what you're making now, but I'm assuming this gym director position is higher. Look, this is what's on the table, and then if we cut it by a quarter to go toward the down payment . . . is that still enough to live on?"

"It is," I say. "Way more than enough." While I knew there was a raise with this position, I had no idea these were the numbers we were talking about. I've never seen that much money in my life, even with the cut. I could cover my bills, and my mom's too, comfortably. Very comfortably. Mom could take a break from the guilt trips. I could put both our electric bills on autopay, even in the winter. I could get a nicer apartment. This kind of salary would be life-changing.

I glance at Cara, who's biting her lip, watching me take it all in. She's so perfect it makes me want to cry.

"Thank you." I smile instead. "A lot."

"Yeah?"

"Yeah, I love it," I say, but I realize then, what I might really mean is—

I love you.

Chapter Twenty-Five

Ready?" Cara asks, giving my hand a squeeze as we stare up at her parents' stately Colonial at the end of a long driveway.

I'm not ready, if I'm being honest, but I need to be, so I nod and pop her car door open. James beat us here by a few minutes, a planned thing, so that at least I'll have a nice friendly face on the inside when the shit inevitably hits the fan. I'm clutching the folder Cara made me like a lifeline, a good luck charm, a magic talisman that's going to make this all okay somehow.

I love her, I think. Followed by, I'm so fucked.

I've been repeating that in my head for the last hour, and I still don't know what to do with it.

Cara smiles at me as we walk to the door, and I feel like I'm walking to my death. Now that we're out of the safe bubble of James's house, the sensation that this is all a very terrible idea is back.

Cara knocks on the door, and we wait on the porch. Weird. I may have a shitty relationship with my mother, but at least she doesn't make me knock.

Stella opens the door, a wide welcoming smile on her face . . . which promptly slides off the second she sees me instead of another,

I don't know, presidential hopeful. "Elizabeth?" she says, knowing how much I hate being called that.

"Hello." I try to sound cheerful as her eyes shoot to Cara's.

"May we come in, Mom?" Cara asks, looking at me nervously.

"Yes, of course," Stella says, opening the door wide and stepping inside. "I'm sorry, I'm forgetting myself. I thought you were bringing the person you're seeing, not someone from the gym."

I bristle at the way she says it, looking down her nose at me, and Cara's hand finds mine again.

"Lizzie is the person I'm seeing," she beams, holding up our linked fingers, "so, I did bring them."

Stella honest to god brings her hand to her chest. I thought pearl clutching was just, like, a saying, not an actual thing, but here we are. And yep, this is going exactly as badly as I knew it would.

"I can go," I say, my eyes pleading with Cara's. "I don't want to ruin your family dinner."

"Nonsense, Elizabeth," Stella says, her face friendly but her tone cold. "No one is leaving." And with that, she turns and disappears into the cavernous house. Cara follows her, mouthing an apology to me as she leads us into the formal living room, all red velvet and cream carpets.

James sits on a large, overstuffed couch while George sits in a giant easy chair across the room, sipping scotch, the expensive-looking bottle carefully placed within arm's reach for easy refills. George smiles when he sees me, confusion crossing his features but not dimming his smile.

"Hi, Dad," Cara says.

"Hi, pumpkin," he answers, getting up to hug her. "And what's this? Is there a problem at the gym, Lizzie?"

"Um, no, I actually came with Cara."

"Cara?" And there's the frown. "I thought you were bringing the new boy you're seeing. I was looking forward to giving him the third degree."

"Well, I did. Sort of. Except it's not a boy and they're not new. At least not to you." Cara smiles weakly. "It's Lizzie."

I watch confusion flit through George's eyes, followed by surprise, before settling on what seems to be a strange sort of reluctant acceptance. In the corner, James snickers, enjoying the show.

I'm going to kill him. I'm actually going to kill him.

George smooths his shirt. "Does your mother know?"

"She answered the door." Cara grimaces, just as Stella comes in with a large glass of wine she's filled to the brim.

Stella takes a long gulp out of her glass and then smiles cheerfully. "Isn't this so nice, George. Our daughter. With our *employee*."

"Mom," James cautions, shifting forward in his seat. I glance over, and I can tell how much her last comment bothered him. After all, I'm not the only *employee* in this room.

"What, dear?" she asks, blinking hard and fast as if daring him to say something else.

"Nothing." He slinks back into his seat with an apologetic look. So much for having my back.

"Smells good in here," I say, hoping that maybe flattery will get me somewhere.

"Yes, that's the prime rib."

"Oh, yum. I hope you didn't go all out on my account."

"How could we have?" Stella smiles. "When we didn't know you were coming."

"Right," I say, and everything gets awkward and quiet. The urge to run ratchets up. "Well, I appreciate the effort regardless. You must have spent all afternoon cooking."

"It's catered," Stella says icily. Like I should know that a family dinner doesn't mean homecooked.

I look at Cara for help, but she's studying the wall. I wonder, for the first time for real, if she's embarrassed by me. She swore she wasn't but this? This is like running a highlighter across our differences and then projecting them onto a movie screen. I don't belong here. I tug at my new button-down. The tag is making my neck itch, but I don't dare touch it. Not with Stella glaring at me, waiting to pounce on whatever trashy thing I do next.

"Well, I'm famished," James says, jumping up. "Mom, can we eat? You were just complaining everything was going to get cold before they got here, and now they're here!"

Stella gives him a look like she wants to strangle him, but settles on a curt "yes, fine" instead.

I follow everyone down the hall to a large dining room. Everything is rich and dark, with padded antique chairs and yes, even more red velvet. It all looks so old and expensive and uncomfortable. I wait for Cara to take her seat and then sit down beside her, looking at all the fancy china in front of me and swallowing hard. Even the row of gorgeous candles burning down the center of this giant teakwood table doesn't make me feel better.

A few moments later, George brings out the prime rib, as James and Stella carry out the few remaining sides and set them on the table. Stella says nothing. She sits in the seat directly across from me, the seat to the right of James, even though the other place setting is at the end of the table opposite from George.

She folds her hands onto the table, watching as I follow Cara's lead and put food on my plate, careful not to take too much.

George places a piece of beef onto my plate, warm and pink and tender enough to give me nightmares. And if that isn't bad enough, this is also the exact moment that Stella notices the green folder in my lap. It's tucked up against my belly because I didn't know where else to put it.

"What's that?" she asks.

"Nothing," I say, when Cara opens her mouth.

Stella leans forward. "Did you bring schoolwork to our family dinner? Shall I hang it on my fridge?"

"It's not—"

Cara sighs. "It's a business plan, Mom. Will you stop being rude?"

I set my fork down, praying Cara stops. Because in her world you can talk back. In her world you can walk away from a fifty-thousand-dollar wedding without blinking. You can be big and brave and loud because *you're* the one people are afraid of. The one they cater to and cower before. You can take risks and swing big because you have the kind of safety net that will catch you no matter how much you miss.

The more Stella glares at me, the more I realize I've definitely already blown mine up.

This was a mistake. This was an epic mistake.

"A business plan?" George asks, setting down his knife. "For what?"

"For the gym you won't even consider her for!" Cara shouts.

Shit, shit, shit.

"This isn't the right time," I say quietly, looking at James for backup but he's just watching Cara nervously.

"You've certainly never had an issue with bringing business to a family event before," Stella says. "Or were you too drunk to remember the last time?"

"Mother!" Cara says and slams down her own fork.

"Stella." George sighs.

Stella lifts her chin. "It's true! Someone had to say it."

"Why? Why did someone have to say it?" Cara argues.

"Cara, be reasonable!" George says, taking a huge swig from the glass in front of him. "You clearly brought her here for shock value; you can't be surprised when your mother takes the bait."

"Shock value?!" Cara shouts.

And oh god, kill me now. Seriously, what the fuck? What the actual fuck?

"Oh, come on," Stella huffs. "We all know what this really is."

"And what is it?" I ask, finally finding my voice and willing it not to break.

"Don't pretend you're here with pure intentions." Stella crosses her arms. "Cara, honey, she's using you! And this was also an obvious plot on your end to get a reaction out of us! Congratulations, it worked."

Cara laughs bitterly. "How, *how* could she possibly be using me! I'm the one who made the file in the first place! I'm the one who told her to keep fighting for it when she said there was no use. I didn't realize how ridiculously petty you are, or I wouldn't have."

Stella raises her eyebrows. "You made the business plan? Of course. If you can't see how she's manipulating you, I'm embarrassed on your behalf. First, she latched on to poor James and when she realized he was just a personal trainer, she decided to move on to the next sibling. She's desperate, Cara. She's after our money. That's probably the whole reason she even went to your wedding!"

"I am not *just* anything," James says, his eyes gone fiery. "And for the record, I forced her to go to the wedding with me! She didn't even want to. She did it as a favor because we're friends."

"Did she, now," Stella says. "Do you really think she would even be 'friends' with you if you weren't set to inherit a chain of gyms, James? Really? Because I don't. People like her are always looking for their next meal ticket and unfortunately my children are both naive enough to fall for it."

"It's not like that," I say quietly, but they can't even hear me, not with both Manderlay siblings jumping into the fray now.

How did this even happen? How did I go from *I need to end this* to *I love you* to being called a gold digger, all in the course of a day? My stomach churns. I need to get out of here.

"She's USING you!" Stella shouts. "Both of you!"

Cara stands up, slamming her palms on the table. "No, she is NOT."

I might as well be five years old again, listening to my mother and her latest boyfriend.

"What about the email, then!" Stella smiles like a cat that caught the canary, and all the shouting stops as the full attention of the room settles on my face.

"What email?" Cara asks me warily.

I shrug and shake my head. "I have no clue what she's talking about." The distrust in Cara's eyes cuts me deep. I knew this was a mistake. All of it. It's what I deserve for agreeing to James's plan in the first place.

"Don't be shy, Elizabeth," Stella continues. "I read all through your inbox while I was debating firing you for theft of company time that day at the gym. The one where your mother went on and on about your new raise and how you would be able to help her more with bills was especially interesting."

"What email? What are you talking about?" I shake my head.

"Oh, did it get deleted? I guess accidents happen when you leave your personal email sitting open like that," Stella says, running her hands over her pearls with a sly smile. "But what raise was she talking about, Liz, the one you're manipulating Cara to help you get?"

Welp, this explains the missing email Mom texted about. Fuck me.

"Her mother is horrible!" Cara yells. "You can't believe a thing she says."

"You don't even know," James adds, backing her up. "She's abusive and—"

"Please, let's leave." I cut him off, desperate to get us all back somewhere safe, back to our own little bubble where nothing else matters. Because I can't sit here and listen to them both splay my deepest shame across the table like an offering.

But again no one hears me.

They shout around me, like I'm not even here. And isn't this how it always is? Just me in the background of everyone else's lives. Scanning their key cards or checking out their groceries or . . . being the rich kids' pawn in a family rebellion. I thought I was a distraction, then I thought I was more, but now I can see that I'm much, much less.

I slide my chair back, and still no one notices.

I'm about to bolt, to race right out of there and keep going until I'm clear on the other side of the world, where I don't have to hear people arguing over me, debating my worth and merits, picking apart my ulterior motives. I'll just tuck myself safely between my weights and my sneakers. Just curl up with my laptop and the soothing sounds of *Annabelle* on the screen. I've well and truly learned my lesson.

But then Cara says it, screams it, really.

"If it wasn't for her, I'd be trapped in a horrible marriage still trying to live up to your ridiculous expectations, Mother. I'd be miserable! You should be *thanking* her!"

I freeze.

"What do you mean, if it wasn't for her?" Stella asks, her voice going eerily calm.

Cara turns to me, startled. "I'm sorry," she says. "It just came out."

"Wait, no, what *does* that mean?" James asks, but he's not looking at Cara. He's looking at me.

"I—"

"Nothing," Cara says, trying to cover her tracks. "I'm just glad I met her. That's all."

"No," James says, looking between us. "You said she saved you from an unhappy marriage, but I thought you two only talked for a couple of . . ."

I look down as his words trail off.

"Lizzie, what did you do?"

"It wasn't on purpose. I . . . I didn't even know who she was and then I tried to fix it. I—" I stammer out.

Stella stands up. "Someone tell me what's going on right now."

"I think Lizzie," James says, betrayal and hurt plain on his face. "Lizzie's the one that convinced Cara not to marry Max. She's been lying to all of us about it. She . . . why would you keep that from me?"

"No," I say.

"It wasn't like that at all," Cara says.

Stella snorts. "I don't often underestimate people, Elizabeth. I'm impressed; a little snake in the grass, right in my own backyard."

"I'm not!" I slam my hand on the table. "I didn't even know who Cara was! I was just hyping up a crying girl in the bathroom. And I tried to fix it but she—"

"Why didn't you tell me? How many times did we talk about it?" James asks, slumping down in his chair. He looks miserable.

"How could I? You were so upset. You kept going on and on about Max's 'social capital.' You were so pissed about how it went down. I was terrified if you knew . . . I was scared of losing you, and my job, and you have to believe me, I didn't know it was Cara in that bathroom."

"You've been lying to me for months!" He groans, staring off like he can't believe this is happening. "And your job? Really? It all comes back to your job, I guess. Maybe my mother's right about you."

My mouth falls open. I can't believe he'd say that. I can't believe he'd even think that. I try to respond but all that comes out is a squeak. And no, I will not cry here. Not over this. Not in front of Stella.

This is why I don't get close to people. They will always, always turn on you.

"I'm glad you're finally coming to your senses, James." Stella practically vibrates as she sits back in her chair with a satisfied look.

. A stricken look crosses James's face. "Shit, Lizzie, wait, I—"

"James, will you shut up!" Cara says, leveling him with a glare. "Lizzie might have said some things in that bathroom, but it was nothing I wasn't already thinking. It was nothing I hadn't already said to *you*, if you had bothered to listen. Max and I were over before we even got engaged. You would have noticed how much happier I've been if you weren't so busy sucking up to Mom and Dad now that you're the little angel. Fucking grow up. And yeah, Lizzie was worried about getting fired. She needs this job! Something your spoiled ass is apparently incapable of understanding. God, I can't handle you sometimes."

"Cara!" George shouts, but James cuts him off before he can say anything else.

"You're so sure you know her better than I do. You think you've got us all figured out, don't you?" James laughs, a bitter look on his face. And oh, oh no. The last time I saw that was on the cruise ship, a second before he threw what was left of his lobster at Jude's face. "I'm not the only one she's been lying to, Cara."

"What are you even talking about?" Cara grabs my hand. "Come on, Lizzie. This is stupid, let's go."

My stomach sinks. Maybe *we* didn't have to blow this up, but I can tell James is about to. I should have known. I should have known it would always come back to this.

"Ask her," James says, folding his hands in front of him. He looks so much like George right now; I want to fling my fork in his face. This whole thing started as his idea. His!

"Ask her what?" Cara snaps, shoving her chair in. And we're caught in the crosshairs, a million miles between us and the door.

"Ask her if she's ever lied to you," James says, looking equal parts pissed off and sad. "Ask her about the fair."

Cara looks at me, confused. "What about the fair?"

"I'm sorry," I say, shaking my head. "I—"

"It wasn't an accident that I didn't show up that day." James takes a deep breath. "I begged her to go and get you off my back about all those stupid dates and all those ridiculous ideas you kept having. Lizzie offered to be a distraction as a favor to me, not whatever this fucking shit is." He gestures to me, Cara, and the now forgotten family dinner. "She's your *babysitter*, Cara. Not your soulmate."

"What?" Cara looks at me, and the hurt in her eyes shatters me. "That's not—"

"She doesn't date people, Cara!" James snorts. "She almost ended it with you earlier just to get out of this dinner." Even Stella looks surprised by his words.

"No!" I turn toward Cara. "I mean, yes, I was scared of coming here with you. But I didn't really want to end it. Jesus, I wasn't—"

Her eyes tear up. "Is this true? Were *we* ever even real?"

"Yes, too real," I say. I reach for her hand, but she pulls it away. "I promise. I tried to tell you when it changed for me, but then you went back to the city and, and, and I knew that you had this whole other life that you used to love," I stammer. "It never . . ."

Cara glares at James. "I can understand my brother coming up with this scheme because he's a fucking asshole." She turns back to me. "But what was in it for you? Was this all just a joke?"

"It's not like that!"

"Then how is it?"

And it's here, the moment of truth. I have to tell her how I feel. I have to make her understand that the only thing that I was ever in it for was *her*.

"Cara, I lo—"

"Please," Stella says, cutting me off. "You can't believe anything that comes out of her mouth."

Cara wipes her eyes. "I actually cared about you. I'm so stupid."

And then I get mad. Really, really mad.

Because I'm not the only one who's been untruthful. They want shock value, huh? Then I'll make sure they get their money's worth. God knows they have enough of it.

"Oh, and what about you, Cara?" I shout.

Cara rears her head back. "What about me?"

"You came on to me first, so don't stand there and act like I tricked you into bed or something. And did you forget that you made it seem like you just had some 'minor business to attend to in the city' when really you were getting your job back? Don't act all high and mighty, like you wanted something real and I was just trying to get into your pants. You always knew you would go back to your old life and forget about me. I'm not the one who strung anybody along here. I'm just the dumbass who thought—"

"No!" she says. "I—"

"Stop pretending I ruined some epic love story." I swallow hard. "You talk about James, but you're spoiled too, Cara. You're all so fucking spoiled. If someone's been manipulating anyone," I say, looking between her and James, "it was the two of you! I've been at your beck and call since you got here, Cara. I've been your shoulder to cry on, your date, and your on-call twenty-four/seven fuck buddy. So, I don't want to hear it!"

James stands. "Don't talk to my sister like that."

"And you?" I say, spinning toward him. "You've made me cover for you and Ramón since the wedding! I've been keeping your secret for months. You begged me to help you out with Cara. You did! And when I refused you guilted me into it! And now you're trying to act like this was something I came up with to manipulate her? Don't jump all over me about honesty and integrity, James, because you don't fucking have any. No one in this family does."

"Ramón?" George finally pipes up, only to sound as horrified as James always expected. "From the *winery?*"

"Enough," Stella bellows, slamming down her wineglass. I cringe at the sound, but even that's not enough to stop me. I'm detonating bombs all over this shit sundae I've found myself in and I'm not about to stop now. I can't.

Hey, Target's always hiring, right?

I turn toward Stella with venom on my tongue. "Jesus, Stella, you're the worst of them all. You put conditions on everything and make your kids fight each other for your approval. Yeah, my mom's a piece of shit, but at least she's honest about it. You walk around like you're the queen, but guess what? You're worse trash than I am. I hope your emptiness eats you up inside because god knows you deserve it. And George, maybe if you fucking looked up from your whiskey glass once in a while, you'd realize how your wife destroyed your family. You're just as guilty as she is."

"Lizzie," Cara says, setting her hand on my arm. I can't tell if it's to comfort me or if it's a warning, but I don't care.

Home is not a person. Blow the whole fucking thing up.

I shake my head and turn back to Cara. "I might not be as rich as your family, but at least I'm not as awful as them either. You are, collectively, the worst people I have ever met in my life. And as you love to point out, Stella, that's really saying something."

I don't even give them the chance to reply before I storm out of their house and slam the door behind me. I'll walk home if I have to. I don't care that it's ten miles just as long as I escape this suburban McMansion hellscape.

"Lizzie. Lizzie, wait!" Cara calls, rushing out the door to chase after me, but I don't stop.

"I can't do this with you anymore," I say, picking up the pace. If I walk any faster, I'm going to have to jog, and I'd like to retain at least a tiny bit of my dignity tonight.

"Wait, Lizzie. Please!" she shouts. "I knew, okay? I knew!"

And that stops me in my tracks. "You knew what?"

"I mean, not all of it," she says, running up to me. "But I saw the texts from Ramón when I messed with James's phone. His password has always been one-one-one-two, even though I tell him to change it." She shakes her head. "I knew he was seeing someone, almost from the start."

"Then why did you keep trying to set him up?"

"Because being absurd runs in our family." She winces. "I hoped it would get him to open up to me, like he'd tell me all about the guy in his life or something. But that didn't happen."

"And you just kept pushing for it anyway?"

"Not exactly." She scrunches up her shoulders. "It became a reason to keep talking to you. I thought I was getting these vibes that you were into me . . . but when I tried to kiss you in the pool and you wouldn't, I thought I misread everything. I was fully prepared to never talk to you again. Like I said, I run. No second chances.

"But then, the fair happened and everything after the fair."

She blushes. "And suddenly running from you was the last thing I wanted to do. Was that your deal too? With the fair? Were we both just being totally ridiculous about each other?"

"I wanted to see you again, however I could and, I don't know, I convinced myself that was the best way. I'm sorry, I should have just—"

"Do I love that we both tricked each other into hanging out? No. But is it maybe a little bit cute?" she asks, pinching her fingers together. "Yes?"

My heart soars. If we were both just playing each other, then doesn't that mean in some demented way we're all on even ground? That this could even be fixable? I don't even know where to start, but if we both want—

"And obviously my mom's wrong about you." She bites her lip. "You wouldn't actually use me . . . right? Like you said, you just wanted to see me?"

And it feels like my heart stops beating with the question in her voice. Like every last drop of blood in my entire body suddenly turns to ice and shatters on the ground.

"Fuck you," I say, the tears coming freely then, unstoppable.

"Lizzie—"

"You need confirmation? Fine. No, Cara. I wasn't using you for a goddamn gym job. I wasn't manipulating you for your money. But the fact that you even just asked me . . . You really are just like your mother."

Cara's eyes go wide. "I am *not* like her. I would never do anything, anything, to make you feel bad about yourself. I—"

"You just did, Cara!" I shout, raising my arms and then dropping them to my sides. "You just did! I can't do this anymore. This is done. *We're* done."

"No, stop." She pulls on my hand. "I didn't mean it like that. I love you, Lizzie. I'm *in love* with you."

I shake my head. "What am I supposed to do with that now?"

"Saying it back would be nice." Cara laughs, but it sounds watery and far away.

I rub my hands over my eyes. "I would have. I tried to, tonight. But there's no point anymore."

"Why?" she begs. She wipes at her eyes with her palms. "Why not?"

"Go home, Cara," I say. "This is over. James was right: people like you don't belong with people like me, but not for the reasons he thinks."

"Lizzie!"

And if I look at her for another second, I know that I'll break. I will. I'll wind up kissing and loving her and telling her so with my mouth and my hands and my body. But I shouldn't. I can't.

Because what's love without trust?

I turn and leave, and I don't look back. If I do, she'll know. She'll know that the only real lie I've ever told, the only lie that matters, is pretending that I don't want her anymore.

Chapter Twenty-Six

I wake up on my couch next to a bottle of tequila. Even with the events of yesterday not totally in focus, I know instantly that I've made a terrible mistake. Maybe if I move real slow then I don't ever have to remember. I sit up, my head pounding, and it all rushes back anyway. Fuck.

Last night was awful, and the Manderlays were horrible to me in their own special ways. But I wasn't much better.

I blew up James's secret about Ramón. Cara said she loved me and I . . . I walked away.

I grab my phone to call her, but see a text from James asking for space to think about things and to stop calling him. But I didn't . . . did I?

Oh shit.

I click over to my call log. There are four calls to James, none of them lasting more than a second. Thankfully none after he texted me—at least black-out-drunk me was respectful. So no, that's not what worries me.

It's the calls to Cara.

All seventeen of them.

One of them lasting three minutes in duration. Did she pick up? Or did I leave a shit-faced voicemail? I'm not sure which one would be more mortifying.

I flop back onto the couch and stare at the ceiling trying to figure out my next step, then I glare at my phone like it's going to bite me before opening it up to my texts with Cara. I send a simple *Sorry about all the calls last night. I had too much to drink.*

She doesn't reply, not even three dots that never resolve. Just nothing. I should have seen that coming. Cara may have plunged the knife into our relationship, but I'm the one that twisted it.

A sharp knock on my door pulls me from my wallowing. I rush over, praying that it's Cara, or even James—but instead I find Stella standing there, clutching her purse tightly like someone is about to rob her. I suppose in her mind, that someone is me.

"May I come in?" she asks.

"No," I say, honestly. Because this is my place, the only place I have in the world that's just mine, and I'm not about to let her invade it. But then she says the one thing that can get me to move.

"It's about Cara. It's important."

I swing the door open wider and step back. "Is she okay?"

"She will be."

"What happened?"

"That's what I'm here to find out. She ran out to talk to you last night and then returned, crying, to grab her keys. She's not answering my calls or texts. Care to fill me in?"

"Not particularly," I say, as she pushes past me into my apartment. She looks around at my ratty couch, at my old laptop, and then zeroes in on the peeling linoleum of the kitchen floor. I have never felt so ashamed, so less than, as I do when she looks back at me and says, "Charming place, Liz."

I steady my chin anyway, praying the hurt doesn't show. She can break me, sure, but she doesn't get the pleasure of knowing she's doing it. "I'm not talking about last night with you. Is there something else you need?"

"There is, actually. I have a proposition for you."

"Oh yeah?" I snort. "Like what? Giving me a choice between quitting and being fired? Because I kinda guessed that was coming already."

"Quite the opposite. The promotion is yours if you want it."

"What?" My mouth falls open.

"You would need to move, of course," she continues. "It's nearly an hour away and I can't have my manager this far from work in case something goes wrong. You would be the primary for everything, including the alarm calls. It would be much more independent than how our other gyms operate."

"Yeah, Cara said you were considering making it a franchise."

Stella raises her eyebrows. "You are an ambitious one, aren't you?" I smile, not realizing until too late that it's not the compliment I think it is. "I have to give you credit. I didn't realize that you were playing such a long con."

"I wasn't—"

She raises her hand to silence me and even though I hate it, it does shut me up. "I don't like that you managed to hurt both of my babies in the process, but I do 'respect the hustle,' as they say. So yes, I'm willing to make it a franchise opportunity. I'll even agree to the terms in Cara's little folder. You can work off the fee, but only until you're able to find financing."

I narrow my eyes. "If you think I'm such a con artist, then why would you ever want to put me in charge of your gym? Why wouldn't you just fire me now and be done with it?"

"Oh, I'm getting to that." She smiles. "In exchange for my unwavering faith in your management abilities, I expect you to be out of my children's lives for good."

I stare at her, stunned.

"Cara *and* James both. You will leave them alone. You will disappear from their lives. I'll see to it that you have a good stable job. You'll have a contract, it will all be on the up-and-up. And in exchange, you will take the job, you will move there, and you will not come back to this town. There is *nothing* for you here."

"I love her." And I hate so much that the first time I say it out loud, Cara isn't around to hear it.

"Make sure she doesn't know that. Give her the clean break she deserves. Let her move on from this mess without complicating it any farther. This is what you've always wanted, isn't it? This is what it was all for?"

"No."

Stella smiles. "Can you really afford to turn me down, dear?"

"What does that mean?"

Stella fixes me with her big fake smile. "Haven't you heard? I'm restructuring our organization. I'm offering you a transfer and a promotion. Should you decide not to take it, you will find that your keys will no longer work at your current location, and you are no longer on the payroll. We've found the front desk manager position at this facility to be redundant."

"So you *are* firing me," I say. Panic sets in as it hits me just how bad this is going to be. My paycheck was barely enough for the bills. Anything I'd managed to save I've already sent to my mother. I won't even be able make rent this month.

"I'm promoting you," she reminds me.

"You're threatening me."

"What do you have to lose, Liz?"

I think: Cara.

I think: James, who, despite last night, is the closest thing to family I have.

I think: our *Bachelor* nights and this shitty apartment that's all my own.

I think: Mina and Mrs. Patel and Mrs. Goldstein.

I think: everything.

I look up at Stella, furious and sad and hopeful all at once, because what she's offering me is a dream, but at the one price that might be too high to pay. There's always strings, aren't there, when you're dealing with a mother.

"They're scared of you. They don't love you," I say. "They won't even if I'm gone."

"Why don't you sleep on it, dear. Take tomorrow off. Paid. I'll expect you at the new work site the day after. I'll even set you up with my realtor, Carson. He'll help you find a new place quickly. A nice one, this time." She glances around my apartment one last time. "I'm giving you a way out, Liz. You should say thank you."

I swallow hard as she looks at me expectantly. She actually wants me to say it. She's going to stand here until I do. Her toe taps against the floor.

"Thank you for the opportunity." My words come out scratchy and quiet. Ashamed. She purses her lips and heads for the door.

"I'll see you soon. Bring your little sketches and we'll see if there's anything we can work with."

I nod.

My home isn't a person, my home is the gym.

Chapter Twenty-Seven

I haven't slept yet. I've been lying on my floor, in the midst of an existential crisis, wasting the hours until it was late enough in the morning that James would be leaving for work.

First, I tell myself that I'm just going over there to get my car, which has been parked in his driveway since the family dinner, but then I catch myself trying to time it just right to get there as he's leaving, so I know that's a lie. I gotta quit doing that, especially to myself.

"You've got a funny way of giving someone space," James says, when he sees me leaning against my car. The morning sun has made the metal already hot against my skin.

"I know," I say. "I'm sorry."

"Are you here for me or Cara?" he asks. "Because she's not here."

I should have anticipated this, but it still hits me like an anvil in the chest.

"Max left a couple days early, so she figured she should head back home. You told her to, after all," he says, and his voice is so hard.

"I'm sorry," I say again, uselessly, because I am, and I know it doesn't matter but I want him to hear it anyway. "I just needed to pick up my car."

He looks at me and his face softens just a smidge. "What are you really doing here?" he asks quietly. "Because you could've gotten your car any time."

"I wanted to say goodbye," I admit, and his forehead scrunches up.

"You're leaving too?"

"Did you know your mom offered me a new job?" I ask, and the confusion on his face proves that at least he isn't in on it. "Yeah, the promotion. She even offered to turn it into a franchise opportunity."

"That's cool," he says slowly, clearly still confused. Good. It would have hurt more knowing he was behind it all. "I guess?"

"Yeah, the catch is that I have to get out of here, and I can't talk to Cara, *or you*, ever again." I laugh bitterly. "I can have everything I've ever wanted, as long as I give up the two most important people in my life. Funny how that works out, eh?"

"And you took it?" he asks, looking even more frustrated and hurt than before. "How could you agree to that? I know I said I needed space, but I didn't mean forever. I meant a small cool-down period! Lizzie, what the fuck? This isn't you. None of this is you."

And the relief of those last words nearly brings me to my knees.

"I didn't." I meet his eyes. "I turned it down."

"Thank god." His face softens. "But then why are you leaving? Where are you going?"

I shrug, trying not to cry. "I haven't really figured that part out yet. She fired me. She said she would, if I didn't take the promotion. And you hate me now, and Cara's gone, and there's nothing really keeping me here anymore. But I couldn't just go without saying goodbye. Thanks for being a good friend—well, when you weren't being a shitty friend."

"I don't hate you, Lizzie, Jesus. What I said to you was extremely out of line. I know you. I know you weren't using me or Cara. I was pissed and hurt and . . ." He rubs his forehead. "You deserve better than that from me. I'm sorry."

"For what it's worth, I'm so sorry for telling your family about Ramón. That was screwed up of me." I drop my head back and look at the clouds. I'm praying that my tears will just roll straight back into my skull, because right now, I feel like if I start, I might never stop. "I'm going to miss you so much," I manage to choke out.

"You're such a jackass, Lizzie," he snaps. And oh, I didn't expect that. "Just the biggest fucking one I've ever met."

And okay, *that* definitely chases my tears away. I look at him, stunned. "I tell you I'm sorry and you call me a jackass? Am I supposed to forget the other night and keep begging you for forgiveness? Because I'm sorry for Ramón, and I'm sorry I lied to you about the goddamn wedding stuff, but I'm not sorry for calling you out on your spoiled brat bullshit and I'm not sorry for falling in love with her! If you want to stay mad at me for that, fine. There's nothing I can do except cut my losses. So this is me, cutting my losses and sparing you the trouble," I say, clicking the unlock button for the car.

"That's not why I said that." He groans. "You're a jackass for thinking I'd want you to leave, and for not trusting me enough to tell me about all that stuff from the rehearsal dinner. It kills me that you didn't think I would understand or listen to you. And I'm furious that you let me keep treating you like you were just some fling or something and not someone who actually had real feelings for my sister."

"Wait, what?"

"Lizzie, come on! It's not the secrets that pissed me off, it's that you felt you had to keep them. I know you don't trust easily, but I really thought I was inner circle. I really thought I had gotten to the heart of you and when I realized I hadn't, I was hurt, and I was mad, and you're right, I was a massive asshole about it. I do owe you an apology. I get that it's on me that you didn't feel safe enough to share those things with me. I shouldn't have lashed out like that, and I hope you can forgive me. You've been there for me, way more than I've been there for you. And that sucks, and I'm sorry."

"I . . . James, it's—"

"What did I do to push you so far away? There was all this major stuff happening between my sister and my best friend and neither of you trusted me enough to tell me what was going on? That hurts."

I look at him, but I don't know what to say. Or how I got things so off course. "You really think I'm worth all this trouble?"

"I know you are." He pinches the bridge of his nose. "I was planning to bring you over some 'I'm sorry I suck' Golden Bird tonight. I've been a shit friend lately, and I get that. I got caught up in finally being 'the good one,' I admit it, but I realized I don't want to be that if it means selling you out." He shakes his head. "And now you're just leaving, and I won't even get the chance to fix it. Fuck. Where are you even going? And if you say back to your mother, I swear, I'll—"

"Not to my mother's. I promise. But I'm not sure where yet. I talked to my landlord and he's being cool. His cousin's looking for a place anyway, so he's going to let me out of the lease. I'm already mostly packed. It's not like I have that much." I sigh and shake my head sadly. "I'm gonna use the refund from my cleaning deposit and drive until I run out of gas. See where I end up and what's hiring. It's not like there's not a Target in every town. It shouldn't be that hard to land somewhere else. It's just, it's better this way, okay? Trust me."

"I don't get it."

"You don't have to." I squeeze my eyes shut. This is hard. *This* is why I don't get close to people. I flew too close to the sun with this family, and now it's time to come crashing back down to earth where I belong, hitting every branch and building on the way down. "There's too many memories here, okay? Too many *almosts* and *what-ifs* and—"

"So, you're running, then, just like Cara," he says, dropping his head back. "You're both such cowards."

"That's not fair," I say, looking away.

"But it's true! You were a coward about applying for the promotion. You were a coward about telling me the truth. You were a coward about your feelings for my sister. And now you're being a coward about your whole damn life. You've lectured me how many times about living my truth and escaping my mother's thumb, but what about you? Because you don't seem very brave and free to me. You just seem scared."

"I am," I say, glaring back at him. "But so what? So what?!"

"It doesn't have to be like this." James wraps me in one of his bear hugs, squeezing me so tight it almost hurts. "Just hold on for a minute. Take a breath. Come inside. Let me make you a shake for the road."

"I shouldn't," I say, taking a step back toward my car.

"Five minutes. Please," he begs. "And then I'll pack your car up myself."

"Alright. Five minutes." And I know I'm just delaying the inevitable, but I can't help it.

I FIND MYSELF sitting at my familiar place at the bar in his kitchen, while he gets to work measuring out various powders and shaking them up with his specially chilled bottled water. I try really hard not to remember the first time I found Cara standing in this kitchen. I try not to remember every other memory of her too.

He finishes up and pushes the shaker bottle toward me with a smile. "For the road," he says. "Although I hope you'll change your mind."

I won't, but I'm sure I'll miss him extra now, after this. Great.

He grabs a sticky note from a pad near his fridge—the one that we used to write our snack wish lists on for *Bachelor* nights—checks something on his phone, and then scribbles some words down that I can't see. He folds the sticky note in half and places it next to my hand.

"In case you want to try running toward something for a change," he says.

I unfold it and stare down at a New York City address. "Is this Cara's?"

He raises his eyebrows, leaning against the counter. "What do you think?"

I suck my lip into my mouth, chewing on it. "I really screwed everything up." I look up at him, swallowing back tears. "And I don't think I can fix it."

"Why not?"

"She told me she loved me," I mumble out with a sigh.

"That's great, then!" His smile falters as he studies my face. "Or . . . it's not great?"

"I . . ."

"You didn't say it back?" He looks confused.

"A little worse than that."

"Shit," he says, and I appreciate that he doesn't pry or try to find out exactly how it all went down. "Was that before or after you told her to go home?"

I hang my head.

"Damn, Lizzie!"

"In my defense, she prefaced it by asking if I was using her."

James shakes his head. "Why does my family always go straight for the jugular? I should text my therapist about this later."

"You do that," I say. "But I didn't exactly go easy on you two either, to be fair."

"Right." James rubs his eyes. "Okay," he says, like he's trying to think of what to do next. "Okay, well. Yeah."

"Yeah." I sigh. "Now you get why I need to move on? You can't possibly still think I have a chance."

"What I think doesn't matter, just what she thinks. But I

guess that doesn't matter either, if you and your low self-esteem are hightailing it out of town anyway."

I roll my eyes. "It's not like I have a choice. I have to be out of my apartment tonight."

"Huh," James says, resting his hand on his chin. "I guess it's really lucky that my roommate left, then. I have a whole furnished bedroom juuuuust sitting there empty, waiting for another sad sack like you to fill it up."

"I couldn't." I laugh nervously.

"Why not? Look, what happened sucked, and you didn't deserve it. Being hurt is no excuse for the way I acted. I know I doubled down and asked for space, but I don't want it. I really was heading to your place today, I swear to god, but you beat me. Because you're the better friend. You always have been. If you truly want to leave, I won't stop you. But you don't have to. My door is always open. You're family. My chosen family, which is way fucking better than the one I was born into."

And I don't know what to say. Leaving felt like the best option when I thought everyone was against me, when I thought I couldn't walk down the street without seeing a missed opportunity or the ghost of a memory. But maybe I'm wrong. Epically, ridiculously wrong.

What would happen if I leaned into the people I love, instead of racing away as far as I could get? What would happen if I trusted someone, well and truly trusted them? It could be fucking awful . . . but what if it wasn't?

"I don't know about moving in," I say finally. He twists his lips like he expected this, but no, no, he's got it all wrong. "What do you think about storing my stuff here for a little while instead? Maybe giving me a ride to the train station?"

He narrows his eyes, the corners crinkling up as he smiles. "Why? You got somewhere important to go?"

I flip the paper around in my hand and stare down at her address.

"Looks like it."

Chapter Twenty-Eight

The steady rumble of the train as it rolls down to the city somehow settles me enough that I fall asleep. My muscles ache after carrying boxes down the two flights of stairs of my apartment building and then back up and into James's spare room, but I find a way to get comfortable enough, tucking my hoodie under my head, resting against the window.

I wake up a couple hours later, drool fully coating the side of my face, when the train comes to a stop. I wipe at my cheek, and stare down at the pink Post-it in my hand. I try not to let the panic well up inside me at the thought of showing up on her doorstep.

It will all be okay, hopefully. And if it's not, I have it on good authority that I have a shoulder to cry on and a place to crash just a little upstate.

Speaking of, I pull out my phone and open the text from James that lays out everything I need to do to get to Cara's apartment. I've only been to the city once and the thought of getting lost on the subway terrifies me. Thankfully, he sent me the directions as if he was texting them to a small child. This is ideal, because I am about as good at directions as I am at telling people I love them. Which is to say, a giant fucking failure.

But that's going to change today.

I get off the train and shove through people, trying to make my way to the street. There's a man selling roses in the corner, and I want to stop but can't decide if that's embarrassingly cliché or not. Is showing up with one rose equal to a grand gesture? Is she even *expecting* a grand gesture? Maybe I should have thought this through.

I know the truth is she's not expecting anything from me. Period. I could get there and find her crying in Max's arms, or doing something else entirely with him or anyone else. I am, in all likelihood, about to get my heart broken. She didn't ask me to come here and a set of directions from her brother isn't actually the engraved invitation and positive sign I've been considering it to be.

Damn.

Better make that two roses, then, I decide, counting out what little money I have left after buying my train ticket.

I step onto the street a few minutes later—two half wilted roses firmly in hand—and find that it's raining out. Perfect.

James's first text says that I need to walk north four blocks. Easy-peasy. Except it takes me two tries to figure out which way is north. And then I forget to count the blocks because I'm so distracted from getting the rainwater in my eyes every time I look up at all the massive buildings surrounding me.

Look, I know it's a newbie thing to do, but have you seen the size of them?

After getting myself incredibly lost, I give up. I type the address into the map on my phone and let Siri's calming voice direct me where to go. I look like the ultimate tourist now, Siri snapping at me to turn right in three-tenths of a mile and all, but I don't even care. Cara is worth it. She's worth the people bumping into me, the people annoyed that I'm walking too slow or suddenly stopping to check street signs. Cara is worth it all.

I know she was out of line for asking me what she did. But I also know how family can mess you up and make all your common sense fly out the window. What happened sucked, but it doesn't negate all the awesome stuff that came before it.

And I'm done sitting on the sidelines of my life. It's time for me to go after what I want. James called it "manifesting," which sounds like a scam, but if daydreaming helps me get Cara back, then, sure, I will "manifest" the shit out of us. Because I want to get this right. Please just let me get this one thing right.

It takes me longer than I'd like to admit, but I do finally get where I'm going.

Cara lives in a large, beautiful building that's been subdivided into apartments. There's a Realtor sign up for one of them, and for half a second, I imagine that she's listed her place. That this is all part of some elaborate plan to run back to me. But deep down, I know it's not. She won't even return my calls.

While James told me how to get here, we never discussed what would happen when I actually did, which now seems like an oversight on both our parts. She doesn't have a doorman and the front door is locked up tight. I think about texting her that I'm here, even going so far as opening the chat to send it, but the unanswered text I sent her on the way to the train station tells me I'm going to need to be harder to ignore than that.

I notice three buzzers on the door—three separate apartments, then. I pull the sticky note out of my pocket, the rain picking up enough to smudge the ink and bend the edges of the paper. James did NOT include an apartment number. Awesome.

I call him, twice, but he doesn't pick up. This is great. This is perfect.

The rain beats down on me as I stare up at her building in a panic, trying to figure out which set of curtains look most like something she'd own. Is she a white cotton kind of woman? Wooden blinds? Navy? Should I throw a rock at each of them? Try to reenact the *Romeo and Juliet* balcony scene? Wait, they both died. I'm looking for more of a happily ever after vibe than a tragic love story thing. No balconies or "light breaking through yonder window" shit is happening on my watch.

I run through my options again. I could call her—but I doubt she'd pick up. I could hit every single buzzer—but that's annoying. Or I could run away forever and fling myself into the sun for not having the balls to say "I love you" back that night even though I did and do and should have shouted it from the rooftops the second I figured it out.

I'd be lying if I didn't say that last one was the most appealing.

I pace back and forth in front of the building for a few minutes, utterly frozen with indecisiveness. I run up to the porch and then back down and then up again. If the neighbors are watching they probably think I'm crazy, and I feel crazy, I do, she makes me crazy in the best ways. I don't want to lose that.

The next time I run up, I slam the buzzer on the first apartment. The voice that answers me is angry and old, definitely not Cara's. "Um, sorry," I say, "I hit the wrong button."

Before I can ask if they know which unit she's in, they've hung up. I try the button beside it. Nothing. I try it again. Still nothing. It occurs to me then that she might not actually be home. That she could be somewhere else, out with city friends or with Max, even. What if this whole thing sent her spiraling back to him. Made him feel like the safer, more stable option. Future First Lady Cara Manderlay, and all that shit.

But there's still one buzzer left.

And so, with my heart on the tip of my tongue, I press the buzzer for apartment three. The navy curtains.

"Hello?" Cara's voice sounds fuzzy through the intercom, and I die a little bit inside. All of my words try to rush out at once, colliding in my throat and making it impossible for any of them to get out.

The intercom clicks off and I stand there in the rain, my head hung. I'm fucking it all up again.

No.

I press the buzzer again, but she doesn't answer. I press it again, and again, and again until finally her voice yells "Stop messing with my buzzer!" through the intercom, like I'm some asshole pranking her instead of the love of her life. Not that I'm the love of her life, but I could be, I want to be, if she'll give me that chance. Because I'm pretty sure she's mine.

The love of my life, I mean, not an asshole.

"Cara," I say, and everything goes silent.

"Lizzie? What the hell?"

Her line clicks off. She hung up. My finger hovers over her buzzer, but I can't. It feels like a violation. Crossing a boundary. She knows I'm here now and she chose to hang up. It is what it is. I should go. I should—

"Lizzie?" she calls again, this time coming from somewhere

up above me. I step back and there she is, in her window, leaning out just enough to see. Okay, I guess we're doing this Romeo and Juliet thing after all.

"Hi," I say.

"What are you doing here?" she asks, and I can't read her at all. I can't tell if she's pleased or pissed. But I know it's time anyway.

Go big or go home, right? And as I currently don't even have a home, going big appears to be the only option I have.

"I love you too," I shout, raising my roses triumphantly.

I hope my declaration is going to be met with a smile. An invite up. Confirmation that I haven't missed the boat. But instead, she crosses her arms and stares down at me, saying absolutely nothing.

"I do," I add, just in case she doesn't believe me. Maybe further affirmation is necessary? "A lot?"

Cara still doesn't say anything. Maybe she can't hear me.

"I said I love you too," I repeat awkwardly. "Hey, can you hear me okay up there?"

That gets a laugh; well, more of a scoff, really. "Yeah, I heard you," Cara says.

"Cool," I say.

Cool? COOL? Surely there was something, anything, in my repertoire besides "cool." I need to do better than this. I need to convince her that we deserve another chance. That just this once, she should break her "no second chances" red flag rule.

"Bye, Lizzie," she says and reaches up like she's going to close the window.

"Wait!" I yell. "Please!" She hesitates, her hand resting on the glass, ready to pull it down at a moment's notice. "I'm sorry I wasn't honest with you from the start. And I'm sorry I didn't know how to handle my feelings for you. I didn't think we could have that, or that you would even want that with me. You're . . . you! Ya know? And I'm so sorry that I let you down. I—" The sound of her window hitting the frame knocks the wind out of me. She's gone, a dark, heavy curtain hanging where the person I loved used to be.

I deserve this. I do. This was always a possibility.

I think about calling out for her again. Of buzzing her buzzer, of begging and pleading with her, but I love her too much to do that. She's made her decision. I need to respect it. She deserves to be happy, whatever that looks like. Whoever it's with.

As much as it kills me, I take a step away.

I'm working up the courage to take another one, and another, my emotions swirling, every cell in my body yelling at me to turn around, to cry, to beg . . . when the door clicks open behind me.

Chapter Twenty-Nine

I had imagined—oh, sorry, *manifested*—our reunion a thousand times and a thousand ways during the trip from my house to hers. However, not a single scenario that I dreamed up accounted for the fact that I'd be standing on a towel in the middle of her apartment, dripping wet, and shivering in my socks.

I'd taken off my shoes by the door, but barely took two wet-socked steps onto her gleaming hardwood floors before she yelped at me to stay still. She disappeared down her short hallway only to return a minute later with a towel.

I thought it was sweet at first, and went to wrap it around myself, until she pulled it back from my hands and set it on the floor.

"You're going to ruin the wood if you drip on it," she said, and then walked back to sit on her couch.

And now here we are, almost five minutes later, both of us staring awkwardly at the captions on her muted TV. She's watching *Walk the Line*, because of course she is, and it's so perfect I want to cry.

"Well?" she asks, finally pausing the movie. Putting me out of my misery.

"I love you," I blurt out, turning to face her but being careful not to step off the towel.

"So I've heard," she says, looking almost bored. "I don't know what you—"

"I love you," I say again, cutting her off. "And I know I keep saying that, but it feels so good even though I know I'm very, very late. Hopefully not too late though. I have other things to tell you too, if you'll listen, but I wanted to get that out of the way first just in case. If you hear nothing else, I wanted you to hear that. That's why I came. That's the only reason I'm here."

Her face softens, just a little, her arms resting in her lap instead of tightly folded against her chest.

"You don't have to say it back," I add. "But I do love you."

"If you keep saying it, it's not even going to sound like words anymore."

"We'll make our own word for it, then, I don't care. Just as long as you know."

The barest hint of a smile tugs at her lips and it feels like I swallowed a lightning bolt. But that's how it's always been with Cara. Electrifying, hot, awe-inspiring.

"I was afraid," I say, and her smile is replaced by a tilted head and a serious expression. "You called me out on it, and James called me out on it, and, hell, I called myself out on it too, but it doesn't change the fact that I was. I don't just mean about the gym or taking chances on my future, I mean everything. You scared the shit out of me, *how I felt about you* scared the shit out of me. I kept waiting for the other shoe to drop. I kept telling myself it was just temporary, none of it was real, don't get attached. And—"

"You walked away, not me. Don't forget that. And after you did, I kept thinking back to the fair. That was our *first time*. I know I hurt you by implying there was any chance that what my mom said was true, but I felt like I had a right to ask, with everything that came out that night." She sighs. "Sherry's pointed out that I was just as much to blame. Like I said, I knew my brother had someone already, yet I kept pretending so that I'd have an excuse to talk to you. I can't really be mad that you were better at playing the same game I was. At least when we started."

"You can be though, it's okay."

"Thanks Dr. Phil." She snorts. "But I've already worked through that."

I notice the past tense. I hope we aren't past tense too.

I take a deep breath and open my mouth to apologize again . . . but she growls, actually growls. "You're making this impossible."

"What?"

"I'm trying to hate you and you're standing there being all hot and apologetic and ugh." She pouts her lips and, fuck, I've missed her mouth. A rush of endorphins hits my brain. I'm love drunk on this woman, and I'll do anything to make sure she knows.

"You're the hot one," I say, all eloquence gone.

"Two people can be hot," she says gently, and I laugh from the sincerity.

"Thank you," I say, deciding to take the compliment. Or at least take it as best as I can. "But you're . . ." I wave my hand in her direction. "You're you."

"Very observant," she says. "I am me. Forget the gym, you have a future in private investigation."

"Ha," I deadpan. "My point is I never understood why you

were into me in the first place. You can have anyone you want. You're funny and smart, and you have a great job. People respect you and you come from a great family."

She coughs. "I'm sorry, have you met my mother?"

"Fine, a respected one at least." I snort.

"And? What's your point?"

"My point is that I'm not that."

"If we're seriously going to make this work, you need to stop with this self-deprecating shit. Seriously, Lizzie, get therapy. Immediately. It's not cute."

"Yeah, once I figure out my next job and stuff, it's top on the list. I'm tired of—wait, did you say 'if we're going to make this work'?" I flash her a confused smile. "Are you open to trying?" I hop forward a little, careful to keep the towel still under me. I *need* to be closer to her for this conversation.

"Second chances aren't really my thing," Cara says and stands up. "But I could potentially be persuaded."

"If?" I say, taking two more giant hops forward so we're nearly face-to-face.

"If you tell me again."

"I love you," I say softly. "I fucking love you so much. I should have said it a thousand times before now. Because I knew from the moment we did the lift in yoga that I was absolutely gone on you and would be for the rest of my life."

"The rest of your life, eh?" She laughs. "What happened to not doing the whole caring and commitment thing?"

"I could be persuaded," I say, tilting my head.

"If?"

"If you say it back."

She looks down and my heart plummets. I pushed too hard, too soon.

"You really hurt me when you told me to go," she says to the floor. The floor that I currently wish I could sink into forever. "I know I hurt you too, by asking what I did. I'd like to think I would have called you up soon and apologized for my part in what happened but . . ."

"But what?"

"But it's so much easier to bolt when things get hard. I'm not good at this. I'm not strong."

"I'll stop running from us, if you do." I give her a soft smile and her eyes go watery.

"I'm terrified you're going to let me down again. What if you—"

"I definitely will," I say, which seems to startle her.

"What?"

"I won't lie to you again, Cara. And that starts now. The truth is, I'll let you down, probably a thousand times if I'm lucky enough to have the chances. I'll forget the milk when you ask me to bring it home or I'll finish the toilet paper roll and leave you stuck when you're already late for work. I'll embarrass you when you take me around your rich friends. And I might even do worse. I'm not perfect. I'll probably let you down at least once in every way except for one. I can only promise you one."

"Yeah?" she asks, her eyes getting a little glassy.

"I'll make sure you feel loved every day of your life for as long as you'll have me." I look her in the eyes, hoping she sees the truth in my words. "Stop running, Cara, and let me catch you. I promise I'll be yours forever."

And that does it. She finally closes the distance, wrapping me in a hug so tight I can barely breathe. "I love you too," she whispers, and my entire body becomes a live wire snapping to attention at the sound of those words coming from her lips. It's overwhelming, it's *everything*, and it ends far, far too soon. Her half step back leaves me scrambling for what to say next. Anything to keep her smiling. To make her say it again and again.

"Speaking of feeling loved," I settle on. "These are for you."

The flowers are a little worse for wear, between the pacing and the rain and getting crushed by her hug. They've lost a good third of their petals.

"Where did you get those?" Cara laughs, setting them on the coffee table beside her. "You're such a tourist. I bet you way overpaid."

"You're worth it." I smile, and she leans into me for another hug. "But now that you mention it, I'd love to know where the cost-effective flowers hide, for future purchases. I mean, I *am* currently unemployed with my entire life in boxes in your brother's spare room," I say softly into her hair.

Cara pulls back to look at me. "You quit?"

"In a manner of speaking."

Cara's face pinches in anger. "Did my mother fire you? Oh, I will *kill* her. I hate that I didn't believe you about her."

"She didn't technically fire me," I say. "She offered me the gym manager job."

"Wait, what?"

"It wasn't worth it. There were . . . it just wasn't the right fit."

"What happened?"

"It wouldn't have worked out." I don't know why I'm tiptoeing around it so much. But it's her mother. *Her mother.* My own mom has practically abandoned me except for when she needs something, and I still pay all her bills. I can't expect Cara to—

"What happened?" Cara asks again, searching my face. And I know what she's really doing. She's asking me to trust her. To tell her what's wrong instead of running away or bottling it up inside or telling another lie or half-truth.

I take a deep breath. I can do this. I *can* do this.

"There was a catch. I would have had to leave town, and leave you and James behind. Permanently. I can only imagine what she'd do if she knew that I basically moved in with one of her kids and took a train to the city to win back the other." I try to laugh, to play it off like it didn't gut me, even though it did.

Cara crosses her arms. "That's disgusting."

"Yep," I say, "but that's how it works sometimes." I shrug. "I wanted that manager job because I'm good at what I do, and I deserve it. I didn't want it as a bribe or a consolation prize. And I definitely didn't want it if it meant losing the two best people in my life."

"I'm sorry," she blurts out. "I'm so sorry for even *suggesting* that my mom could be right about you. I don't want that in your head, ever. I know it's not true, and I knew it that night. Everything got so mixed up and heated at dinner, and I had no right to—"

"It's okay."

"It's not. It's really not," she says. "I've been too lost in my own hurt to sit with what I said to you. You were right to tell me to fuck off. You'd be right to say it again now."

I pull her tight against me. My eyes tear up at the familiar scent of her skin. It's only been a few days, but it's felt like forever. Is this what it's like to truly care for someone? To let them all the way in. I nuzzle deeper into her neck and mumble, "I'd rather say something else."

"Because you still love me?" she asks, and I lean back enough that our eyes can meet.

"Because I hope I'll always love you," I say softly. And she's so close now, but still not close enough. "I want to kiss you."

"Then why aren't you?"

"Can I?" I ask. "Are you sure?"

It's Cara who leans in first.

And finally, finally.

"We better get you out of these wet clothes," she says.

And yeah, we better.

Chapter Thirty

I love you," I whisper again, pressing each word into her skin with a kiss. I run my hand down her bare shoulder and pull her tighter against me, the little spoon I never want to set free.

The morning sun peeks in between the cracks of her navy curtains, and the busy sounds of a city waking up flood the room around us. I watch her sleep in my arms. There is a nonzero chance Cara will wake up with regrets today, so I intend to savor this moment while I have it. Maybe there is something to this manifesting thing after all.

I run my free hand down her side, the dip of her waist, the curve of her hip, trying to memorize everything. I kiss along the side of her neck, moving up, up, up, until I feel her lips smile against mine.

She rolls over sleepily, a happy yawn as she tucks her head against my chest, slotting our legs together and chasing away my fears with a single kiss to my collarbone. "Good morning," she hums as my fingers drift lower, and lower, searching out the warmest, softest part of her. God, I love this woman.

"I wish I could have seen my mother's face when you said no," Cara says over a breakfast of egg and cheese bagels, and a side of fruit that she had delivered from her favorite deli.

"To be fair, I texted her so I didn't see it either."

"You texted her?" Cara practically cackles. She's in an oversize T-shirt advertising some crypto company, her legs pulled up underneath. It's probably Max's and for the first time I don't care, because at the end of the day, I got the girl. *I got the girl.*

"I wasn't going to show up at her house and say, 'Oh, hey, yeah, I can't take the job because I decided I'm actually gonna head down to the city and bang your daughter instead.'"

"Oh, was that your plan? You just came to bang? Because I seem to remember a lot of tearful 'I love you, Cara's last night."

I scowl but there's no heat behind it.

Cara laughs. "You're a sap, admit it."

"I have no idea what you're talking about."

She hops off her chair and straddles my lap, her T-shirt riding up in delicious ways. "Admit it," she says, her voice low as she arches her back.

"Only for you," I say, as she leans in for a kiss. She takes her time, like she's savoring it just as much as I am, and then turns to grab a strawberry off my plate. She swipes it through whipped cream and holds it up. I bite it slowly, never breaking eye contact, as she grins.

"Not to be all queer woman–cliché," she says. "But how about you and me head upstate and rent a U-Haul? Make this situation a little more permanent?"

I choke on the strawberry—I'm pretty sure I just felt one of those tiny seeds shoot out of my nose—but if this is how I go, it was totally worth it.

"Arms above your head," she says, enjoying my reaction. She wipes at my watering eyes and trails her hand down my face as I catch my breath.

"Is that a yes?"

"Hell yeah, it's a yes."

"Excellent," she says, and then kisses me hard so I know she means it.

LESS THAN A full day later we find ourselves in James's living room. We didn't actually need to rent a U-Haul; I don't have that much stuff. Ramón, bless him, let us borrow his pickup truck for the move, even though he couldn't get the time off. The three of us—me, James, and Cara—are going to drive it down to the city tomorrow since we all realize my shit car won't make it. James is gonna sell it off for me once I'm all settled in. But tonight is for reconnecting and starting fresh.

"I knew you guys would figure it out," he says, leaning his head on my shoulder after the third time he's made me dramatically reenact asking Cara if she can hear me over the rain during my first "I love you" speech. He finds that part exceptionally hilarious and honestly, it's so nice to all be together again that I don't even mind.

James cracks a joke later that we're all in the "bad moms club," and pulls another long swig from his beer, which opens the floodgates between him and Cara. Before I know it, they're hugging and crying and promising each other to drop this competitive nonsense and not let Stella and George come between them anymore. It's nice. It's really nice.

We all go quiet then, and I think about my mom, and about how I'm finally ready to take steps to be free of her. Cara and I even spent the whole train ride up applying for a bunch of payment assistance programs for Mom, so I can finally quit paying her bills without feeling like a monster. I'm done looking back, I am manifesting my future, and it doesn't include people like her.

I look at Cara and James and think of everything we've been through, smiling that we made it, even though it was hard.

This is my family. This.

James nudges my leg with his own when Cara grabs our empties and heads to the kitchen. "I'm sorry you lost the gym though," he says.

"It probably wouldn't have worked out anyway. Hopefully I can find one in the city and start working my way back up."

"Yeah," he says. "Starting over sucks though."

I glance at Cara fishing through his fridge and smile. "Not always."

He follows my gaze. "Dude, you're really in love with her, aren't you?" James stage-whispers. "God, I'm good."

"You?!"

"Yeah! If I didn't take you to her wedding, then—"

"Anyway," Cara says, jumping over the back of the couch and practically landing on both of us. "Enough of that. I was thinking. What if you didn't have to work your way back up somewhere?"

I crinkle my forehead, confused.

"And what if *you*," she adds, shoving her brother, "didn't have to tie yourself to Mom and Dad anymore? They couldn't hold your job over your head if you got a new one."

"How would that even work?" James snorts. "I'm a personal trainer. I need somewhere to work out of. It doesn't make sense for me to pay usage fees somewhere when we own the gym."

"What if you weren't paying rent? What if you were building equity?"

James and I look at her, both totally bewildered. "What are you up to?"

"I've been looking to acquire some more investment properties," Cara says. "I wanted to diversify my portfolio a bit more, and I found a great gym space a little outside the city. It would be farther away from Ramón, but not too much," she says, fixing her eyes on James. "And if you guys got serious, I'm sure we could find a position there for him too."

"What?" James and I say in unison. "When did you even have time to look?" I ask.

"I actually found out about it right before everything happened." Cara shakes her head. "I was going to tell you after dinner with my parents if we needed to," she says. "I figured if things didn't go well, and if my mom was unwilling to see how amazing you are, then we'd take your business plan—"

"It was your business plan anyway," I say.

"No, it wasn't. It was always yours. I just translated it from napkins and scrap paper to business-speak," she says. "Anyway, I made a few phone calls when you were getting ready this morning and it's still available."

"I don't know," I say, because this feels like too much, too fast. "I mean, it's amazing, you're amazing for even thinking of it, but this is a lot."

James pats my leg. "If Lizzie's out, I'm out. But thank you."

I look at him. "Why? You and your sister could totally crush it. Don't hold back because of me."

James shrugs. "I don't want to do it without you. It's your dream. Besides, I'd probably put the cardio bunnies in the middle of the weight room and then everyone would be pissed off. I don't have your vision, and I know Cara isn't worth shit in that department. I mean, have you really looked at her apartment yet?" He mimes puking. "Once you rip those love goggles off, you're gonna be asking yourself, 'Why would you ever pair navy with that much green?' And it was her, it was alllll her. Don't even let her *try* to blame it on Max because when he got wasted that night, he said—"

"Oh, get wrecked." Cara laughs, smacking him with a pillow. "But seriously, Lizzie, you're not even a little bit interested?"

"I just think it would be weird," I say, rubbing the back of my arm, "with you being my boss and all. I don't know. Maybe it would be fine, but just in case it's not? I appreciate you so much," I say, taking her hands, "but you don't have to buy me a gym to work at just because your mom fired me."

And dude, rich people. They really are like a whole other species, aren't they?

"Oh, babe." She laughs, passing me a bottle of water. "I'm not buying you anything."

"Huh?"

"I love that you think my grand gesture is buying you a whole gym. That's the cutest shit I've ever heard, but no, that's not what I'm offering here."

"You lost us," James said, and for once I really don't mind him talking for me.

"I'm proposing a partnership. The warehouse is a good investment. It's in a good area, a real up-and-coming place. If you don't want it for a gym, I'm still going to buy it and rent it out."

"Okay?"

"In fact, if you don't even want to be partners, I'm happy to back out of the gym completely and just be your landlord. You and James can figure out the gym side and pay me for the warehouse rental. But," she smiles, "if you do want to be partners, then I thought we'd split it three ways. I can handle the numbers side, James can handle setting up the programming and personal training, and Lizzie, you can design and run it. We could make it a warm, diverse place, meeting a variety of needs, just like you wanted. I'm imagining it running the gamut from powerlifting to drag queen cardio to Mommy and me yoga. We could make it amazing, I know it."

"Partners?" I ask quietly, swallowing hard as I realize my bank account is empty. I want to but . . .

"You'd each have to come up with your share of the buy-in," Cara continues. "But Lizzie, I can help you secure financing for that. I'd say I'd loan you the money, but as you mentioned it really isn't best to mix love and business, at least not in a way that gives one person more power than the other. I have a lot of people we can talk to in order to get you set up. Helping my clients figure out financing is often part of my job. If you want to do this, I'm confident we can get it done."

"You want to be partners?" I ask again, a smile breaking across my face.

"I would love to be your partner," she says, leaning closer to kiss me. It starts off fast and happy but then takes a turn. My hand barely drifts under the hem of her shirt, when our faces are gently but firmly pried apart by her brother. We both laugh and look at James, whose face is scrunched up in mock disgust.

"Get a room," he says in a singsong voice, "before me and my partnership change our mind."

We laugh, nearly falling off the couch as we sit up. He heads to the kitchen for popcorn, and I grab the remote, pulling up *Annabelle Comes Home* from my list of favorites.

I sneak a glance at Cara, curled up in the corner of the couch, already looking right back at me.

"You really want to do this with me?"

"I do," she says. "There's just one thing I need to do first."

Chapter Thirty-One

If I had realized that "one thing" entailed driving back to the place where it all went to shit, I'm not sure I would have agreed . . . but here we are.

I'm sandwiched between James and Cara in the cab of Ramón's pickup truck. Both of them have gone creepily still now that we're in the driveway and it's like I've slipped into one of my beloved *Conjuring* movies, only without the benefit of having Ed and Lorraine Warren here to exorcise the demon waiting inside.

"You want me to come with you?" James asks, all of us staring up at the imposing figure that Stella and George's house cuts across the darkening sky.

"No," Cara says. "I've got this."

"Do either of you want to tell me what we're doing here?" I ask nervously.

Cara pops the door open. "Taking care of some unfinished business."

I look over at James and he just shrugs. I wait for a half a second and then climb out after her. Whatever she's about to face, I'm not letting her go through it alone. Family doesn't do that to each other.

The front door swings open before we even make it to the

porch, and Stella steps out. She must have been watching from the window after we pulled up. Cara stops abruptly on the sidewalk, and I shift beside her, dreading whatever comes next.

And why, why are we here? A tinge of fear creeps up my spine. Does Cara think we can all make up? Is that what this is? My stomach flips, a nasty voice in the back of my head warning me that despite the stack of boxes in the bed of the truck behind me, nothing in life is a done deal. I could lose Cara right now, the same way I lost her the last time I was here.

But no. No. I have to trust her. Trust us. No more running, no more excuses, for either of us.

"Cara," Stella says, her voice guarded. "I didn't realize you were in town. What a lovely surprise. And Liz, I certainly didn't expect to see you so soon either."

Cara reaches for my hand, and I slip it in hers in an instant.

"Don't worry," Cara snaps. "I'm heading back to the city, later tonight."

She said "I," not "we," and I hate it, but I do my best to squash down my insecurity. Stella flashes me a smug smile, and I bet she thinks she's won. I bet she thinks Cara is leaving me behind. But she's not. I have to believe that she's not. I have to learn to trust her, I have to trust *us*.

And if that means giving her my shaky hand while we stand in front of the person who tried their best to keep us apart, then I will. Because sometimes, home *is* a person.

"Well, I'm glad you stopped by for dinner while you were still in town." Stella pulls the door open even wider, unmistakably gesturing for us to head in. Cara squeezes my hand tighter, but neither of us moves.

"I'm not staying, and I'm definitely not coming in. I just wanted you to see that your plan didn't work."

"What are you talking about?" Stella gapes. "Has she—"

"Whatever you're going to say, Mom, don't," Cara says, her posture going unbelievably straight. And wait, is my girl . . . is my girl standing up for us?

My girl, I say again inside my head. Not to get sappy, but goddamn, I love the sound of that.

Stella frowns. "Well, I'm sorry but I don't know what plan you're talking about. Come inside, the both of you; we'll get this straightened out."

"Technically, there's nothing straight about this, Mom," James calls from the truck and then holds up his hands when we turn around to look at him. "Sorry, sorry, she set it up and I couldn't resist."

I smile back at my best friend. I needed that.

Stella squints into the sun, clearly just noticing now that we didn't come alone. "James? Is that you? What are you doing in that truck? Get out of the hideous thing and come inside. Quickly, before the neighbors see."

"We're fine," Cara says and maybe she is, but I'm anything but. I'm doing all I can not to tremble, and judging by how tight Cara is squeezing my hand, I think she feels at least close to the same.

You would never know by looking at her though.

Stella waves to someone over our shoulders—a couple of neighbors watching us curiously as they walk by with the biggest golden retriever I've ever seen. "Cara." Stella grits her teeth, continuing to wave. "The Masons are staring. Will you and your . . . guest . . . be reasonable and get inside? Now, please."

"Oh, I've been reasonable, Mom. I *am* reasonable." Cara shakes her head. "I just wanted you to know that I'm aware of what happened the morning after I left. I know that you offered her the promotion to keep us apart."

"Cara!" George's voice booms as he emerges from the darkness of the house to stand beside his wife. "What has gotten into you lately?!"

My instinct is to shrink back, but Cara's hand keeps me grounded, warm and steady.

"Did you know about this, Dad? Because if you did, and you didn't stop it, you're no better than Mom is."

"Whatever you've heard, I'm sure it's been distorted by this unfortunate—"

"Did you know," Cara raises her voice, "that Mom offered Lizzie the new gym as long as she never talked to me or James again?"

"Is that what she told you?" George asks, turning his attention to me. "You know damn well that my wife only went to your place to see if Cara was there. We were worried sick. And then you tried to blackmail her into giving you a job."

"No," I say, looking at Cara. "That's not what happened." And please, please, please don't let her believe any of this. Don't let her have to ask me again if—

Cara flashes me a quick smile as James gets out of the car and comes up behind us, and I realize that both Manderlay siblings really are finally done with their parents' bullshit.

"Mom lied to you, Dad," Cara says. "And I'm sorry you can't see the way she's manipulating everyone. But at this point, I don't really care."

"Cara—" he begins, but she cuts him off.

"I love Lizzie, Dad," she says, but before I can even process that she just said that *in front of her parents*, a torrent of other pent-up feelings seems to rush out of her. "I've loved her for a while now, you know, but I was way too scared to tell her. And after everything that happened . . ."

James shakes his head and places a hand on each of our shoulders to rub reassuringly. A physical embodiment of *keep going, I've got your back*.

Cara takes a shaky breath. "I spent my whole life doing what you two expected of me, regardless of whether it made me happy or not. I couldn't even escape you, Mom, when I moved down to the city. You were constantly in my head, even after I got promotion after promotion. Even after I stopped coming home, I was still scared of disappointing you somehow. And it wasn't because you raised me to always be the best version of myself and I didn't want to let you down, or some other stupid, noble reason. No, Mom, you raised me—"

"Raised us," James interjects.

"You raised *us* to believe that love always comes with strings. That it can be revoked at any time, for any reason, but especially if we do anything, *anything*, to ruin people's perfect image of us, the perfect show that you put on for the neighbors. For the senator. For anybody you think is worthy. Well guess what, Mom, I'm sick of it. I'm sick of being your fucking puppet. The only one here not good enough is you."

"That is not true, Cara. I—"

"It is true, Mom," James says. "And not only that, but you had me thinking of my own sister as the enemy. You made me so desperate for . . ." He shakes his head. "I'm not proud of how I behaved when I finally got my moment in your sun after Cara called off the wedding, but at least I realized how fucked-up it was before I lost my sisters, *both of them*, for good."

His sisters. Plural. He called me his sister. I bite my cheek to keep from crying and lean into him so he knows I heard. Knows how much it means to me.

George looks between his kids. "Are you punishing us for wanting the best for you?"

"That's not what this is about." Cara takes a deep breath, and levels her eyes at her parents. "I didn't come here to tell you what a shitty job you did raising us, even though it's true. I came here to tell you that I'm done living my life trying to please you. I'm done looking backward. Lizzie is my future, and I'm not giving her up for you or anyone else. So get on board, or get the hell out of our lives."

And holy shit. Holy shit, my girlfriend is a badass.

"Come on, Lizzie," she says with a smile. "Let's go home."

Epilogue

One Year Later

"What if she doesn't come?" I ask, my mouth going suddenly dry. I'm standing in the mirror trying to fix the bow tie on my very white pantsuit, nervously getting ready beside James.

Cara and I fought over who got to have him as best man, but I won out in the end, saying I really had no other family to stand up for me. She relented and upgraded Jane from bridesmaid to maid of honor. It seems fitting in a weird way, that we're doing this now, that we're doing it like this.

It's been a year of ups and downs, but mostly ups. As promised, I've already let Cara down in a thousand ways, from forgetting to text back to taking the last tampon. But I've also done a lot of good things: held her hand while she stood up to her mom, hid sticky notes in her briefcase with pervy stick figure drawings of what I wanted to do to her when she got back home to me, woke her up every Sunday with breakfast in bed . . . and, oh, a few months ago, I held out a ring and asked to make this partnership a little more permanent.

Which is how I got here, in my fitted white tux.

"She'll be here," James says, pushing my hands away from the bow tie and adjusting it himself.

"What if she's crying in a bathroom right now and some supremely hot girl is about to whisk her away?"

"Do you want me to go tell her she can't pee?"

"I mean, would you?" I ask, and he looks at me like I'm ridiculous. I know I am, but most people don't get the kind of lucky that I've been living lately. Most people don't find the love of their life in a bathroom stall. Most people don't have their dreams come true. And I just . . . I don't want to take any risks.

"You know she's like madly in love with you, right, dude?" James snorts. "She's probably been standing at the end of the aisle since the sun came up."

"Well, that's impossible," I say, "because I drove by this morning to try to sneak a peek and I didn't see her."

James shakes his head, setting his heavy palms on either side of my shoulders. "This is going to be so good, Lizzie. Now take a deep breath and enjoy the hell out of it."

My eyes water; he's such a good friend. And I don't, I can't, so I pull him into a tight hug. "What did I do to deserve you?"

"I think it was when you deadlifted one hundred and seventy-five pounds and then offered to spot me the first day we met."

I laugh and wipe at my nose.

"Now don't go turning into a blubbering mess," he says, giving me a stern look. "Save it for your bride."

"Okay," I say, taking a deep breath. "Okay, I think I'm ready."

James grins. "Let's get you two married, then."

JAMES TAKES HIS place in the center of the little stage—he got himself ordained just to be able to officiate for us—and I take my place beside him under the makeshift trellis we set up in front of the new gym. There's a giant white ribbon covering the front of the door behind us that wasn't there this morning. When I look at James, he just grins.

It's taken almost a full year since that fateful night Cara first mentioned working together, but now it's here, and what better way to celebrate the fact that we did it than like this.

Cara has been largely secretive about the wedding planning, her and James scheming in a way that I thought was endearing . . . until the panic started to set in. But I have to say, they pulled it off.

On either side of the sidewalk leading through the front lawn to the gym are small sets of folding white chairs. Beside me, a couple violinists are seated, who smile and wave at me as I take my place. "Friends of Jane's," James murmurs into my ear at my confusion. "She said to consider this your wedding present, but then Sherry slapped her arm so I don't really know. You may get a toaster out of them yet."

I laugh. I can't help it, some of the tension broken as I shift from foot to foot.

Stella and George are reluctantly sitting in the back row. Cara wanted to invite them, since they've both apologized to us—which I suspect was more George than Stella, if I'm being honest—but neither of us wanted them front and center. We've carved out a shaky small truce. We'll see if it holds.

I opted not to invite my mom at all, and I feel strangely good about it. People who aren't there for the bad times don't deserve the good. People who hurt you on purpose don't also get to celebrate with you. It's not being toxic or holding a grudge, it's actually just healthy. At least that's what my therapist says.

This is our moment, Cara's and mine, and we're not taking any chances.

A classic limo pulls up and I hold my breath as the door opens. Suddenly Cara appears at the end of the sidewalk and it's like the whole world can start again. She's in a sleek white jumper, all lace and beads and silk. Her hair is pulled back into a bun, and she towers on satin stilettos adorned with tiny crystals. She's so beautiful it hurts, and I bite my knuckle to keep from all-out crying.

"Told you she'd show up," James murmurs into my ear, and I nod with a watery laugh.

The violinists begin to play beside me when Cara takes her first step. I lose it, trying to play it off while I wipe at my eyes, but then she's here in front of me, taking my trembling hands in hers.

"You're shaking," she whispers.

"You're here."

She grins even bigger. "I wouldn't miss this for the world."

"Thank you all for coming." James clears his throat. "It's my understanding that this incredible bride in front of me . . . and Cara," he deadpans, "have written their own vows, in order to steal my thunder as their officiant. Ladies, I guess you may proceed."

Cara smacks his arm, and our little crowd of loved ones laughs. Mina's baby squeals at the sound and we both grin.

"Lizzie." Cara squeezes my hands and takes a deep breath. "I used to think we met by chance, but now I know it was because we were meant to be. Since that day in the bathroom, where you performed your legally required girl code duties to the best of your abilities, you have filled my life with laughter, love, and just the right amount of chaos to keep things interesting." She smiles, and I look away for a second, overwhelmed. "You're my best friend and my love, and I will never take it for granted that, from this day forward, I will also get to call you my wife. I promise you, like you once promised me, that I will show you every day how loved you are, how good you are, how worthy you are of our life and our love. I will forever encourage you to chase your dreams, because every time you do, good stuff happens for the both of us."

I laugh, trying so hard not to cry, my entire body trembling.

"And I will always be there to hold your hand, to wipe your tears, and to let you watch *Annabelle* on repeat, even though I hate that doll, because for some godforsaken reason you've chosen that to be your comfort movie."

Everybody laughs, and I shrug like *what can you do.*

"But above all, I vow that I will be loyal and loving and faithful for the rest of our lives and then some."

I stare at her, nearly speechless.

I can't believe I get to be with this woman. I can't believe this woman loves me.

I can't believe I didn't write anything down.

I tried, I did. I wrote a thousand vows, scribbled on pieces of paper the way I used to draw this very gym we're standing in front of, but none of them felt quite right. I didn't want it to be rehearsed. I wanted to look at her, to be here, in this moment with her, feeling it all, and hoping the words spill out half as well as I knew hers would.

"I didn't write it out," I say, and then stop to reset. "Like yours are really great. Mine probably won't be that great. But bear with me." Our friends politely chuckle around us, and I take another deep breath. "The first time I said I love you out loud was after we broke up, or actually . . . I don't know. Can you break up with someone you're not even officially dating?" Someone in the crowd coughs. "But yeah, the first time I said it out loud was after I had really screwed things up. I blurted it out, like the second I saw you again, in case you shut the window in my face. Which I would have deserved, but I'm so fucking glad you didn't. Okay, well, technically you did shut the window, but then you opened a door. Which is kind of like that saying, but whatever."

And okay, I didn't have saying "fuck" in my vows on my wedding bingo card, but here we are.

"But I realized how important you were to me long before that and I was terrified. I was so scared of losing you that I almost never got to have you—I convinced myself I *couldn't* have you. And that's a mistake I will happily be paying for with foot rubs and that horrible pistachio ice cream you love for the rest of my life. I hope I've done a good enough job showing you how much you mean to me, how much I love you." I rub my eyebrow and take a deep breath, trying to stave off more tears. Cara squeezes my arm, her own lip trembling, urging me on with a little happy nod. "My vow to you today is that I will never push you away again. I will always be here for you, fighting for us, even if it's hard. No strings, no lies; you're stuck with me now. And I promise that never again will you be the one doing all the heavy lifting in this relationship. Even though you're the one who said those three words first, I've been feeling them, with every cell in my body, from the start."

Cara jumps forward, wrapping me in a hug.

"Too soon! Too soon!" James shouts, pushing us apart. "You have to wait for me to say, 'You may now kiss the bride.' Here, put these on."

He holds out our rings, forgotten on the tiny pillow. We shove them on each other's fingers as fast as we can and then look at him impatiently. He tilts his chin up, building suspense. "By the power vested in me by the state of New York after googling how to get ordained, I now pronounce you . . . married!" he shouts, jumping up and down. And just as we're leaning forward to kiss, he grabs a comically large pair of scissors and shoves them between us. "But wait, there's more! You may now kiss the bride *while cutting this ribbon!*" He yells that last part, like he's hosting the best infomercial of his life.

I look at Cara, confused, and she just shrugs. "He was so excited about combining the ribbon cutting with our kiss, I couldn't say no."

I shake my head as we each take one side of the giant scissors. I wonder if James is the one who wrapped them in lace.

"Three, two . . . one!" he says and we snip the ribbon, laughing, as we finally get our kiss. The whir of the photographer's camera echoes around us, and our guests clap, but right now, in this moment, Cara's the only one I'm focused on.

At least until James screams, "Oh my god, you're married!," in our faces while Ramón struggles to drag him away. We smile, both of our eyes teary, as Jane and Sherry invite our guests into the gym for our reception.

We follow everyone inside a short time later, after taking about a hundred too many photos, and I discover the entire space transformed with streamers and flowers and waiters and food.

I'm not sure how the health department will feel about this but given that we don't open for another week, I'm sure we'll have plenty of time to address it.

The wedding cake, a gorgeous white tiered affair, is set on a beautiful table beneath the squat rack, which is festooned with a garland made of real vines that I'm definitely taking back to our apartment after. On the top of the highest tier, surrounded by ornate lacing and flowers, sits what looks to be a topper of Ed and Lorraine Warren, as played by the incredible Patrick Wilson and Vera Farmiga in the Conjuring and Annabelle series.

"Is that . . . ?" I ask, turning to Cara in awe.

"You always say they're relationship goals."

"Fuck, I love you so much."

"I know," she says with a wink.

I look around and try to take it all in, soaking up the feeling of contentment that washes over me. Our friends, our gym, our wedding. It's perfect. It's *home*.

"What do you think?" Cara asks, as our future spills out before us. "Do you love it?"

I look at her, overwhelmed and in love. "Yes," I say. "I do."

Acknowledgments

So many people have played important roles in getting this book into your hands, and while I could never thank them enough, I'm certainly going to try!

Massive thanks to:

Sara Crowe for being the best agent in the business, I'm so glad to have you by my side on the wild ride. And to Sylvan Creekmore for believing in this book from the start and making this entire editorial process fun. Also, to my copyeditor Karen Richardson and proofreader Amy Reeve for polishing this book and helping to make us all look good.

To DJ DeSmyter, Jessica Cozzi, and Jessica Lyons, for all of your hard work making this book a success, I am so grateful for all of the time and energy you've put into this! To Monika Roe and Amy Halperin for creating such an incredible cover! And to the entire team at Avon Books: I am so lucky to have found such a wonderful home for my books.

To all my friends for always being there for me, cheering me on, and/or commiserating with me, and for watching both horror movies and Hallmark movies in excess whenever I beg. To crab nation, without which I would surely be lost. (But also, I need to take this opportunity to say that Blake H. and Aaron are both just doing their best actually!) To my family, for your support and understanding when I have to lock myself in a room for hours on end to make up stories. To my cats for always knocking things over and keeping life interesting. To my fish, who has listened to me read this book out loud more times than any self-respecting fish should have had to.

And last but definitely, definitely not least, a massive heartfelt thank you to my readers, this is all for you.

About the Author

JENNIFER DUGAN is the author of the young adult novels *Melt With You, Some Girls Do, Verona Comics,* and *Hot Dog Girl.* She is also the author of the YA graphic novel *Coven.* She lives in upstate New York with her family.